"There's something you need to understand, Matt."

Liv folded her arms over her chest. "You might be able to charm yourself out of a multitude of situations, but you aren't charming me. Sometimes, despite charisma and good looks, the answer is no. And that's what it's going to stay. No."

He bit down on the corner of his lip before saying, "Aren't you going to threaten me with your father again?"

"Dad's busy cutting hay."

"About time."

"He's been sick."

"Sorry to hear that." He didn't sound one bit sorry and he made his lack of sympathy clear when he said, "This isn't over, Liv. I'll hire a lawyer."

"Andie's dad already advised me, and he said he'll give me all the help I need to keep Beckett."

"He's my horse."

"Not according to the State of Montana." Liv lifted her chin. "This is the last time we're having this conversation."

Dear Reader,

Ah, secret high school crushes…remember those? My heroine, Liv Bailey, certainly does. She spent months tutoring hot high school rodeo star Matt Montoya so that he could remain eligible for competition, only to have him ask her sister out once his grades improved. Although Liv didn't realize it at the time, the situation with Matt helped spark her initiative to stop being the quiet, nice girl who bent over backward to keep everyone happy.

Ten years later, when the story opens, Liv is no longer the make-no-waves person she was, and when Matt once again needs her help, he's surprised at how much she's changed. Matt has also changed, but not by choice. He's dealing with a career-ending injury and has to learn how to deal with the situation. Like many men, he starts with denial…

I wrote this book because I'm fascinated by the idea of reinvention, whether by choice or circumstance. I especially like it when people rebel against their assigned niche (remember how everyone was assigned a niche in high school?). Then there's the matter of unrequited love. Who hasn't fantasized about running into that crush and having him or her realize just what they missed? It was a lot of fun giving Liv that chance and it was also satisfying changing Matt from a self-absorbed guy obsessed with reclaiming his career into a caring hero who realizes there's more to life than winning.

Thanks for reading *Once a Champion!* I love hearing from readers. If you have questions or comments, please contact me at jeanniewrites@gmail.com.

Jeannie Watt

Once a Champion

JEANNIE WATT

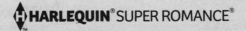
HARLEQUIN® SUPER ROMANCE®

Recycling programs
for this product may
not exist in your area.

ISBN-13: 978-0-373-60781-5

ONCE A CHAMPION

Copyright © 2013 by Jeannie Steinman

Printed in U.S.A.

H HARLEQUIN®
™ www.Harlequin.com

ABOUT THE AUTHOR

Jeannie Watt lives in rural Nevada with her husband and many animals. For many years she sent her (now grown) children to visit their grandparents in Montana, where they would experience ranch life firsthand. Her kids still talk about the fun they had teaching calves to lead, branding, driving tractors and fencing. She and her husband still talk about the peace and quiet they enjoyed while the kids were leading calves and driving tractors.

Books by Jeannie Watt

HARLEQUIN SUPERROMANCE

1379—A DIFFICULT WOMAN
1444—THE HORSEMAN'S SECRET
1474—THE BROTHER RETURNS
1520—COP ON LOAN
1543—A COWBOY'S REDEMPTION
1576—COWBOY COMES BACK
1628—ALWAYS A TEMP
1647—ONCE AND FOR ALL
1690—MADDIE INHERITS A COWBOY
1749—THE BABY TRUCE*
1755—UNDERCOVER COOK*
1761—JUST DESSERTS*
1821—CROSSING NEVADA

*Too Many Cooks?

Other titles by this author available in ebook format.

Acknowledgment

I'd like to thank Kari Lynn Dell and Myrna Gallian for bringing me up to speed on rodeo competition and calf/tie-down roping. I love watching rodeo, but, as with all sports, there's so much more to it than meets the eye. Thanks so very much, ladies!

CHAPTER ONE

WHAT ON EARTH had happened to the Bailey Ranch?

Matt Montoya slowed his pickup to a crawl as he drove over the cattle guard that marked the northern boundary of the property, taking in the sagging fences and weed-choked hay fields that should have been cut at least a week ago. What the hell?

He hadn't been to the Bailey Ranch in years, not since he'd come to look at some cattle after he and Trena had first married. The place had been immaculate then. Well-farmed, well-maintained. This was not the ranch he remembered.

Matt stepped on the gas and continued down the drive to the ranch house, half a mile away. A few steers stood in the pasture, heads down, tails swishing as they ate. At least they looked fat and well fed, but again, the last time he'd been here, Tim Bailey had had at least a hundred Angus in this field that now held ten.

So was his missing horse here, on this disturbingly run-down ranch? If so, Matt didn't know why. Tim had never been a horseman, preferring to do his cattle work on a four-wheeler, but one of the local team ropers had insisted that he'd seen Matt's gelding here when he'd come to repair a gas line.

All Matt could do was hope. He'd been looking for Beckett for over a year now and this was the first solid lead he'd had. Ironic if the missing horse had been on this ranch, two miles from his own home base, all this time. Ironic and aggravating.

After parking under the giant elm trees that shaded the old ranch house, Matt got out of the truck, moving carefully to avoid banging his healing knee, and then for a moment he stood, getting the feel of the place. It wasn't good, smacking of neglect and abandonment.

White paint hung in tattered strips off the sides of the house and the once blue trim was now mostly gray wood. Weeds poked their heads up through the gravel and the lawn looked as if it hadn't been cut in about a year. Or maybe two. Matt felt as if he were standing square in the middle of a deserted ghost town, except that this place wasn't deserted. Two trucks and a small white sedan were parked next to the barn. Someone was there. But where?

If he couldn't find Tim, Matt wasn't above exploring the pastures and barns on his own. He needed to know if Beckett was on this ranch and if he was, then he had to formulate a plan to get him back. Tim Bailey was a notoriously stubborn guy, so it might take some work, but Matt was going to reclaim his horse. He needed him.

Matt had just reached the sidewalk when the front door of the house swung open and a slender woman with a long reddish-brown ponytail stepped out onto the porch. She closed the door behind her with a gentle pull, as if trying not to disturb someone inside. Matt stopped dead in his tracks.

"Liv?"

It'd been a dozen years since he'd seen Tim's daughter, his former tutor who'd helped him maintain his GPA so that he could compete in rodeo during high school. He missed so much school being on the road that he'd had to get some kind of help to keep from flunking, and brainy Liv Bailey had been the perfect person for the job. Shy, but no-nonsense when it came to studies, she'd guided him through the first semester of his senior year, had helped him make grades. Liv had always been there for him and now here she was again.

Life had suddenly got easier.

"Matt," she replied coolly, shifting her weight and taking a stance in front of the door as if guarding it from an intruder. Or from him. Not the greeting he'd expected.

"How are you?" Matt asked, taking a couple more steps forward.

Liv folded her arms over her midsection in a defensive motion, causing her breasts to swell against the blue chambray shirt and making Matt suddenly aware that she'd changed a bit since high school. She pointedly glanced down at her chest, where his eyes had briefly held, then back up at him, making him feel like a middle-school kid who'd been caught looking at a girly magazine.

"I didn't expect to see you here," he said with an easy smile. In a strange way, he'd enjoyed their tutoring sessions back in the day. She'd worked hard to pound the knowledge into him, but since she was so shy, he could easily fluster her with a smile or joke—which was exactly what he'd done whenever he'd wanted a break.

"Why not?" she asked in a reasonable voice. "It's where I grew up."

"Last I heard, you were in college."

"I've been out for a while." There was a definite edge of sarcasm in her voice.

"I know. I was just saying…" Nothing important. "Are you living here now?"

She nodded, but did not elaborate, choosing instead to stare at him as if he'd crawled out from under the proverbial rock. This was not the Liv he remembered.

"Why are you here?" she asked.

"I'm here about a horse," he said, figuring it was time to focus on the matter at hand, since he and Liv were obviously not going to have a touching reunion.

The color faded from her already pale cheeks. "A horse?"

"Yes. It's a long story, but to shorten it up, I left a roping horse with my now ex-wife. He disappeared. I'm looking for him."

"Disappeared?" She reached up to touch her earlobe in the same self-conscious gesture he recalled from their tutoring sessions.

"Without a trace."

"Before you were divorced?"

"Yeah. But we were separated. The divorce was in the works." And should have happened a lot sooner than it had. It would have happened a lot sooner, had he known that Trena was not spending her nights alone.

For a moment Liv pressed her lips together and stared down at the weathered porch boards. There didn't seem to be anything on this ranch that wasn't weathered. Except for Liv. Liv looked...good.

She also looked threatened.

"Do you have my horse?" he asked.

She met his eyes then, hers as blue as the winter sky on a sunny day and just as cold. "I have *my* horse."

Her horse.

Matt hooked a thumb into his pocket. "Can I see *your* horse?"

Liv drew in a breath that made her chest rise—not that he was looking—and changed the subject. "What are your plans for the future?"

"Excuse me?" he asked.

"Simple question. What are your plans for the future?" She used the same voice she'd used while trying to help him learn calculus. A voice geared to hide her innate shyness.

"I injured my knee a month ago in Austin. I'm here

to finish healing up, train a little and then I'll go back onto the circuit." He figured another week of ground work and then he'd get back on his horse and start some serious training. Hopefully his doctor would agree when he saw him in a few days.

Liv didn't so much as blink when he'd said he had to heal, maybe because he'd been plagued by so many injuries the past two years that hearing he had another meant nothing. Not that he thought Liv was following his rodeo career; it was just that when a hometown boy made good, the locals kept track.

"How long will it take your knee to heal?"

Matt shifted impatiently, wanting very much to put an end to the questions by saying, "Why do you want to know and where's my horse?" but instead responded with the more congenial, "Time will tell."

There was another long pause, and for a moment she stared past him out into the pastures behind the barn. He almost turned to see what she was staring at before realizing she was making a decision.

Which told him that Beckett was definitely on this ranch.

"I have a horse," she finally said. "With a brand inspection and a bill of sale to go with it."

"Is it my horse?" Matt asked quietly.

"I bought him from Trena."

Relief surged through him, even though he knew he had some work ahead of him.

"Trena had no business selling him."

"Maybe she did, maybe she didn't." And from the

expression Liv now wore, she apparently believed Trena did have a reason to sell. "That doesn't matter. If the horse was sold before the divorce, he was community property and the sale is legal. Trena's name was on the papers."

Well, shit. Matt took a moment. One thing he'd learned over the years was that expressing anger solved nothing. There were other ways to get what one wanted.

"She had no right to sell, Liv." He spoke in his most reasonable voice, no easy feat under the circumstances. Trena had skewered him every way she could prior to their divorce, but selling his horse had been her vengeful coup de grâce. "Beckett was home recuperating from an injury."

"I'm aware," Liv said stonily.

"And you would keep him, my horse, even though you know that he shouldn't have been sold."

"Legally—"

"I'm not talking legally, Liv. I'm talking about a vindictive person trying to hurt another by selling what was dear to him."

If he'd expected the speech to make a difference in her demeanor, he was disappointed. She continued to stare at him as if he were a nasty slug or something.

Matt rubbed a hand over the back of his neck, feeling like he'd stepped into the twilight zone. Who was this woman? Where was the Liv he'd once known? That nice kid who'd saved his academic life?

Probably scared to death that he was going to take

Beckett away from her—which he was, once he figured out how.

"Can I at least see him?"

"No."

"Why not?"

"Because he's my horse, Matt. I'm keeping him." Once again anger started to rise, and once again Matt tamped it down. He needed to be careful, not burn bridges.

"What did Trena tell you?" Because it was pretty damned obvious that Trena had told her something that wasn't true.

Liv shrugged carelessly, but her expression was taut as she said, "It doesn't matter. I bought the horse. I'm keeping the horse."

"Liv…"

"It's time for you to leave."

"Liv—"

"Now."

Matt exhaled, told himself to calm down. Not blow this. "I'll buy him back," he said. "For ten percent more than you paid."

She smiled a little at that, the first smile since he'd arrived and it was more of a smirk—an expression he'd never seen on Liv's face before. "I'm not selling."

There was a noise from inside the house and Liv glanced over her shoulder then back at Matt. "My dad is not well," she said, finally explaining why she was guarding the door, "but I think he'd take a good shot at kicking your ass if you don't get out of here.

So unless you want to fight an ailing older man, I'd
get into that fancy truck of yours and get the hell out
of here."

And with that, Liv turned and walked back into
the house. For a moment Matt stood, staring at the
door she pulled shut behind her.

Realizing that standing on the front walk wasn't
doing him any good, Matt started back to his truck,
striding down the cracked sidewalk and across the
weed-choked gravel, his knee throbbing with each
step. Anger solved nothing, but he was pissed as hell
when he climbed into the cab of his truck. Yeah,
he could hammer on the front door and maybe Tim
would try to kick his ass, or he could go home, re-
group. Think this through. Figure out a way to get
his horse back.

He was going with plan B. It'd be easier on both
him and Tim in the long run.

An unexpected shiver ran through Liv as she watched
Matt Montoya turn his truck around and drive past
the barn. Delayed reaction. She rubbed her hands
over her upper arms. She would not let Matt have
Beckett.

"Who was here?" Her father's deep voice sounded
from behind her. She'd hoped he'd sleep through
Matt's visit, and he had, so thank heavens for small
favors.

"Matt Montoya."

"Did he need a calculus lesson?"

Liv turned back to her father and smiled a little. Rarely did her father make jokes, and even less so now that he was not feeling well. He was tall and lean, his dark hair streaked with silver, and normally he held himself in an almost military posture. Right now, though, his shoulders were slightly hunched, as if he were in pain. Liv hated seeing him that way, hated that he was pretending he was merely recovering from the flu.

"My horse. He had questions about him." Liv took one last look at the rooster tail of dust from Matt's truck, then moved away from the window. "Seems he wasn't in favor of Trena selling Beckett."

"Good thing she did," was all Tim said. "Did Matt give you any grief?"

Liv shook her head.

"Good thing," Tim repeated as he sat in his leather recliner, a chair that had been in the house ever since Liv could remember. He leaned his head back, closed his eyes. Seeing her father in a chair during the day had shocked Liv when she'd first moved home from Billings a week and a half ago—almost as much as the fact that he hadn't cut the hay on time. Not that he'd let her cut it for him. That would be admitting there was something wrong instead of pretending it was a conscious choice on his part.

She needed to get him to a doctor, but there was no forcing Tim Bailey to do anything he didn't want to do. They both knew the ranch was a wreck, that it was due to health issues, but he resisted all of Liv's efforts to discuss the matter. Finally she'd stopped trying—at least until she had more of a handle on the situation.

"I'm feeling better today," he said, keying in to her thoughts. "Whatever this bug is, I'm finally getting the better of it."

Liv didn't believe him.

"You're dressed for town," Tim commented. Meaning that she was wearing slacks instead of jeans and sandals instead of running shoes.

"I'm having lunch with Andie." Her doctor friend who had the clinic where she was going to start providing physical therapy services. She was just glad she'd still been at the ranch when Matt showed up looking for Beckett. She hadn't expected that to happen, not in a million years.

"Don't know why you left an established business in Billings," Tim grumbled. Liv knew he suspected it was because of Greg, her ex-fiancé, but that wasn't why she'd left.

"I wanted to come back to Dillon." She didn't dare say "to be closer to you and find out what the hell is going on because the ranch is a wreck and we both know it." Out loud, anyway.

Her parents—polar opposites—had divorced when she was five. She'd spent every summer with her father on the ranch, and even though she loved him, she didn't really know him. She didn't know if Tim Bailey let anyone truly know him—even those he loved.

Living with her father had never been uncomfortable, merely silent. Sometimes they talked, but usually about small things. Things that didn't require Tim to open up. And when they weren't talking, they'd worked together on the place. Every morning Tim would have a written list of chores and Liv would do her part, some in the house, some outside, mostly what her father considered to be girl stuff, not hard labor. She'd often wondered if her father wrote a list to be organized, or so he wouldn't have to talk. She'd wanted to talk. She still wanted to talk.

Fat chance.

The man was sixty-three years old. He wasn't going to change, but maybe they could develop more of a relationship, somehow, if he didn't keel over first.

"If you have thoughts of discussing me with Andie, don't."

Liv just smiled and grabbed her sweater. Silence could work for her, too. She wasn't going to argue with him and she was definitely going to discuss him with Andie.

"I mean it," he called as she headed for the door.

Wow. Two sentences in a row. He was serious.

And Liv was worried.

Anxiety knotted her stomach as she walked to her truck—and then past it to the barn. Beckett had free access to the stalls from the pasture and by some miracle he'd been inside, out of the sun, when Matt had arrived.

The big sorrel raised his head when Liv opened the

man door on the opposite side of the barn and nick-ered a soft greeting.

"Good to see you, too," Liv said as she walked across the dusty floor to the stall. "No treat today," she murmured as she slowly raised her hand to rub the horse's ears—something she hadn't been able to do when she'd first bought him, because the horse had been so head shy. It'd taken her months to get to where she could raise her hand without the geld-ing flinching.

Beckett leaned into her hand, bobbing his head as she hit the sweet spot behind his ears. The scarred areas on his back and shoulders were now marked only by white hair that showed starkly against his rich copper coat. When she'd bought Beckett, the areas had been gruesome saddle sores where the hair and, in some places, the skin, had been worn off by a poor-fitting saddle and too many hours of use. The sore on his shoulder had been infected with maggots and the memory still made her shudder.

When Liv had expressed her outrage, Trena had only nodded, keeping her mouth carefully shut as if saying too much would betray Matt, her then hus-band. Trena wasn't without guilt—she should have tended to the wounds, kept them from becoming in-fested—but she was afraid of horses and Matt was responsible for the wounds themselves. Well, some-one had to take care of the horse, and that had been when Liv had been certain she was buying Beckett, regardless of what her then fiancé, Greg, decreed. Her life had changed that day as she stood up to Greg and hadn't backed down in the name of peace and harmony. He'd been stunned. And so had she.

It had felt wonderful to finally stand her ground... and terrifying.

Liv gave Beckett one last pat, then took a few backward steps, debating about closing the access door to the pasture and keeping Beckett in the barn, just in case Matt came back.

She decided against it. Beckett needed space to move and if Matt came back, what was he going to do? Load the horse and leave? Steal him?

Probably not. He had a reputation to maintain and stealing a horse from the rightful owner was not going to help his image. But she could see him trying to charm her into selling. Charm had always been Matt's strong point. It'd been the reason she'd been so duped by him back in the day.

As she walked back to the man door, she pressed a hand against the side of her face, remembering the one time he'd kissed her—on the cheek—and grimaced at how ecstatic, yet disappointed, she'd been. She'd been such a damned fool where men had been concerned back then, and had remained a fool for about ten years after. It'd taken Greg's controlling behavior and a horse that needed her care to make her wake up and see the truth.

CHAPTER TWO

BECKETT WAS ON the Bailey Ranch. That was the good news. The bad news was that, unless Liv did a 180, getting Beckett back was going to be a challenge and Matt didn't know what he was going to do about that. But he was going to do something and he was going to do it soon. He'd been off for four weeks and figured he had another six before he could trust his knee enough to compete—just in time for the Bitterroot Challenge, the richest rodeo in Montana. He needed to start racking up earnings again.

The injury in Austin had put a major crimp in his comeback season, a season that until that point had been gold. Hopefully, because of his winning streak, he'd earned enough to hold his qualifying position for the National Finals Rodeo in Vegas, but he wasn't taking chances. The year before, while dealing with his divorce and all the shit Trena had thrown his way, he'd missed qualifying by four hundred dollars. Four hundred lousy dollars—after winning the world title the previous season. It'd killed him, and it hadn't helped that his brother, in his debut season, had done so damned well.

He needed to get that championship back.

He sank down into his chair and stretched his bad leg out in front of him. When he'd wrecked his knee this time, he'd done more damage than usual. In the past he'd injured his right knee, the one he used to brace against the calf when he threw it to the ground. This time, however, the left knee had gone, the one he used to mount and dismount. The emergency room doctor had been blunt and told Matt he'd roped his last calf, but Matt had heard that before and had proved the doctors wrong three times so far— and that was only on his right knee. It simply made sense that he had at least two more goes on his left. If he spaced them out.

Matt eased off his boot. Life without roping was not an option—at least not yet. It was the reason he got up in the morning, the reason he needed Beckett back. They shared chemistry, he and the horse. If Trena had truly wanted to hurt him—and she had— she couldn't have come up with a better way to do it. He leaned back in his chair, closed his eyes.

Honestly, even if he never roped off Beckett again, Matt wanted him back because, until he had that horse, Trena would remain the victor in their private war.

And Matt did not take losing well.

The sound of a truck pulling into the drive brought Matt out of his chair and for one wild moment he thought that maybe Liv had decided to take his offer. Beckett was worth many thousands of dollars and he was certain that Trena would have gotten as much out of him as she possibly could, since the sale of the horse, as well as his truck, old tractor and two of his hunting rifles, had apparently bankrolled her exit. Ten percent over what Liv had paid would make for a tidy profit for her and he could see where after some thought she might have come to her senses.

But the visitor wasn't Liv.

Matt instantly recognized the battered red pickup when he glanced out the window. His cousin, Wilhelmina, or Willa to anyone who didn't want a black eye.

Willa was practically on his doorstep when he opened the door and a kid of maybe thirteen or fourteen was shuffling up the walk behind her. When had her son gotten so old?

Matt and Willa were not the closest of relatives, despite the fact that they lived in the same area, but that was mainly because he was always on the road and Willa was too prickly and mean to let anyone get too close to her.

"Hey, Willa. What's up?" he asked, knowing it couldn't be good. His cousin was all of five feet two inches high and had a squarish build, with blond curly hair and intense blue eyes. The kid was three or four inches taller than his mother with light brown hair and those same blue eyes peering at him from behind horn rim glasses. He smiled at Matt with a hint of apology that sent red flags popping up—then ambled a few feet away and pulled a phone out of his pocket.

Willa dove straight into her request. "I got a job working on a dude ranch up north and I need a favor."

Yep. Bad news. "What kind of favor?"

"Crag needs a place to hang for a while."

Crag? He'd thought the kid's name was Craig. "Why with me?"

"Because you owe me," she said in a low voice so that her son wouldn't hear.

"I don't owe you enough to be a babysitter," Matt hissed back.

"Yeah, you do." Willa stated it as fact, and he grudgingly had to admit she had a point. Willa had been the one who'd called him in San Antonio and warned him that a lot of his property seemed to be disappearing shortly after he and Trena had officially separated. She'd seen someone driving the old Studebaker pickup he'd bought to restore and had looked into the matter since, close or not, Matt was her cousin. He just wished she'd noticed before Beckett had been sold.

But… Matt eyed the boy, who candidly stared back…he knew nothing about kids.

"Like I said, Crag needs a place to stay and he needs something to keep him busy. Sorry about the short notice, but—" Willa shrugged "—not much I can do about it. I'm supposed to be there tomorrow."

"What's the rush?"

"One of their wranglers got hurt and this is a big opportunity for me. If I can get on full-time, I'll get regular living quarters and then Crag can come live with me, but I have a probationary period."

No. No. *No.*

"Willa…"

"He won't stay here the entire time," Willa said. "I'm making other arrangements. I just hit a snag and I have to get up there ASAP—"

"I get it." Matt didn't want to ask how long she wanted him to keep the boy, not with the kid standing there, but he needed some idea, since he didn't plan to be there for much longer than six weeks himself.

"Please?" She practically mouthed the word, she said it so quietly.

"What are we talking here time-wise?" Matt asked. "I have some plans for later in the month. And a doctor's appointment in Bozeman tomorrow."

"One week, tops." Willa scuffed the toe of her dusty work boot on the deck in a way that made him wonder if she was being totally honest. "That's when my friend will be back from visiting her boyfriend in Seattle and she said Crag can stay with her. I can't let this opportunity pass." There was a note of desperation in her normally no-nonsense voice.

"I get you." Matt wasn't happy, but he did understand. Willa had a college degree in animal science, which had exactly zero job potential. Working as a horse wrangler on a dude ranch was a golden opportunity.

"All right." Matt attempted to smile at the kid, who

didn't appear to be fooled by the lukewarm effort. He didn't appear to be insulted, either. Just…accepting.

"Great. Thanks!" Willa turned to her son. "Go get your suitcase. I think you'll like staying here."

"No doubt," the kid said flatly before getting to his feet and heading back to the beat-up truck.

Willa turned instantly back to Matt. "If he tries to go stay with his friend Benny don't let him," she said as soon as her son was out of earshot. "The kid's not bad, but there are six other kids in the family and the mother never knows what any of them are doing. I think she's on tranquilizers."

"I would be," Matt said. "Anything else I should know?"

"Nope. I think you two will get along great. I'll email and call when I can, and here's my cell number—" she handed him a card that read Willa Montoya, Horse Specialist "—so you can get hold of me if you have any questions. But other than Benny's family situation, I can't think of anything you need to know." She dug into her pocket and pulled out some folded bills. "I have a hundred bucks I can give you for food."

Matt shook his head. "No need."

"Do you have any idea how much an adolescent eats?"

"If he eats too much we can settle up later." He didn't feel right taking money from a woman so desperate to get a job—even if she was putting him in a position here.

Willa smiled and pushed the money back into her pocket. "Thanks, Matt. For everything."

"No problem," Matt said, hoping it sounded at least a little sincere.

A few minutes later, after Willa had said a few words to her son and then hugged him goodbye, she waved to both of them and then drove away.

Matt and Crag stood awkwardly next to one another, watching Willa escape to her new opportunity, and then Matt let out a long, silent breath.

This day was not turning out at all well.

The kid glanced over at him. "You know, if you don't want me around, that's okay."

No, it wasn't. Matt did not take commitment lightly and he'd just made one.

"I have a friend I could stay with—"

"Benny?"

"Mom got to you, eh?"

"Listen, Crag—"

"Call me Craig. Please." The kid rolled his eyes as he said the last word. "I mean, come on. If your name was Wilhelmina, would you name your kid something as dumb as Crag?"

Matt felt like smiling. "No. I wouldn't do that," he agreed.

"Me, either. I just ask people to call me Craig and hope that the majority of them think my mom has an accent or something."

This time Matt did smile. "Good plan." He gestured

at the duffel. "Let's go inside. I have a spare room with a bed, but it's not fancy."

"It wasn't like you knew I was coming."

Amen to that. Matt held the door open and let Craig walk in ahead of him. The kid seemed okay. Not prickly like his mother.

Only a week. He could do it.

He hoped.

"So you're coming to watch practice tonight, right?" Dr. Andrea Ballentine reached for the check the server had just set on the edge of the table and Liv took hold at the same time. Liv gave a tug. They'd just finalized arrangements and Liv would start seeing patients next week, so she was technically employed and could technically pick up the tab.

"Only if you'll come to drill practice tonight," Andie said as she let go of the ticket.

"I'll come." Even though Liv had concerns about joining a mounted drill team that had a reputation for speed. She and Beckett had belonged to a sedate parade team in Billings comprised of ten women who drilled at a jog. It was pattern work, but slow pattern work. Flying around an arena at high speed in intricate patterns with eleven other riders? Liv wasn't so sure about that.

It wasn't that she wasn't a decent horsewoman. In fact, she was quite comfortable on horseback, but while her stepsiblings, Brant and the wildly popular Shae, had both been members of the high school rodeo team, Liv had never joined. Why? Because she'd been shy and self-conscious and didn't like people watching her. She wasn't a huge fan of speed, either. According to Andie, the Rhinestone Rough Riders had only one speed and that was as fast as they could go. Intimidating, to say the least, but Liv needed to do something to build a social life now that she was back in town and she was determined to explore new horizons—something she'd wanted to do but hadn't for the first twenty-some years of her life.

"Promise?" her friend asked as she counted out dollar bills for the tip. Andie had always fancied herself the guardian of Liv's social life, which was kind of funny, since Liv's social life had always been practically nonexistent—especially in high school. Andie, on the other hand, had somehow straddled the line between being popular and walking amongst the common folk. She always included Liv in everything, even if Liv had been practically invisible in most social situations. She'd been so afraid of screwing up, saying the wrong thing, doing the wrong thing... afraid to let her true self show.

"Yes. I promise I'll come to practice tonight. Eight o'clock, right?"

"Seven-thirty, but we don't start riding until eight. You might want to come a little early, meet the other riders. You're going to love it."

Liv hoped so. She had a ton she could be doing on the ranch to get the place back together before she established her practice, but since Tim bristled whenever she suggested that she do some real work, like, say, painting the house, she had free time that was driving her crazy. In a way she sympathized with her father. All he wanted was to be left alone while he pretended nothing was wrong, and Liv had ruined that by moving home. Maybe a few evenings to himself during the week would help.

"So what's up?" Andie asked as she closed her purse and set it on the table.

"Up?"

"Yeah," Andie said, picking up her coffee cup. Apparently lunch was not yet over. "As in distracting you. We've hammered out a deal, gossiped and ate the best cheesecake ever, but your mind is somewhere else." Her eyes narrowed suddenly. "Greg hasn't been in contact again?"

Liv snorted. "No."

The last time Greg had attempted to contact her, Liv had told him in no uncertain terms what she would do. A few of her threats had involved law enforcement. One had been more directly aimed at his private parts. That had shocked him. Quiet, cooperative Liv threatening violence. And she'd been serious.

"Then what?"

"I'm worried about Dad."

"With good cause," Andie said. "Keep working on him. Try to wear him down."

"It's like trying to wear down granite with a toothbrush," Liv muttered. "But what's really bugging me is that Matt Montoya stopped by the house."

Liv hadn't intended to talk about the situation with Matt and Beckett because she was halfway hoping it would resolve itself; that once Matt had time to think, he'd realize that legally he didn't have a leg to stand on and that Liv meant it when she said she wasn't selling. But deep down she knew that wasn't going to happen. Matt was nothing if not persistent. She'd seen it when he came to her twelve years ago, determined to pull substandard grades up not just to passing, but to As, and she'd also seen it in his rodeo career. Not that she was following it.

No. This probably wasn't going away.

Andie's face darkened. She was one of the few people who knew what had happened to Beckett. "No kidding. Why?"

Liv folded her napkin and set it next to her plate. "Apparently Trena sold the horse to me without Matt's permission."

"Of course she did. To save the animal."

"He wants Beckett back."

Andie set down her cup with a thunk. "You're kidding. After what he did? What are *you* going to do?"

Liv shrugged as casually as she could. "Nothing. Beckett was community property, so Trena had a right to sell, and I'm not letting him go."

"How'd he take it?"

"I don't know, and that's what's bothering me. I have a hard time believing that he took no for an answer so easily."

"Doesn't sound like Matt," Andie agreed.

"He's tenacious." And confident, which had ended up biting him in the butt in high school, when he'd been overly confident in his ability to miss a huge amount of school due to rodeo and stay current in his studies. After being placed on academic probation, he'd asked Liv for help catching up on his studies.

She was smart. She lived close by. She had a wild crush on him. Three things that made the situation perfect for Matt. She would have done anything for him. Liv didn't know if Matt had been aware of the crush, but looking back, she didn't know how he couldn't have been. She could barely finish a sentence when he was around, unless that sentence involved derivatives or vectors.

When he'd asked her for help, she'd thought she'd died and gone to heaven. Spending her evenings with Matt Montoya! Maybe he'd come to see her as a person. Maybe they'd become friends...and more.

"More" had been a big part of her plan, but it hadn't worked out. Once he was caught up and his grades were back where they belonged, he'd smiled and thanked her with a kiss on the cheek, followed by a bouquet of thank-you flowers delivered to the school. Liv had waited breathlessly for him to ask her out, now that they were no longer "professionally" involved.

Less than a week later, he'd asked Shae to go to Rodeo Prom.

Even now it made her cringe. Shae had known about Liv's wild crush on Matt and she'd said yes to him anyway. To Shae it had been a matter of being realistic. If Matt had been interested in Liv, he would have asked her out. He didn't and therefore he was fair game.

They'd dated for all of two months and then Shae had dumped him and moved on. Shae was hell on men. Liv kind of wished she could be the same way.

"Well, you know," Andie said, "if you have any problems all you have to do is call."

Which was another reason she hadn't said anything. Andie was wildly protective. Liv didn't need protecting. Not anymore.

"I won't have any problems," she said.

"Are you sure?" Andie asked with a slight frown.

"Yes." Liv tilted her chin up. "I'll handle this on my own." She'd handle everything on her own—her dad, Matt, anyone else who might want to tangle with her—and not by using her old strategy of trying to negotiate peace and keep everyone happy, except for maybe herself.

WHEN LIV ARRIVED at the drill team practice that evening, there was a variety of horse trailers parked in the lot—fancy trailers with living quarters, small two-horse trailers and a long aluminum stock trailer that looked as if something had tried to fight its way out from the inside.

She parked her truck in the last space, next to the stock trailer, and pocketed the keys as she walked over to where Andie was saddling her horse, Mike.

Liv felt awkward and out of place, and was nervous, even though she wouldn't be riding tonight—all in all, she was feeling way too much like the old Liv.

Those first months after she'd walked out on Greg had been sheer hell as she fought to let herself be less than perfect. She was better, much better, but still had her moments...like when she was faced with the unknown.

"Glad you came," Andie said as she set the saddle on the bay quarter horse's back. "Gretchen isn't going to make it and we need someone to shoot video. Linda's husband does a terrible job."

"I can do that." Liv had never filmed anything in her life other than a few minutes of phone video here and there, but, realistically, how hard could it be? And how perfect did she need to be? Not perfect at all.

She needed to remember that.

Andie finished cinching up, then slipped the halter around the horse's neck and eased the bridle onto his head. "I'll introduce you to the group."

The group consisted of ten women besides Andie. Liv knew some of them—Susie Barnes, who'd graduated the same year as she and Andie; Ronnie and Melody Churchwell, twins who'd been a few years behind her—and others she didn't. At least four of the women were well into their fifties and Liv instantly lost track of names. She took note of what each one looked like so that she could quiz Andie later.

"Well, ladies," a smallish woman on a big buckskin horse said in a commanding voice, "it's time to ride!" She moved her horse forward, saying to Liv as she passed, "You're going to film for us, right?"

"Yes," Liv replied.

A bald man instantly held out a video camera with an expression of relief. "I never do this to Linda's liking," he confided as the group rode in the arena.

"I probably won't, either," Liv said, again ignoring a twinge of performance anxiety. She reached out and took the camera, turning it over in her hands. "How does it work?"

The man gave Liv a brief rundown of the camera operation, then said, "You need to go up to the announcer's booth and when the music starts, you film. *Don't* forget to turn the camera on." Then with a quick, tight smile, he headed for a truck parked next to the stands, walking quickly as if afraid that Liv was going to relinquish her responsibilities to him if he didn't get away.

Liv climbed the rickety steps up into the arena announcer's stand and for the next hour watched as the women rode, stopped, argued, discussed, rode again, turning the camera on and off. On and off. She only forgot to turn it on once, and she was fairly certain that with the miles of film she'd recorded, no one would notice.

By the end of the practice, she had a good idea of the dynamics of the drills. Whether she and Beckett could do them was another matter. At one point she'd caught her breath when it appeared as though the riders were going to run smack into each other, only to have the horses weave together in a long serpentine pattern. There was a lot of splitting and joining, rollbacks and spins—all at high speed.

"So what do you think?" Andie asked after Liv had joined her at her trailer. She pulled the saddle off her horse and lugged it to the tack compartment. Liv automatically picked up a brush and started working on the bay's sweaty back while Andie unbridled the horse.

"I think it looks challenging."

"We all screw up out there, you know."

"Yes. I know. I have it on film," Liv said.

"Did you get the flaming argument between Linda and Margo?"

"I tried for close-ups," Liv said with a straight face.

Andie laughed and leaned against the trailer. "So?"

"I can't wait to get started," Liv lied. She was intimidated as hell, but determined to try new things, face new challenges. And give her poor father an evening or two to himself.

MATT HAD NOT in any way, shape or form, ever expected to become a babysitter—which was exactly what he was, even if the kid was fourteen.

Craig seemed a lot more comfortable being in a strange place than Matt was having him there, which made him wonder how many times the kid had been dumped into someone else's care…and why none of those someones were available this time.

"I'm kind of curious as to why your mom is having you stay here," Matt finally said after setting a grilled cheese sandwich in front of the kid at dinnertime. "Surely she has other friends in the area?"

"She tried a bunch of them, but there were problems. Vacations, visitations. One of her friends, Gloria, had just gotten back from rehab—"

"I get it."

Craig peeled back the edge of the sandwich to inspect the cheese. "This is a good opportunity for my mom. It's hard to get horse jobs, which is probably why she has to cut hair on the side." He spoke so earnestly that Matt hoped Craig didn't think he was trying to get rid of him.

"Do you like horses?" Matt asked as he sat at the table. They'd spent a long, silent afternoon together as he'd worked on his quarterly tax report and Craig had played games on his phone. Matt had needed that time to get his bearings, get used to the idea of sharing his house with a teenager, but the silence was getting old. And uncomfortable.

Craig made a face before he bit into his sandwich. "Horses? No," he said with his mouth full.

"Roping? Rodeo?"

"Uh-uh," Craig answered through another mouthful of sandwich.

"Oh." Well, that squelched talking about roping techniques with the kid. "What do you like?"

"I read a lot and there's some TV shows I like. Have you ever seen *Star Crusher*?"

"I don't watch a lot of TV."

"But you do have satellite, right?" Something akin to panic lit the kid's eyes.

"Yes. So…what else do you like?"

"The video games my mom allows, which aren't many," he said with a disgusted twist of his lips. "No exploding heads."

"Can't blame her there."

"And I think old trucks are kind of cool."

Score. Maybe they *could* talk. "I had a Studebaker truck once that I was going to rebuild." And it still stung that he didn't have it.

"I know," Craig said excitedly. "I've seen it. That was what clued Mom in about your ex selling your stuff. Kirby Danson driving your old truck around."

"You know all about that?"

"Well, Mom and her friends talk a lot."

"And you listen." Great.

"Well, she and I talk a lot, too. It's just, like, the two of us, you know? That was bogus what your wife did to you."

And not something he wanted to discuss with a fourteen-year-old, not even one whose eyes were now ablaze with indignation on Matt's behalf.

"What are you going to do while you're here?" Matt asked. "Besides play on your phone."

Craig shrugged. "Whatever, I guess."

Matt finished his sandwich and sat back in his chair. He would have liked to have had a beer with his meal, but didn't know if that was allowable with an impressionable houseguest under his roof.

"If you have any work or anything that needs to be done around the place, well, I could do that."

"Work?"

"Mom thought it would be a good idea. Keep me busy."

Damn, this had to be tough on the kid. The problem was that Matt's place was well-kept. He had a cleaning lady and the guy who fed his livestock when he was on the road also did the maintenance.

"Yeah. I can use some help." Or come up with something. "I'd pay you."

Craig shook his head. "No. You're giving me a roof and food."

"Your mom paid for the food." Or had tried to.

"A roof, then, and she didn't pay for that."

"We'll negotiate later, okay? You want to watch TV now?"

"In the worst possible way," Craig said. "Mom says I can't watch someone else's TV unless they invite me to."

"Consider yourself invited," Matt said. "For as long as you're here, the TV is yours."

"Thanks," Craig said, gathering up his plate and heading for the dishwasher. Matt watched in surprise as the boy loaded his dinnerware, then added the dishes that had been soaking in the sink. A quick swipe of the dishcloth around the sink after he'd rinsed it, then Craig headed to the living room. Wow. Willa had taught her son well.

As soon as the television came on in the next room,

Matt opened that beer and sat at the table drinking it. Talk about a strange day. Found his horse, got an unexpected roommate—with whom he had nothing to talk about.

Matt reached out and grabbed the newspaper off the sideboard where he'd stacked all the stuff that'd been on the table when he'd cleared it to feed Craig. He flipped it open with one hand and looked at his brother—make that his half brother's—smiling face on the front page and almost closed it again. But he didn't.

Ryan Madison. The darling of the Montana rodeo circuit, who'd just done a charity roping clinic for the local kids, and who was also within striking distance of qualifying for the NFR for the second time in a row.

Matt shoved the paper aside.

Not that he didn't want Ryan to qualify. He enjoyed beating his brother. He wished he'd had a chance to beat him last year, except he hadn't because of four hundred lousy dollars. Ryan had come in a respectable fourth, which wasn't bad for his first NFR and considering he'd been on a borrowed horse.

It'd killed Matt to sit on the sidelines and watch.

He and Ryan had been roping rivals since they were ten or eleven, and by the time Matt was fifteen, the two of them had developed an animosity that bordered on legendary—they'd also had no idea they were related. As far as Matt knew, Ryan was still in the dark—which was just fine with him.

CHAPTER THREE

THOUGH SHE TOLD herself she wasn't going to think about it, Liv tossed and turned that night, and when she finally did fall asleep, she dreamed about searching for Beckett. She found tracks and bits of mane and tail hair clinging to branches and fence wire, but no horse. She woke up with her heart pounding.

A dream.

Even so, she got out of bed and walked over to the window looking out over the pasture and felt a wave of relief when she saw Beckett grazing near the barn. Her horse was still there. Hers. She couldn't imagine losing him, not after everything they'd gone through. He was the reason she'd been able to stay strong against Greg, stick up for herself, let her true feelings show even if they were at odds with the people around her. It had been so very hard in the beginning....

Liv slipped out of her pajamas, folded them and put them under her pillow before she pulled on jeans and a Montana State T-shirt. After that she straightened the covers and opened the curtains all the way.

If she hadn't tried to buy the gelding, if Greg had succeeded in forbidding it, she might now be Mrs.

Gregory Malcolm, bending over backward to do whatever her husband wanted her to do. Be who he wanted her to be. During their relationship she'd had moments when she showed some backbone and argued her position, but ultimately she'd always backed down, as she'd done for her entire life—as her mother had done for her entire life—and let him have his way. Because if you made waves, people might abandon you.

The thought made her shudder.

A clattering of cutlery greeted her as she walked into the kitchen. Tim was already there, dressed and standing straighter than he'd been the day before. He put a couple more knives into a drawer, then turned.

"Coffee's on," he said. "I'll be in around noon if you don't mind getting me some lunch then."

"Where are you going?" Liv asked.

"To salvage what I can of the hay."

"You're feeling better," she said flatly. He was standing taller, but his color was still off. "And you can spend a day on the tractor."

"Yes."

"Are you sure?" Initiating confrontation still did not come easily to her—even after months of post-Greg affirmations and years of practice with her patients, who often did not want to do what they had to do in order to heal—but she was so much better at it than she'd been before.

His thick black eyebrows came together. Tim was

not used to being challenged. He was used to living life alone, his own way.

Tough.

"I wouldn't be going out if I wasn't sure. I have work to do." He grabbed his battered cowboy hat off the table and jammed it onto his head before stalking out the back door.

Liv let out a breath and then poured herself a cup of coffee, her movements automatic, mindless. Confrontation or concern? Which had her stomach in a knot?

She heard the tractor fire up as she took her first sip from the heavy ceramic mug. She had five days at home before she started seeing patients. Five days to keep a full-time eye on her father to make sure that he really was recovering and not just blowing smoke.

MATT CALLED WILLA at 6:00 a.m. to see if she'd made it safely to her new job and to find out if she was okay with him leaving Craig alone for the day while he went to his doctor's appointment in Bozeman. The connection was awful, cutting in and out, and Willa had been on her way out the door—in fact she was late—but no, she didn't have a problem with Crag spending the day alone. She'd hung up before Matt could ask about what day the kid would be leaving so he could make some plans.

The drive to Bozeman took almost two hours, which gave Matt a goodly amount of time to stew about the issues in his life while his knee stiffened up. His mom had called right after Willa had hung up, inviting him to a family dinner that Sunday. Matt had said yes, even though he hated formal family dinners, and mentioned that he might be bringing a guest. His mom had instantly gone on alert, assuming he meant a woman, and he'd had to tell her no. It was a kid. He was babysitting.

There'd been a strangely awkward silence after that and Matt had quickly filled her in, wondering what had made her go so quiet. Perhaps the fear that he'd fathered a kid, just as her husband had?

Except that Matt was pretty damned certain that his mom knew nothing about Ryan. It was a total fluke that he'd found out, and only because he hadn't been where he was supposed to be on that fateful trip to Butte fifteen years ago.

Whatever the deal was, he and Craig would be having Sunday dinner on the ranch. Craig seemed okay with it, but then the kid seemed okay—no, he seemed beyond okay—with just about everything thrown his way. Dishes, housework, living with a cousin he barely knew—nothing seemed to bother him.

Matt wished he possessed that ability, but that wasn't how he was wired. He had issues that needed resolving and he wanted them resolved now. His knee, his career, his horse. He had goals to meet, rodeos to win.

After dealing with the doctor, he was going to have to make another move in the horse game. He'd consulted with his lawyer and legally he didn't have a leg to stand on, but morally Liv was in no better shape.

Maybe she hadn't been aware of what Trena had been doing when she bought Beckett, but now that she did know…well, if their positions were reversed, Matt would like to think that he'd sell the horse back to Liv.

His knee was throbbing by the time he got out of the truck in Bozeman. He idly rubbed the sore area along the side, wondering if he was going to be in a brace permanently, or only for a while. A brace would slow him down, but it beat blowing his knee out altogether. The guy he was seeing was supposed to be good and was replacing Matt's former doctor, who'd recently retired. Matt had fully expected the new doctor to warn him against using his knee too much, as the old doctor had, but he hadn't expected him to be so utterly adamant about it.

"If you plan to continue roping, then plan on getting another doctor." Dr. Fletcher pulled his pen out of his pocket after examining the knee and clicked it.

"That's a bit rash, wouldn't you say?" Matt shifted a little, making the paper covering the examination table rip beneath him. Damn but he hated doctor's offices.

"I just did say it," the doctor said after making a few notes and then closing the folder. "And I meant it. If you put this knee under undue stress and strain, you risk destroying the joint."

"What about physical therapy?"

"I'm prescribing PT, but that doesn't mean your knee is going to ever get good enough to throw a calf."

It wasn't the answer Matt wanted. More than that, it wasn't an answer he was going to accept.

"Listen to me," the doctor said with a quiet intensity that broke into Matt's stubborn thoughts. "I know this isn't easy to swallow, but facts are facts. Your knee won't last if you continue roping. You're too young for a knee replacement, but if I did end up replacing the joint because of stupid behavior, you still won't be able to rope because the joint won't stand up to lateral pressure.

"I'd like to see you again in two weeks," he said as he handed him the chart to take back to the reception desk where he'd settle his account.

"Right," Matt said. But he didn't plan on coming back. There were other doctors. Knee specialists. Alternative medicine. Doctors with more open minds.

Matt settled his hat on his head as he left the office ten minutes later and several hundred dollars poorer. He'd seen some of his rodeo compadres come back from rugged injuries not only to compete, but also to win.

He had every intention of doing the same.

Matt ran a few errands, then started the long drive home, keeping his thoughts as positive as possible. He *was* going to rope again. He *was* going to finish out the rodeo season. He *was* going to get his horse back.

The rodeo arena parking lot was full when he pulled off the freeway in Dillon and Matt slowed, then drove in. It'd been over a year since he'd stopped by the Tuesday night roping to talk with the guys he'd grown up with, rodeoed and partied with. He used to hit the roping every time he was in town, but when Trena had turned his life upside down, he'd stopped going. Then, when he'd failed to qualify for the finals for the first time in seven years…well, he just hadn't felt like socializing after that. He'd stayed home and trained, then headed to Texas to start what had been a golden season right up until his foot had hung up in the stirrup in Austin.

He parked and felt a stir of anticipation as he watched a steer leave the chute at a dead run and the horses and riders charge after it a few seconds later. The pickups and trailers parked next to the fence blocked his view, but he could see the cowboys' loops swinging.

Okay, maybe this had been a mistake. All it did was remind him of what he couldn't yet do. Maybe in a week, two at the most, he'd be roping from horseback, but for right now he was stuck on the ground roping the dummy for hours on end.

He needed to get out of here. He'd meet up with his friends at another time, another place. Just before he turned the key in the ignition, he was startled by a knock on the passenger window. Wes Warner waved at him through the glass and Matt put the window down.

"Should you be here?" Wes asked with a smile that barely showed under his thick mustache.

"I was just discussing that with myself," Matt said. Wes, a former bronc rider whose career had been cut short by a car accident, was no stranger to injury or the disappointment of losing a promising career.

"Want a beer while you carry on your conversation?"

"Sure." Craig had assured him that all was well when he'd called the house half an hour ago so one beer wouldn't hurt.

Wes gestured with his head and Matt got out of the pickup and followed him to the tailgate of his truck, which faced away from the arena.

"Did you find your horse?" Wes asked as he pulled a longneck out of the cooler and handed it to Matt. "I heard he was on the Bailey Ranch."

"He is," Matt said, twisting off the top.

"Why does Tim have a horse?" Wes opened his own bottle, which foamed over the top and onto his pants before he took a long pull.

"Not Tim. Liv."

"Liv has your horse?" Wes wiped the back of his hand across his mustache, clearing it of foam. "Quiet Liv Bailey? I didn't even know she rode."

"She rides," Matt muttered. Shae had once told him that Liv was actually an accomplished rider, but lacked the drive to be a real competitor. Funny words from a girl who was mainly interested in competing in the queen contests and not in the events.

Wes leaned back against the side of the truck. "How'd she end up with your animal? Isn't she living in Billings?"

"She's on the ranch right now, and I have no idea how she ended up with him."

Wes scratched the side of his head. "She and Trena weren't friends or anything, were they?"

Matt snorted. "As far as I know they weren't." Trena and Liv had traveled in different circles. Way different circles. Almost to the point of being on different planets.

Trena had moved to Dillon at the beginning of their senior year, a California transplant. Blonde. Beautiful. Not a rural bone in her body. She'd arrived with the kind of splash that would have sent shy Liv running for cover, instantly making the girls jealous and the guys pant. It'd taken her almost a nanosecond to hook up with the king of the football team, Russell Marshall.

Matt had been doing his damnedest to pass his classes and stay on the rodeo team, thus the tutoring sessions with Liv, and hadn't made a play for her back then. He'd been more focused on his own kind— rodeo girls such as Liv's stepsister, Shae—and that had remained his focus until his early twenties when he and Trena had run into each other again when he'd come back to Dillon during the hiatus after the NFR. They'd clicked in a big way, and the next thing he knew, they were married. Happily. For a while.

Trena had sworn that she wouldn't mind going on the road with him, but the reality, even with a state-of-the-art live-in trailer, had been too much for her. She'd wanted to rent motel rooms, eat out, fly everywhere. Spend money as fast as he made it. He made good money, too, but not enough to spend like that.

The next year she didn't go on the road with him. That had spelled the beginning of the end, although Matt hadn't known it at the time.

The gate banged shut behind them and a few seconds later a cowboy Matt didn't know rode by. He nodded at Wes, who nodded back.

"There's a get-together later tonight at the Lion's Den," Wes said. "We're making some plans for the Fourth of July rodeo."

"I have to get home," Matt said. "I'm, uh, baby-sitting."

Wes coughed. "You?"

"Me. For Willa's kid."

"Does he rope?"

"He loads the dishwasher."

"That's a handy talent," Wes said.

"Even if I wasn't taking care of the kid," Matt said, "I'm not feeling all that social right now." He set the bottle on the edge of the truck bed. "I thought I was, but...I shouldn't have come down here yet."

"So what are your plans?" Wes asked quietly. "Now that you're back in the area."

"My plans are to heal my knee in time for the Bitterroot Challenge."

Wes sent him a dubious look. "Is that possible?"

A twist of the knife. "I won't know unless I try."

"That's right," Wes said. "You gotta try."

"I've seen guys come back from worse injuries than this," Matt said, not liking how defensive he sounded.

"Me, too."

Matt swallowed the last of his beer and tossed the bottle into the trash can near the fence. "I've seen guys come back from broken backs and climb back up on a bull again."

"You kinda gotta wonder if they got kicked in the head one too many times."

"You're missing the point," Matt said.

Wes smiled from beneath his mustache and took another drink of his beer. "Other than healing, what are your plans?"

To rodeo for another five years. He was thirty, single and not ready to settle down. When he did settle down, it might not even be in Dillon. His mother would hate that, but sometimes he thought it would be best if he didn't settle too close to his dad.

"And I mean other than rodeo."

"I don't know."

"You could start a babysitting business."

"I could punch you in the face," Matt said conversationally and Wes smiled. "I don't have any set plans," he admitted. "Other than the one I just told you."

"You might want to come up with one. Just a bit of advice from one injured rodeo man to another."

Coming up with a backup plan felt like admitting defeat before he'd even started to fight the battle.

"You could go back to college. Here at Western."

Matt made a dismissive gesture. He didn't want to go back to college. Not at his age. He had no idea what he wanted to do with his future.

"I'll come up with some kind of plan." It'd probably involve raising hay and roping horses, which sounded pretty damned boring. He wasn't ready to go that route yet.

"And the horse?"

"I'm getting the horse back," Matt said. It was a matter of changing tactics.

He'd shown up on Liv's ranch without warning and indicated he wanted Beckett back. Of course she'd felt threatened. But under normal circumstances, when she wasn't pressed into defensive mode by a surprise attack, she was a nice person. A good person. Not a person who kept a guy's horse.

He'd wait a couple days, then drop by and they'd talk again, under less stressful conditions.

NOT AGAIN.

Liv pressed a hand to her forehead as Matt Montoya's distinctive two-tone silver-and-black Dodge pulled up under the elm tree and parked. Thank goodness Beckett was behind the barn where he couldn't see him.

She moved back from the window as Matt got out of the truck and stood studying the house for a moment, as if gauging his best means of attack.

Plan all you want, Montoya. You aren't getting my horse.

Finally he started toward the house, his gait uneven due to the brace he wore, and Liv quickly crossed the living room and opened the front door to step out onto the porch. This time, though, it wasn't to keep Matt from waking her father. Tim was out on the baler, trying to salvage the hay. He looked like hell, but still insisted he felt better. Liv didn't believe him, but was at a loss as to what to do. She was frustrated and more than willing to take it out on Matt. In fact, she was kind of looking forward to taking it out on him.

She closed the screen door behind her and drew herself up as Matt approached, looking like a cowgirl's wet dream. Her seventeen-year-old self would have never believed that the guy could have looked hotter than he had back then, but she would have been wrong. Matt was taller, his shoulders broader, and he had a sensuality about him that he hadn't had back then.

Looks fade. Integrity lasts.

As far as she was concerned, Matt had no integrity. He'd shown that when he'd used her to get his grades up and then never spoken to her again, and he'd shown it when he'd misused Beckett.

Her eyebrows rose slightly as he stopped on the bottom step.

She very much wanted to say, "No," before he started speaking, but figured that wouldn't get her what she wanted—his carcass off her property.

"I'm sorry about the other day," he said with rather convincing sincerity.

"What part?"

He looked surprised at her comment. "All of it. I mean obviously you had no idea of the truth, and I just kind of sprung it on you."

"I know the truth, Matt. The truth is that I bought that horse fair and square. I've had him for over a year and I love him."

"I happen to be fond of him myself."

Yeah? Then why was he in the condition he was in?

But Liv wasn't going there. It would only prolong the conversation. "You must have dozens of horses."

"Practice horses. I only have one other rodeo horse and he's not as good as Beckett."

"That didn't seem to slow you down when you won the World."

"My times could have been better."

"It's all about the time?" Obviously it was all about time. And him. Not about the horse or his wife.

"Some of it is about Trena selling my horse behind my back and some of it is that I happen to like that horse—my horse—and I'd like him back." He spoke calmly, reasonably. The picture of the charming cowboy who'd been done wrong and the fact that he could stand here and pretend he cared about the horse that he'd hurt through lack of care…well, it was all she could do not to walk down the three steps that separated them and smack him a good one. For Beckett.

Liv folded her arms over her chest. "There's something you need to understand, Matt. You might be able to charm yourself out of a multitude of situations, but you aren't charming me. Sometimes, despite charisma and good looks, the answer is no. And that's what it's going to stay. No."

He bit down on one corner of his lip before saying, "Aren't you going to threaten me with your father again?"

"Dad's busy cutting hay."

"About time."

"He's been sick."

"Sorry to hear that." He didn't sound one bit sorry and he made his lack of sympathy clear when he said, "This isn't over, Liv. I'll hire a lawyer."

"Andie's dad already advised me and he said he'll give me all the help I need to keep Beckett."

"He's my horse."

"Not according to the State of Montana." Liv lifted her chin. "This is the last time we're having this conversation."

"Or?"

"I'll call the sheriff and tell him you're trespassing."

"Really." He said the word flatly, telling her he wasn't buying in to her bluff—which meant it may not be a bluff much longer. Liv no longer allowed people like him to walk over her.

"Yes. Really. Now please leave." *Before Beckett steps out from behind that barn.*

Matt's face became cold and blank. "This isn't over, Liv."

"Yeah, it is. Come back again and I will call the sheriff."

Matt turned and walked back to his truck without another word. Liv held her breath until he fired up the engine and swung the truck in Reverse.

Round two to her. She truly hoped there wouldn't be a third round.

CHAPTER FOUR

HE SHOULD HAVE waited longer before talking to Liv, because all he'd succeeded in doing was to put her on the defensive. Again. Now he was worse off than before, and the thing that killed him was that he wasn't by nature impulsive. He'd simply thought that she'd had time to think about the situation, what was fair, what wasn't. Liv had always been reasonable—until now.

Stupid move.

But, as he'd told her, this wasn't over.

When he pulled into his driveway Matt realized that his jaw was aching because his teeth were clamped so tightly together, but he made no effort to relax the taut muscles. Let his jaw ache. Maybe it would distract him from the ever present pain in his knee.

He parked the truck next to the barn then crossed the driveway to the back door, his knee throbbing with each step. Through the clear glass storm door he could see Craig sitting on the sofa, reading.

It was so damned strange to come home to someone in the house after so many solitary months. He pulled the storm door open and took all of two steps inside before he slowed to a halt, noting the evenly spaced striations across his very clean carpet.

"Did you vacuum?"

Craig looked up from the book. "Yeah. The place needed it."

No argument there. The cleaning lady had bailed on him last week and wasn't due again until next Thursday.

Matt gave a small shrug. "Thanks."

"No problem. The hardest part was finding the vacuum."

"Where was it?" Matt asked as he pulled off his hat.

A look of surprise flitted across the kid's face. "In the garage."

"Ah." Matt was about to toss the hat onto the nearest table when he noticed that the top had been dusted. The old ropes he'd been collecting in the far corner of the living room were coiled and stacked.

"I have a cleaning lady," he said as he crossed to the rarely used hat rack and hooked his ball cap over the spurs hanging there. "She complained about too much stuff in the hall closet, so I told her to put the vacuum wherever she liked. I never asked her where she kept it."

"You never use it?"

"Not if I can help it. I take it you do some of the cleaning at home?"

A quick shrug. "Someone has to. Mom works. A lot."

"You don't have to do this to earn your keep or anything."

"My mom told me to help out where I could." The kid spoke with a hint of challenge. Okay, he needed to make himself useful. Matt wouldn't fight him.

"Well, I appreciate it." Matt glanced again around his now-tidy living room, then walked down the hall to his room—right across from the extra bedroom. He paused, then nudged open the door. The bed was made, the blankets taut, and all of the kid's clothing was folded and packed in his suitcase, which lay open against the far wall. Ready for a quick getaway?

More likely the boy was used to living out of a suitcase.

Matt rubbed a hand over his forehead. How rough was Willa's life? He had a suspicion that she was getting no child support, but how bad off was she? Or was he reading more into the packed suitcase than he needed to? Maybe Craig was just a neat freak. The evidence seemed to point that way.

Matt pulled the door almost shut and went into his own room, where he sat on the bed and took off his brace, wincing as he pulled the Velcro tabs. If anything the joint hurt worse than usual. Not the promising sign he was hoping for.

Once the brace was off he put on sweatpants and a black T-shirt, then went into the living room, trying to walk normally.

"Are you okay?" Craig asked.

"Fine." So much for walking normally. He sat

down in the chair opposite the kid and stretched his knee out. "Hear from your mom?"

"No." Craig shut his book, leaving his index finger inside to mark his place. "I tried to text her, but it never delivered. She must not have service there."

"I think the area is pretty spotty. When I called her she kept cutting out."

"Maybe that's part of being a pretend cowboy," Craig said before focusing back on his book. "No cell service."

"Yeah. Maybe."

For a moment the silence hung heavy between them. Then Craig said in a matter-of-fact voice, "I know it's weird having me around."

"It's not a problem." To Matt's surprise, he meant it. "But I confess that I haven't had a roommate for a while."

The kid's lips curved up slightly. "And probably weren't expecting one."

"No, I wasn't. But we're family." Matt's experience with family, with the exception of his mom and Willa, wasn't stellar, but there was no reason it couldn't improve a little.

"Yeah?"

Matt sensed the need to tread carefully. "Yeah. Of course we are."

Craig put his book down. "My mom is doing the best that she can."

"I know she is." Craig seemed to be pretty together, so Willa had to be doing something right. "And I also know that life has a way of throwing curveballs." He rubbed a hand over his knee. "People have helped me out. I'm happy to help out you and your mom."

Craig focused on something behind Matt for a moment, then cleared his throat and said, "I have a feeling that I might need a place to stay for longer than a week."

"Your mom said—"

"I think it's only fair to tell you that she always says that. She means it, too, but Mom…Mom's kind of, I don't know…optimistic?"

"I don't care how long you have to stay." Matt's gut tightened as he said the words. What was he getting himself into? And what if he needed to get out?

Craig snorted. "We'll see."

"It doesn't bother me," Matt reiterated. Really, what did it matter? So he didn't have as much privacy as he was used to. Big deal. He had a clean house and someone to talk to. All he had to do now was to find common ground so they could have a conversation. Maybe he'd have to watch that *Star Crusher* show the kid kept talking about.

"Montoya has brass, I'll give him that." Andie checked her cinch before dropping the stirrup back into place. "I can't believe he gave it another shot."

"I'd love to think that he got the message this time," Liv said, slipping the bit into Beckett's mouth, "but somehow I don't think so." She pulled the head-stall up over the horse's ears and buckled the throatlatch, her fingers clumsy because of nerves. Tonight was her first high-speed practice and she hoped she survived. She'd studied the drill on paper, had practiced alone in the pasture, but felt less than prepared all the same.

"Then to top off a grand day," she continued, refusing to let the nerves get to her, "Mom called and we're all meeting in Missoula this Saturday to look for bridesmaid dresses." Liv had long known the day was coming, but that didn't make it any easier to face.

"Shopping with Shae. How fun."

"Yes," Liv said, her voice straining as she tightened the cinch, "I'm *so* looking forward to it." She sighed. "It's not that I hate shopping with Shae or anything. It's just that I—"

"Hate Shae. I know."

Liv laughed in spite of herself as she dropped the stirrup. "You know I don't hate Shae. We've had a few close moments."

"Like when?"

Liv considered. They had never been enemies— just residents of different planets forced to live as sisters. "Once she needed help with a class." And Liv had helped her, because she'd known how hard it'd been for Shae to ask. She'd helped Shae, helped Matt. Then they'd dumped her and started dating. No one, not even Andie, knew how much that had hurt.

At the time, Liv had simply pretended that, after working closely with Matt, she'd come to realize that he didn't have much substance. "Not crush-worthy" had been her exact words to Andie. She hadn't mentioned that she'd cried into her pillow the first time Matt and Shae had gone out.

Wasted time. Wasted tears.

Even though she could look back and shake her head at what had seemed like the end of the world, she also felt vestiges of anger at being so damned used.

Shake it off.

"To be honest," Liv said, putting a foot in the stirrup and mounting, "I never hated Shae. I was just jealous of her. She seemed so...perfect." And Liv had felt so far from perfect when they'd lived together. Shae was confident and bossy and on the occasions when she and Liv argued, Liv inevitably backed down—mainly because her mother would insist that she did.

"Shae is perfect," Andie said airily. "Just ask her."

Liv smiled fleetingly before saying in a flat, adamant voice, "I don't want to go tomorrow." What's more, she didn't want to go into the arena right now. "I don't know why I'm even invited. Shae will pick what she wants whether I'm there or not."

"Your mother probably insisted." Andie mounted as she spoke.

"My mother never insists on anything from anyone except me."

"Then your mother manipulated."

"That's probably closer to the truth. Frankly, I wish she hadn't wasted the effort. Shae's having a small wedding, but I don't doubt for one minute that she's going to bully me into buying the most expensive dress on the rack."

"But it will be in impeccable taste."

"No doubt. Am I being too much of a bitch?"

"You're probably just tired of Shae walking over the top of you."

"Could be, could be."

Andie laughed as she gathered her reins. "Well, there's nothing like an evening thundering around an arena to work out your aggressions."

The knot in Liv's stomach, the one she'd been trying to ignore by focusing on the other stresses in her life—Matt, bridal shopping, her father—tightened. "I've never done a drill faster than a trot."

Andie's eyebrows went up. "That will not happen often with this crew."

"But—"

"You'll learn the drills in no time. I did."

"You were a barrel racer."

She and Andie turned their horses to follow the other riders to the arena gate. Linda called for attention once all twelve riders were there, and then Andie leaned close to say, "You will screw up. Everyone does. If someone yells at you, ignore it."

"They're going to yell at me?" Liv whispered back.

"Oh, yeah."

"I didn't sign on for—"

"Ladies!" the woman on the buckskin barked. Liv jumped as if she'd been caught talking during a test.

Get a grip.

Yes, she could do this. It was just different than what she and Beckett were used to. She'd joined the sedate drill team in Billings as a way to meet other horsewomen and to get Beckett back into the arena in a way that didn't stress him out. They'd both loved the easy-paced practices and leaving the Billings drill team behind had been one of Liv's regrets. Those easy practices were obviously a thing of the past.

Andie's eyes were straight ahead, focused on Linda, but she wore that small I'm-not-taking-this-serious smile that made Liv wish she wasn't, either. Drilling with this bunch would be a great way for her to learn to lighten up. Make some mistakes.

Linda described the strategy for the practice, and Liv had little to no idea what she was talking about. "We'll do the first run-through at a trot to bring Livvy up to speed."

Liv send up a silent prayer of thanks and nudged Beckett forward. His ears pricked at the gate, as always, and his eyes rolled a little, but he went in quietly. Linda immediately bellowed at Liv to turn to the left and circle the arena at a fast trot behind Susie, who'd entered just before her. Liv urged Beckett into a trot and did as she was told. Linda continued to yell instructions: follow Andie, pair up with Margo, cut to the center, roll back—*roll back? really?*—reverse and head to the center. Slide to a stop....

By the time she finished, the back of her shirt was

damp and her jaw was tense…but she'd done okay. A couple more times at a trot and she'd be good to go.

"Okay, ready to do it at a canter?" Linda asked.

"No!" Liv ignored the fact that it was a rhetorical question as her survival mechanism kicked in. "Not even close."

"You'll do fine," Susie said.

"Define fine," Liv muttered, turning Beckett to join the rest of the women as they left the arena.

Liv did not do fine on the next run, but she did survive. Her knee hurt from making a wrong turn and finding herself on a near collision course with Becca. They banged knees as they passed, but at least the horses hadn't crashed together.

As the practice continued, there was lots of yelling, but none of it, she realized, malicious. Just loud attempts to get her back on course before she creamed someone—again—which wouldn't have happened if they were trotting.

"Well done," Linda said as she rode up next to Beckett.

"Really?" Liv asked flatly. "I almost killed Becca."

Linda waved a dismissive hand as if killing Becca was not a major concern. "But you didn't. And you catch on fast. You did good for the first time."

"You didn't do *that* good," Andie said as Linda rode away, making Liv smile.

"Thanks for the reality check." But actually, now that it was over, Liv did feel a sense of accomplishment. She and Beckett could do this and

Beckett seemed to enjoy it more than the slow parade drills—probably because he was born to run. Charging after a calf wasn't all that different than charging after a teammate who was opening up a gap in the pattern.

"Anytime, my friend. But you know what?"

"Mmm?"

"It's good to see you stepping out of your comfort zone."

"You like to watch me suffer?" Andie might be her closest friend, but she had no idea just how much time Liv had spent out of her comfort zone over the past year. Some things Liv just didn't talk about.

"If I wanted to watch you suffer," Andie said as they joined the group riding out of the arena, "I'd come along on the shopping trip tomorrow and watch you try to hold your own against Hurricane Shae."

"Hey," Susie Barnes said, catching up to Liv and Andie. "Isn't that Matt Montoya's horse?"

"My horse," Liv said automatically.

Susie's forehead creased. "But…he used to be Matt's, right? I recognize that spot on his belly, but it took me a while to remember why I knew him."

"Matt once owned him," Liv admitted.

Susie smiled. "I knew it. He and Pete rope together sometimes when Matt's home." She frowned. "Isn't this the horse that disappeared?"

Tread lightly. Liv did not want to alienate a team member with a snarky reply. Thankfully she had years of experience repressing true thoughts.

"You know, I don't really know the history," she said pleasantly. "He was for sale last year and I bought him."

"Oh," Susie said. "I see." Although she didn't. "Well, the two of you did great for the first drill."

"Thanks," Liv said. "Can't wait for the next practice." She might be a little sore and mentally exhausted, but it was going to be a lot more fun than shopping with Shae.

DINNER AT MATT'S parents' ranch was canceled on Friday due to an unexpected storm that delayed his mother's flight home from Las Vegas, where she'd been visiting her best friend from college. Matt was beyond grateful.

Not only was he avoiding an uncomfortable family dinner, but Craig also wouldn't have to watch Matt and his father stiffly interact. Craig was an astute kid, and Matt was certain he'd key in on the dynamic between him and his dad—and he'd also ask questions. Questions Matt didn't feel like hearing or dealing with.

"So what are we going to eat?" Craig asked upon receiving word that they would be staying home for supper.

Craig might be a fourteen-year-old cleaning wonder, but he wasn't much of a cook. Unfortunately, neither was Matt, but one of them had to put food on the table. When he was alone, Matt usually grazed or ate out. When he did cook for himself, he fried up steaks or burgers, dumped some lettuce out of a bag and called it a salad. On special occasions he might bake a potato.

Right now, though, he was out of steak, burgers and potatoes.

"I think we should go out for a pizza," Craig announced. "I'll buy."

Matt didn't think that was a bad idea—the pizza part, not Craig buying.

"Let's go," he said.

"We're going out for pizza?" Craig asked, springing up off the sofa. Matt remembered when he used to be able to move like that. Hell, he'd give just about anything to be able to move like that again. Almost thirty-one years old and he felt like he was sixty-one. Or older.

But he'd get it back. Soon.

"We're going to the grocery store. We'll stock up on some frozen pizza and whatever else you like to eat."

"Mom gave you money, right?"

Matt grunted and hoped it sounded like an affirmative. He was in a lot better shape financially than Willa. "Can I drive?" Craig asked as they walked to the truck.

"Sure. In about a year and a half."

"Mom lets me drive all the time."

"I'm sure she does."

"Once I was the designated driver when her designated driver failed in his designated task."

Matt smiled without looking at the kid. Craig's use of vocabulary slayed him.

"So what shall we get?" he asked a half hour later as Craig pulled a cart out of the line.

"We start with some real cereal."

"Wheaties aren't real?"

Craig shook his head and grabbed a box of Cap'n Crunch.

"Would your mother approve?"

"She practically has stock in the company. Check her purse. You'll find a plastic bag full of the Cap'n." Craig looked over his glasses. "For emergencies, of course."

"Of course," Matt said, adding a box of Wheaties to the cart. "What else?"

Craig led him through the aisles. In addition to his usual staples—steak, hamburger, salami, bread, eggs, milk, cheese, Pop-Tarts—Matt bought crackers and peanut butter, chocolate milk, frozen pizzas…lots of frozen pizzas…Hot Pockets, frozen dinners and a watermelon. Willa was allergic and never bought watermelon, so Matt gave in and bought a melon that the two of them would never get eaten. Not alone anyway.

"Is this everything?" Matt asked before they got to the checkout stand, a bit in awe of the sheer amount of food in the cart—most of it of the snack variety.

Craig's expression changed. "Did Mom give you enough money?"

"More than I need," Matt said. "I was being literal. I hate shopping and don't want to come back."

"If you let me drive—"

Matt just shook his head and started for the nearest checkout stand, wishing he'd seen that Dirk Benson, the assistant manager of the store, was behind the register before he'd pushed the cart to the stand.

"Hey, Dirk," he said, pulling out the wallet he wouldn't be needing for a while, what with the amount of food Dirk was going to ring up.

Dirk called for backup, aka a courtesy clerk, and started sliding items over the scanner. He was almost done when he asked, "So what's going on with you and Ryan Madison?"

And just when Matt thought he was going to get out of there without an inquisition. He should have known better. Dirk's son had rodeoed with Matt and Dirk and took local rodeo very seriously.

"In what way?" Matt asked, knowing full well in what way, but not wanting to talk about it in front of the kid.

"In the way that he did a lot better than you did at the NFR last year, what with him qualifying and all."

Matt nodded congenially, determined not to let the guy get to him. Dirk had never forgiven Matt for being a better athlete than his own son. Add to that the fact that Dirk's kid and Ryan had buddied up in college and, yeah, Dirk was no Matt Montoya fan.

"And now he's pretty close to qualifying again and even though you've got a lot more earnings, doesn't look like you'll be adding to them."

Matt smiled tightly, then swiped his card with a

quick motion that he hoped conveyed his feelings, as in...*shut up, Dirk*.

"There's a big purse for the challenge," Dirk continued. "And Madison will probably win." He blinked innocently at Matt. "What with you being injured and all."

"Don't write me off." Matt shoved his wallet deep into his back pocket and rearranged two of the bags that were balanced precariously on top of the load in the cart.

"You saying you'll be able to come back in time?"

"Take it however you want," Matt said as he loaded the last bag—the one Dirk had missed because he'd been so busy talking. And yes, he'd be back. He had a month and a half.

"What's he talking about?" Craig asked as they walked through the automatic doors and he tried to keep up with Matt, who was moving pretty good despite his knee.

"Nothing."

"Sounded like something."

"Sounding like something and being something are not the same thing," Matt muttered.

"You don't want to talk about it."

Matt hit the unlock button on his keys. "Who's cooking tonight?"

"I cooked last night."

"Pop-Tarts don't count."

"I can't cook."

"As I see it, you have all day to learn. Maybe a little internet research. We got a lot to work with here."

"What are you going to do while I research recipes?"

"Practice." He spent hours every day roping a dummy from both the ground and horseback. Next week he'd start roping calves again.

"For your big comeback?"

Matt exhaled. "Yeah. For my big comeback."

"I DIDN'T EXPECT you to get home so late." Tim slowly got up from his chair as Liv walked through the front door. He was trying hard to look normal, but wasn't quite succeeding. Pain pinched his features.

Liv hadn't had a chance to talk to him before she'd left for practice, since he'd still been on the baler proving himself to be hale and hearty, so she'd made dinner and left it in the warming oven, loaded Beckett and left. It had taken everything she had not to march across the hayfield and rap on the tractor door to tell her father that he'd made his point—he was getting better—and he didn't need to kill himself to prove it.

But she hadn't. Maybe once he got the hay knocked down, he'd set a more reasonable pace. One thing she knew for certain was that if she made a big deal, or continued to make a big deal, then her father's stubbornness would kick into overdrive.

"Did you eat?" Liv asked, walking past him and into the kitchen. The dishes were done and the food was put away. She turned back to find her father standing in the doorway, looking pale. "Don't do the kitchen stuff," she said sternly. "That's my job."

"I'm used to doing the kitchen stuff."

"Well, then there's no reason we can't switch off for the day. I'll handle the hay and you can take care of the cooking."

Haying wasn't rocket science, but Tim had always insisted on doing it himself. When she was younger, Liv had thought Tim did everything around the ranch because he had an old-fashioned notion of men's and women's work, but now she suspected it was because he didn't like to delegate. He was a man who depended on himself and only himself—end of story. He'd let her work by his side, which he had done while she'd stayed with him, finding it a way they could spend time together but not have to talk. But he flat out refused to let her take over operations.

"I'll do the field work."

Liv leaned back against the counter, folding her arms over her chest as she studied the closed-off man standing near the table.

"How're you feeling?" she asked flatly. Liv was not a fan of direct confrontation, thanks to all those years of training from her mother, but she'd just spent an entire evening out of her comfort zone, so a few more minutes wouldn't hurt.

"How am I feeling?" Tim asked stonily. Liv couldn't say his barriers went up, because with her father they were never truly down, but he wasn't in any hurry to answer. It was as if he hoped that if he stared her down long enough, she'd say, "Oh, never mind." She didn't, even though it was tempting, and he finally said, "Tired, after a day on the tractor. I think that's understandable."

Liv sighed, but before she could clarify that she meant overall, not just today, Tim said, "What did Matt want yesterday?"

The sudden change of topic had the exact effect that Tim had no doubt been hoping for. "How'd you know he stopped by?" she asked. She certainly hadn't told him.

"Walter told me when he came to borrow the auger."

Walter lived directly across the county road from the Bailey Ranch and filled his hours watching the coming and goings of his neighbors—when he wasn't borrowing stuff from them or doing odd jobs.

Liv gave a small shrug. "He wanted the same thing as last time and I think he got the point this time."

"Well, if he didn't—"

Liv pushed off from the counter. "I can handle Matt. It isn't like he can do much about the Beckett situation."

"I don't want him harassing you, like that other guy that you didn't want to tell me about."

"Two visits are not exactly harassment." And she wished Tim didn't know about "that other guy." The only reason he did know was because Greg had the chutzpah to call Tim looking for her after she'd stopped answering his calls.

Her father raised one eyebrow and she took his point. After Matt's first visit, during which she'd taken a firm stand, there was little call for a second. At least not in person. Phoning would have done just as well, but Matt had probably figured he'd be more persuasive in person. And he was, but Liv was not falling for it.

"If he starts harassing me, I'll let you know." She didn't like lying to her father, but she wasn't going to let him fight her battles, either. "By the way, I'm going to Missoula tomorrow to shop with Mom and Shae."

"All that way to shop? Why doesn't your mother meet you in a more central locale, like Butte? Surely you could shop there."

Tim and Vivian had been divorced for almost twenty years and there was no lingering bitterness between them. In fact, Liv had never noticed any bitterness whatsoever. Even her mother, who clung to people with a death grip, changing as necessary to please them, had come to realize that she couldn't change enough to stay married to Tim. He was a man who had difficulty allaying fears, reaffirming his commitment, saying the words "I love you," and Vivian was a woman who needed those reassurances. Often. It hadn't hurt that she'd married David McArthur within a year of divorcing Tim.

"The wedding, Dad. We're shopping for brides-maid dresses and Shae wants to shop in Missoula."

"Right. The wedding. I forgot about that." The

words were barely out when a yawn seemed to catch him by surprise. Liv pretended not to notice, folding a dish towel before hanging it. He'd had a long day proving he was on the mend. She only hoped it didn't send him into a relapse.

"Shae has promised to keep it a small affair." Tim cocked his head as if waiting for the punch line. "Reed, her fiancé, is the sensible type." Liv read her father's face and smiled. "Yeah. I know. What's he doing with Shae? Opposites attract, I guess."

Silence hung between them for a second and Liv had a strong feeling that they were both thinking the same thing. That opposite thing hadn't worked out so well with him and her mother.

"Reed is a good guy and smart. He knows what he's doing." Liv pushed a few strands of hair away from her face, grimacing at how stiff it was from arena dust.

"Let's hope" was all Tim said. He seemed to be growing paler before her eyes, reminding her of how far she'd been sidetracked from the issue of his health. Even though she wanted to take him by the front of his shirt and shake him, demand that he tell her what was going on with him, she figured right now a full frontal assault would do more harm than good.

She was going to have to wait. Wait and worry. Then maybe in another couple of days try again if he was still doing his impression of the walking dead.

"I'm going to bed, Dad," she finally said, well

aware of the relief that flickered across his stern features, there then gone. "Why don't you do the same?"

"I will."

Of course he would. Just as soon as she did.

CHAPTER FIVE

LIV PULLED OFF her ball cap as she walked into the bathroom and then released her hair from the elastic band. It barely moved. Her former drill team had never stirred up so much dust during a practice, but then her old drill team hadn't ridden hell-bent for election during practice, either.

She waited a moment at the sink, studying her dusty reflection, wondering how long Tim was going to stay up to make his point. A long time, apparently.

Finally, after she'd shucked off her dirty clothing and was about to crank on the shower, she heard her father walk down the hall toward his room at the far end of the house. His door closed and the house fell silent.

Thank goodness.

Liv turned on the water and a few minutes later stepped under the spray, letting it beat on her, washing dust out of her hair and, hopefully, working tension out of her shoulders. Murky water swirled around her feet before going down the drain, but the stiffness in her shoulders barely abated.

Stress. Oh, yes. Her perpetual friend, back with a bit more force than usual after drill practice and the unsuccessful confrontation with her father. Add to that the shopping trip tomorrow, starting a new job in a few days and Matt trying to finagle her horse away from her and no wonder her muscles were seized up.

She rolled her shoulders under the spray, closing her eyes and making a conscious effort to relax. She could deal with this stuff—even if most of it took her well out of her comfort zone.

Liv sighed as she reached for the shampoo. Maybe in a year or two it would be easy. Or easier. Right now it was a constant effort to hold her own, not take the easy way out and become invisible and/or compliant. She just wasn't certain how much was enough when it came to standing your ground.

The water was turning cold by the time she turned off the faucet, and her shoulders felt only slightly better. She put on her threadbare flannel pajamas and headed to her bedroom, combing her hair with a large wooden comb as she walked. Liv did not own a blow-dryer—hers had given up the ghost shortly before she moved home and she had yet to replace it—so instead of trying to sleep, she propped herself up against the headboard and started reading her new patients' case files as her hair dried. Shopping with her mother and Shae meant having hair that didn't look as if it had been slept on wet. It would be amusing to see their expressions if she showed up with bent hair, but Liv couldn't do it.

She finally closed the last file close to midnight and

snuggled down into the sheets, closed her eyes. And realized she was nowhere near being ready to sleep.

Was her dad asleep? A few nights ago she'd heard him pacing his room, but it was silent tonight.

She flopped over onto her side.

Was she up to watching her mother fall all over herself tomorrow trying to make Shae's special day even more special? She hated seeing her mom doing everything in her power to keep Shae happy, because she knew why she was doing it—to please David, her husband and Shae's father.

Liv pulled in a breath, closed her eyes even tighter.

Would Matt make yet another attempt to get her horse? And if he did, how was she going to handle it without upsetting Tim? She'd think of something.

Liv rolled onto her back, resolutely tried to close off the racing thoughts, then after another ten minutes, gave up. How many nights had she spent like this over the past year and a half? Awake and wondering, worrying?

Too many after breaking up with Greg.

Liv pulled the flashlight out from under her bed and silently left her room, creeping down the hall to the mudroom where she eased her feet into her barn shoes. When she left the house, she didn't quite shut the heavy door behind her. Her father had excellent hearing and the last thing she wanted was for him to get up to investigate the sound of the front door closing.

Gravel crunched beneath her feet as she crossed

the driveway, the sound unusually loud in the still-
ness of the night. Once inside the barn, out of view
of her father's window, Liv turned on the flashlight
and grabbed a brush out of the grooming box. Beckett's stall was empty, so she headed for the rear man
door, clicking off the flashlight as she went.

Beckett, familiar with the late-night ritual, nick-
ered softly as Liv started across the pasture to where
he stood under the Russian olive tree, moonlight bathing his back. He ambled over to meet her halfway
and then stopped, obligingly turning his side toward
her, waiting for the grooming to begin.

Liv started on his neck, following each flick of
the brush with a stroke of her hand. She worked her
way over the healed saddle sores on his withers and
lower back, now evident only by the white hairs that
covered the scars. It still angered her to think about
his wounds. Did Matt think a horse was just a tool to
be used and abused for his benefit? Did he even care
that the saddle he was using didn't fit or that Beckett's mouth had been injured from too large of a bit
and the way Matt had handled him?

Liv gritted her teeth, the brush flying over Beckett's coat in quick, agitated movements before she
suddenly stopped and leaned against the horse,
squeezing her eyes shut as she inhaled deeply. A
moment later, Liv set the brush on the ground and
started working the tangles out of Beckett's mane
with her fingers. The gelding pulled in a deep breath
and then exhaled. A horsey sigh, which Liv echoed.

Beckett didn't like having his mane untangled, but he endured, as he'd endured his abuse.

Now Matt wanted the horse back. Fat chance. If he was stupid enough to come back a third time, Tim would not be the one dealing with him. No. She didn't want anyone dealing with Matt Montoya except for herself. Andie and Tim…they meant well, but Liv would fight this battle alone. This was one area where she had no qualms about standing her ground.

Once she'd finished with the mane, she ran her hand over Beckett's nose and the horse pushed against it, snuffling for a treat. She had nothing, but smiled as she ruffled his mane, then wrapped her arms around his neck and pressed her cheek against his solid muscles.

If it hadn't been for Beckett needing to be rescued, she may not have realized how closely she'd been mirroring her mother's behavior, or how damaging that could be, until it was too late.

Vivian's one need in life was to have a man to keep her secure, and in order to hang on to her man, she would become indispensible so they would keep her. *Don't make waves, Liv.*

And Liv hadn't. She'd been the picture of compliance and cooperation for most of her life. Until the situation with Greg had come to a head.

Something inside of her had snapped after he'd essentially told her to choose him or a horse. In a life-changing moment of clarity, Liv had said she chose the horse. She could still see the shocked expression on Greg's handsome face, feel the twist of her gut as she'd realized what she'd just done. Then he'd laughed. A reprieve, a chance to pretend she'd been making a joke.

She hadn't felt even a flicker of temptation to recant, which was in itself stunning because until that point she'd considered herself to be madly in love with the man. Maybe she was in love, she'd told herself. Maybe they just needed time to work this out.

Or maybe she'd finally realized that she'd allowed herself to be manipulated and controlled for way too long.

Minutes later Liv had been in her car, driving away, well aware that Greg expected her to return in short order with an apology and the admission that he was right.

Didn't happen.

But not because Liv wasn't tempted. Part of her was hopeful they'd work things out. Part of her was outraged that Greg hadn't discussed the matter—he'd made a decree. She told herself that their relationship would ultimately be better because she had taken her stand. After all, she needed a say in things. But when she told her mother what had happened, Vivian had been horrified. Give up the horse. Go back.

Another of those clarifying moments.

Two days later, Greg called and essentially asked Liv if she'd come to her senses. His tone was gentle and teasing, but the message was still there—do as I say. The difference was that now Liv heard the message, whereas before she hadn't—or if she had, she'd chosen to ignore it. Liv told him once again that she chose the horse and hung up, her hands shaking, as she wondered if she were giving up her chance for happiness. They were so perfect together...because Liv never asserted herself. She was cooperative, agreeable, didn't rock the boat...

Greg called back the next day and told her she could keep the horse. He hadn't realized how important it was to her.

This time it wasn't so difficult to hang up. It'd taken him three days to "realize" that she was serious and the horse was important to her? Then give his permission for her to buy Beckett? Why did she need his *permission?* They weren't yet married.

Liv felt so damned stupid for having not seen the warning signs of a controlling relationship a long time before. And then, when Greg's campaign to win her back began, Liv became more and more aware of the bullet she'd dodged.

He started off nicely enough, flowers with a note. A stuffed horse left on her desk at work with a please-forgive-me card.

Liv stayed strong. He called. He met her in unexpected places. He even cajoled her into dinner and Liv had gone, thinking that maybe she could convince him she was serious. They were over. But he needed someone compliant in his life and Liv had fit the bill. He was not giving up.

Everywhere she went, Liv expected to run into

Greg, to the point that she'd considered a restraining order. When she'd heard word he'd gone out on a date with another woman, she'd been thrilled, until he'd phoned to tell her that no one compared to her. She shuddered to think about it.

If it hadn't been for Beckett—caring for him, grooming him, riding him, pouring out her guts to him—she didn't know if she would have made it through those long months. Beckett had helped her stay strong when Greg had pushed his hardest.

And then it struck her.

It wasn't the stress of wedding shopping or her father's health that was keeping her awake, or even fear of losing Beckett. It was Matt—Matt, who was behaving just like Greg, refusing to take no for an answer. Pushing.

Déjà vu all over again. She was not going to tolerate a replay of the Greg months. This time it might be over a horse instead of her future, but she didn't care. Matt was pushing and she was instinctively protecting herself. And rightly so—especially after he'd indicated the situation wasn't yet concluded to his satisfaction.

"Yes, it is, Montoya." Beckett's ear flicked back as Liv spoke. The situation was over and if Matt showed up again, she'd make good on her threat to call the sheriff.

Finally she patted the horse on the rump and headed back to the house, picking her way across the field in the moonlight. The front door was slightly ajar, just as she'd left it, and Liv slipped inside, holding her breath as the heavy oak made a distinctive scraping noise just before the latch caught.

Liv held perfectly still for a few long seconds, her hand still on the doorknob. Then, when no sound came from her father's room, she walked silently down the hall.

She yawned as she got into bed, hoping now that she'd figured out what was bothering that she could sleep.

It was her last conscious thought.

LIV OVERSLEPT.

She would have slept even longer if her father hadn't knocked on her door and asked if she wanted him to fuel up her car before she left. Liv grabbed the clock, which she'd turned toward the wall the night before, and yelped when she saw the time.

"Liv?" Tim called through the door.

"Uh, yes. Thanks. I'll be out in a minute."

Thanks to a lack of early-morning traffic and highway patrol officers, Liv arrived at Malinda's Bridal Boutique only a few minutes after it had opened. She was not surprised to find her mother and Shae already at the racks.

Liv fended off the associate with a quick I'm-with-them gesture, then started across the highly polished parquet floor, feeling awkward, as if arriving at a party late after everyone else had already settled in. As she approached, Shae held up a dress, said something, and her mother laughed, her need-to-please agreeable laugh. Excellent.

"You're here," her mother said to Liv, beaming as she reached out to hug her while still holding a beaded oyster-colored dress in one hand. "Right on time."

Shae smiled and also gave Liv a perfunctory hug, enveloping her in a subtle cloud of fragrance. "Glad you could make it." She pushed her long dark hair over her shoulder, and Liv couldn't help but notice how perfectly cut it was.

"Me, too." Liv had no illusions as to why she was in Shae's wedding—because it wouldn't look right if she weren't. She and Shae were sisters, after all. Stepsisters, but they'd lived together since they were fourteen and should have been closer than they were.

It was hard to be close to someone who intimidated you, however, and from day one, Shae had intimidated Liv—because Liv had allowed herself to be intimidated. She and Shae had little in common, valued different things, and Shae was so very popular while Liv was not. Of course she'd been intimidated.

Their only common ground was that their parents were married, which added to the problem. Vivian wanted her husband happy and her husband's children happy, so on the occasions when Shae and Liv had disagreed, Liv eventually backed down. For her mother.

To add to the tension, Shae, under coercion, had made a few futile attempts to include Liv in her social activities, but neither had been comfortable with that, so eventually they settled into living parallel lives in the bedroom they shared. There'd been moments when they'd acted like sisters—shared a secret or two, groused about a teacher—but for the most part it was every girl for herself.

"This is the preshop," Vivian explained, as if Liv weren't already aware.

"Yes," Shae said, hanging a pink silk dress. "You can imagine what a free-for-all this would be with seven bridesmaids giving their opinions."

"We're going to narrow it down to three choices today," Vivian said, rejoining the hunt.

Seven bridesmaids? "I thought Reed wanted a small wedding," Liv said as she casually flipped through a few dresses, wincing at the price tags and realizing that it would be almost impossible for her to come up with seven friends to serve as bridesmaids—not unless she included Beckett and her father.

Shae laughed, that confident yet somehow seductive laugh that Liv envied and had occasionally tried to emulate with little success. "Reed doesn't know what he wants."

"He seemed like he knew what he wanted last time I talked to him," Liv said conversationally. They'd had a fairly decent discussion at the family Easter Sunday dinner. Liv liked Shae's fiancé, a handsome, mild-mannered guy who still had a backbone. Shae had made a good catch there.

Shae's smile shifted slightly. "We've talked and

he's beginning to see things my way. After all, you only get married once."

"Unless you're one of the seventy-five percent of divorcées who remarry," Liv muttered.

"How on earth do you know that statistic?" Shae asked in the same voice she'd used when Liv had actually known the answers to the questions on the history exams in high school.

"I made it up."

Shae laughed. A real laugh. Then she turned back to the racks and pulled out a pale green sheath. "How about this?"

"Not bad," Liv murmured. *Except for that six-hundred-dollar price tag.* Surely Shae wouldn't do that to her seven friends. Liv glanced over at her mother and recognized the frozen smile, the make-Shae-happy look.

Shae looked at the price tag. "Wow."

Liv held her breath.

Shae shrugged and put the dress back on the rack, looking over her shoulder at Vivian as she did so. "This is a possibility."

Liv felt the air whoosh out of her lungs. Really? A six-hundred-dollar possibility? She made an effort to bite her tongue—for her mother's sake. This was not a matter of Greg or Matt trying to control her. This was Shae. Shae who always got her way.

After two more racks, Shae turned to Liv and Vivian. "Shall we move on to the next place and see what else we can find?"

"Please," Liv said with feeling, earning herself a sharp look from her mother. "I think we should explore all options," she added on a more upbeat note. Vivian's frown relaxed.

At lunch, Shae shook her head as she dipped a tea bag into a cup of hot water. "I think it's pretty obvious that it's impossible to find a decent dress for under three hundred."

"Can you find something you can tolerate?" Liv asked. She'd seen more expensive dresses than she wanted to think about in the past three hours. Each place they went hammered home the point that the wedding industry was all about spending as much as possible to celebrate what? A union that may or may not last? It was a shameful exploitation of a solemn occasion and Shae was plunging in with both feet, practically shouting, "Here I am! Take my money and provide me with an illusion that has nothing to do with reality!"

Her stepsister's green gaze snapped up. "A wedding is not about tolerating. It's about making a beautiful statement to the world."

"And what would that statement be?" Liv asked with a slight frown as she took a sip of her Coke.

"That Reed and I love each other and want everything to be perfect."

"Can't you love each other and make everything perfect on a budget? Because I've got to tell you, paying over two thousand dollars for dresses worn for less than six hours is heinous."

"The cost is split," Vivian quickly interjected.

"Well, to me that makes it even worse."

"How so?" Shae asked, eyes narrowing slightly. Liv recognized the expression well. The few times that she'd given Shae a bit of advice, this had been the exact reaction she'd gotten. The how-the-hell-could-you-know-anything-about-my-world look.

"You're asking your friends to pay a ridiculous amount of money for a dress they'll never wear again."

"It's common practice."

"So is cheating on taxes and not tipping. It doesn't make it right."

Vivian dropped her napkin on the table and jumped to her feet. "I need to powder my nose. Will you excuse *us,* Shae?"

Liv groaned, the heavily emphasized "us" making it clear that she was to accompany her mother to the john. Well, she wasn't going. She smiled at Shae and was about to say that she'd be happy to do some internet research on reasonably priced dresses, when her mother took her by the arm and practically lifted her out of the chair.

In order to avoid being frog-marched into the bathroom, Liv stood and allowed Vivian to steer her across the dining room. The bathroom door was barely shut when Vivian said, "What are you doing? You're ruining the day!"

"I'm pointing out some things for Shae to think about." Other than herself.

"Don't make waves, Liv. I want Shae to have a nice wedding."

"Mom, a person can have a nice wedding without strong-arming her friends into extravagant purchases."

"It's common—" Vivian's mouth snapped shut.

"Practice?"

"Olivia...please?"

Liv finally let out a breath and glanced off to her left, away from her mother, toward the elaborate silk flower arrangement next to the far sink. "Fine. I'll scrape up enough money for a dress I'll wear one time."

"It's tea length."

Liv almost laughed. "Come on, Mom. How many bridesmaids dresses are fit to be worn twice?"

"Why are you being like this?" The desperate note in her mother's voice sent a stab of guilt through her. It was then she noticed the tears welling up in the corners of her mother's eyes. Her mother was no stranger to tears, but she cried only when she was truly upset.

"I—" Liv made a frustrated gesture "I'm sorry, Mom."

"I don't understand this."

"What?"

"Why you're being so stubborn."

Liv leaned back against the counter, thoroughly glad that no one else needed to use the restroom. "I was cooperative all morning."

"You're not cooperating now."

"I am tired of letting myself get pushed into things." And Shae was almost as good at pushing as Greg had been.

"Do you have to make a stand now?"

Liv exhaled. This was not the time to rebel. What purpose would this serve? She could come up with three hundred dollars for a dress. Four hundred if she had to. But she was drawing the line at five.

Vivian opened her mouth, but Liv raised a hand. "I want Shae to have a nice wedding, too. And I'll buy a dress—the dress of Shae's dreams—as long as it's not over four hundred and fifty dollars...without making any more comments."

"Thank you." Vivian took a tissue out of her purse and dabbed at the corners of her red-rimmed eyes. Liv waited while she reapplied lipstick, then led the way out of the restroom, hoping it wasn't evident that Vivian had almost started to cry.

Shae made an effort not to look at Vivian too closely, so Liv figured that it was indeed obvious that she had been a bad daughter and made her mother cry.

The waiter appeared with a tray of desserts, giving Vivian time to fully compose herself and by the time he left, she smiled and said, "Where to next?"

Shae cut a quick look at Liv who blandly met it, determined to make the best of the day and to not upset her mother again. *Go ahead, Shae. Rape my bank account in the name of love and making a statement.*

"The Bon," Shae said with a touch of challenge in her voice.

Liv shrugged and then shouldered her purse. "Sounds good."

Vivian beamed.

BY THE TIME Liv got home, her head was throbbing from smiling and holding in her thoughts for her mother's sake. Shae had her list narrowed down to three dresses, all between two and three hundred dollars, surprisingly, and now she was going to consult with the other bridesmaids before doing what she darned well pleased.

The tractor was parked next to the barn and when Liv went into the house, she noticed that Tim's door was shut.

Was he napping again? Another bout of exhaustion? Or maybe he knew that she planned to have a frank discussion with him and was avoiding it.

Liv dumped her tote bag beside the door and went to change into her riding clothes. She needed some time in the saddle and maybe a beer to help her destress. The ride would come first.

She went into the barn and scooped up the grain, a little surprised that Beckett didn't come ambling into the open part of the barn when he heard the grain. Maybe he was out in the belly-deep grass.

"Hey," Liv called as she opened the man door that lead to the corral and pasture beyond that. Something was wrong. The corral was empty, as was the pasture.

Not one sign of a horse. There was only one gate to the twenty-acre pasture and it was next to the barn, closed and latched.

"That son of a bitch."

CHAPTER SIX

LIV DROPPED THE BUCKET then stormed back to the house. She was almost to the door when she realized that she didn't have Matt's phone number.

No problem. She'd go see him in person.

Except that she didn't know where he lived.

Damn.

She grabbed the phone book out of the drawer and flipped through it. Montoya Land and Ranch...no, she was certain he wasn't living at home. He had some kind of an issue with his father, nothing he spoke of, but something she'd picked up on during their semester of studying.

The only other listed Montoya was Willa.

Muttering a dark curse, Liv slammed the phone book shut, then opened it again and dialed Willa's number. Out of service. Then she dialed the number to the ranch and got an immediate answer—a sweet, feminine voice.

"Mrs. Montoya?" Liv ventured, hoping it was indeed Matt's mom, who'd always liked her.

"Yes?"

"Hi. This is Liv Bailey." How on earth did she

sound so calm and pleasant? She should get an Oscar for this performance. "I'm trying to get hold of Matt."

"Liv!" Mrs. Montoya sounded delighted. "I heard you'd moved back."

"Yes, I'm living with Dad and setting up a practice here."

"That's wonderful. I may have to get Charles in to see you. He's been having some terrific lower back issues. What exactly do we have to do to set up an appointment?"

"All I need is a referral," she said. *And Matt's phone number...*

"Are you affiliated with anyone?"

"I'm renting a space in Andrea Ballentine's building."

"So we should go to Andrea?"

"Any doctor will do. I just need the referral for insurance purposes." Liv twisted the cord in her hand. *Come on. The number. Give me the number.*

"Wonderful. Now, you were saying you need to talk to Matt?"

"I need his advice on a livestock issue."

Mrs. Montoya laughed. "Well, it isn't like he doesn't owe you. Do you want his cell or the house?"

"Both," Liv said sweetly as she twisted the cord even tighter. Oh, yeah. He owed her. And once she hung up, her big debate was whether to involve the sheriff now or later.

Later. Right now she wanted a piece of him. It took another few minutes to finish her conversation with Mrs. Montoya, who had a lot to say, and then she instantly dialed the first number she'd written down—the house.

It rang six times and she was ready to hang up when an adolescent voice said, "Hello?"

Liv hesitated, wondering if she'd dialed wrong, or if Mrs. Montoya had given her the wrong number. "May I please speak to Matt?"

"He's out practicing. I'll take a message if you want."

"No. Thank you." Liv hung up without saying goodbye or asking when the horse thief was expected to finish practice. She dialed the cell and Matt answered on the fifth ring. Apparently she'd caught him midswing.

"This is Liv," she said flatly. "Where's my horse?"

"What are you talking about?"

"Beckett is missing."

"Missing?" There was a brief stunned pause and then Matt asked in a steely voice, "You think I took him?"

"The gate is closed and latched. The horse is gone."

Matt muttered a curse, barely audible, but Liv heard it and couldn't say she liked the tone. "You know what?" Matt said in the same quiet voice. "You've got a hell of a lot of nerve, calling me and accusing me of stealing."

"You said this wasn't over," Liv said.

"And that means I stole your horse."

"You want him and he's gone."

"I don't have him."

"I don't believe you."

"Well, I don't care what you believe. I don't have Beckett and you're wasting time on the phone when you should be out checking your fence lines."

"He didn't get out through the fence."

"Yeah? Well, if your fences look anything like the rest of your place, I bet he did. He could probably step over them they're sagging so low."

Liv put a hand to her head. She hated that he'd just made a viable point. The fences weren't bad close to the house, so she hadn't walked the perimeter before releasing Beckett into the pasture. What did the far fence look like?

"This isn't over," she said.

"You're damned ri—"

Liv hung up before he could finish the sentence. She pulled an elastic out of her pocket and gathered her hair into a low ponytail as she headed out the door. If Beckett had walked over the fence, it was a matter of calling neighbors.

Matt probably has him.

Although he had seemed genuinely outraged at her accusation. But perhaps he was a consummate actor. He certainly had a way of telling people what they wanted to hear so that they would do what he wanted. How many times had she blushed when he'd given her a charming offhand compliment as they had studied together?

Matt and Shae. Definitely a pair. At least Shae had

always been honest with her, through both words and actions.

Liv let herself into the pasture through the gate, then started walking the fence line, noting that after she turned the corner and started north that the wire was loose—but it didn't sag and certainly not enough for a horse to step over. She continued walking, keeping a hand on the smooth top wire as she went, trying not to think about what she was going to do if the fence was intact.

Call neighbors. Put up notices. Ask the sheriff to check Matt's place. As if he'd be stupid enough to keep the horse there. All right, check his parents' ranch.

She was approaching the second corner-post set when she saw the rooster tail of dust in her driveway. Tim was home. She pulled out her cell to call him, tell him what was up, when she saw the glint of silver as the truck pulled to a stop.

Matt. Great.

She put her head down and kept walking, which was difficult, since the back fence line did not border a field, but instead ran along an unfarmable draw. Willows and tall grass had grown up along the stretch. She'd only made a few yards when Matt let himself through the gate and headed out across the field toward her, his strides long and purposeful for a guy with a knee injury.

Liv sucked in a breath, telling herself that there was no need for her heart to be hammering. But it didn't help. From the way Matt was stalking across the pasture toward her she had a strong feeling that he was not the guy who'd stolen her horse.

MATT COULDN'T REMEMBER the last time he'd been so totally pissed, which was something considering the turns his life had taken lately. What was up with this woman?

They'd studied together for half a year, intense sessions three times a week, and he'd thought he'd known her—or what there was to know. Liv had been a shy girl who made academics the focus of her life. Well, she wasn't so shy anymore and had no qualms about making accusations with a vehemence that surprised him.

He and Liv were going to have a talk, he was going to find out what the hell was going on and they were going to find Beckett.

Liv tilted her chin up slightly as he approached, a stubborn expression on her face. Or maybe it was defensive. Whatever, it wasn't welcoming.

"How'd you get here so fast?" she asked, firing the first shot.

"I only live two miles away. Did you find where he got out?"

"No. The fence seems fairly tight and I'm not yet convinced that he *got out*." She gave a small challenging jerk of her chin with the last words, but he could see doubt in her eyes. Maybe Liv was starting to rethink her accusation. Good.

Matt walked past her to the fence and took hold of the top wire, lifting it a good three inches. "Yeah. Tight."

"Too tight to walk over," she muttered.

He shook his head and started along the fence line, not trusting himself to say anything else. It took a few seconds, but he heard Liv fall into step behind him. If there wasn't a hole in the fence—

He barely started the thought when Liv's cell phone rang. He stopped and turned toward her when she answered it.

"Hello," she said without looking at the number, and then she squeezed her eyes shut as if in pain. "This is kind of a bad time—" Another grimace. "Yes, the lavender was nice…the green, too…no, I don't mind the extra fifty bucks. Shae—" She fell silent and listened. "Can I call you back? Beckett's gone and I'm—" she met Matt's eyes before continuing "—dealing with it. Sure. As soon as I know something. Thanks."

She'd barely pocketed the phone when it rang again, only this time she did look at the caller's number. Her eyes widened slightly as she put the phone to her ear. "Dad, hi."

Her tight expression began to change as she listened to her father. A hand went up to her forehead as she studied the ground. "Really?" Once again her eyes, very blue and very conflicted, came up to meet his, held briefly, then dropped again. "No. I'm home now."

"Find your horse?" Matt asked softly. Liv turned

her head away and put a finger in her ear so that she heard only her father.

"He's all right? No wire cuts?" The sun moved out from behind a cloud as she spoke, warming Matt's back and making Liv's reddish-brown hair dance with glints of gold in a rather spectacular way. He didn't remember her hair being that particular color, but they'd usually been inside, under flat incandescent light. "Good. I'll see you soon," she said.

Liv's shoulders dropped as she pocketed the phone. She gave her head a small shake, then resolutely looked up at Matt. "I owe you an apology."

Matt didn't respond after she stated the obvious and color started to rise in her cheeks. Ah, the curse of pale skin.

"Beckett got out and went over to the Raynor place. They called, and Dad went to get him." One corner of her mouth tightened briefly. "He thought I might get home and find him and Becket gone and worry, so..." She held up the phone.

"Too bad he didn't call sooner."

"I said I was sorry."

"Yeah." Matt looked around the field. "That makes it all better. I guess I'm lucky you didn't call the sheriff on me." His eyes narrowed. "You didn't, did you?"

"No." Liv shifted her weight, and he couldn't help but notice that she looked pretty damned good in her worn-out jeans. Again, he couldn't remember her ever wearing anything like that when she'd tutored him, but...maybe he didn't remember much about

Liv, except that she'd been kind of sweet and smart. And handy.

"But you were going to?" he asked, thinking that was all he needed to make his life complete.

"The thought had crossed my mind," she said coldly.

"You honestly thought I'd come here and steal Beckett."

"You said this wasn't over," Liv said. "And I happen to know that you're not above doing what you have to in order to get your way."

"What does that mean?"

Liv shrugged but did not elaborate.

"What did I ever do to you to earn such a low opinion? I can't think of one freaking thing."

Again the color rose in her cheeks, but her mouth was clamped so tightly shut that her lips were starting to turn white. Matt waited a couple seconds, and when she remained silent, he said, "I'd better go."

He needed to get out of there before he said something he regretted. He hadn't given up on getting Beckett back and he was so damned close to burning this bridge...

He started across the field, leaving Liv standing next to the fence. There wasn't one single thing he understood about what had just taken place between them.

LIV CONTINUED TO WALK along the fence as Matt strode toward where he'd parked close to the barn. She refused to let herself watch him go although each step he took made her feel that much better. By the time she found the low part in the fence, where Beckett had most likely escaped, Matt was in his truck and on his way down the driveway.

Okay. Maybe she'd jumped the gun. She wanted to blame stress from a long day with Shae and her mom, but really there was no excuse for flat out accusing Matt without getting more facts. But what was she supposed to think?

Tomorrow she'd tighten the fence with the small tractor while Tim was out in the field doing men's work, and tonight Beckett could spend the night in his stall so he didn't wander off in search of equine company again. Horses were herd animals and Beckett was all alone. Maybe she'd get him a goat for company.

As she started to walk the last stretch of not-too-bad fence leading back to the barn, her father's truck and trailer pulled into the driveway. Long day for him and it was her fault. She should have checked the fence before she released the horse, but never in her life had she seen any fence on the property loose enough to walk over. Tim was fanatical about upkeep.

Was.

Liv's stomach knotted as it always did when she wondered about just what was going on with her father. How long had he been sick and was he ever going to admit he wasn't getting better?

Maybe when pigs started flying.

That point was driven home when he got out of the truck and started to the back of the trailer to open the door. Not knowing that Liv was there, he winced as he opened the latch, then stopped and stood for a moment with his hand pressed against his side.

That was the last straw. Liv banged open the gate and he instantly went back to unloading the horse.

Liv held back the "Dad, are you all right?" already knowing how he would answer—untruthfully—and instead said, "I can't believe he left the property."

She held the wide trailer door open as Tim went inside to get Beckett. He led the big sorrel out of the trailer, wincing again as he made the step down onto the gravel, but not slowing his pace. Liv walked beside Beckett, stroking a hand over his neck as he moved.

"Yeah. Mrs. Raynor wasn't exactly happy to see him since he tromped through her rose garden on his way to her yearling pen."

"I was just thinking I should get him something for company."

"Can you afford another horse?"

I'm living rent-free, so yes.... "I was thinking along the lines of a goat."

Tim's face contorted. "I hate goats. Think of something else."

"Why do you hate goats? They're small and cheap to feed."

"They eat everything in sight and they tend to stand on top of the vehicles. Scratch the paint."

"Maybe we could keep it penned."

"Maybe you could think of something else."

"All right. But for right now, we need to stretch the fence. It's so low along the east side that Beckett walked over it." Just as Matt had said he'd done, damn him.

Tim nodded without looking at her. "I'll get on that."

"I'll help you, Dad."

He opened his mouth, then closed it again. "Right now would you mind getting me a plate of leftovers? I was about to eat when I got the call."

"All right. I'm going to keep Beckett in the barn until we fix the fence."

A year ago, Tim would have crossed the field and worked up a temporary fix so that the horse didn't have to be contained in a smallish stall, but tonight he simply said, "Good idea."

Fifteen minutes later she put a hot plate of food in front of her father, then sat at the table with him.

"Nothing for you?"

"I grabbed a bite on the drive home." Even if she hadn't, she wouldn't have felt like eating after the encounter with Matt. Why was it so damned upsetting to be in the wrong?

Maybe what was so damned upsetting was that Matt was in the right…and she'd set up the situation.

"How's your mother?"

Tim always asked, and Liv answered automatically. "In a tizzy over the wedding."

"I can imagine. She was forever worried about what people would think." He shoveled a forkful of spaghetti into his mouth.

"How did you two ever get together?" It was a rhetorical question, but Tim surprised her.

"By lying to ourselves."

"Yeah?" she asked slowly. Both he and Vivian were matter-of-fact about the failure of their marriage, something Liv had once marveled at, until it occurred to her that her mother may not have been as accepting if she hadn't married David so rapidly. But Tim had never talked about it before.

"What can I say?" he asked. "Dave is better for her than I ever was." He pushed the plate away, then met his daughter's eyes and said, "Don't get a goat."

Liv laughed at the sudden change of topic, but she knew it was brought on by the fact that Tim had almost given her some insight into his relationship with her mother. She picked up his plate and carried it to the sink. "I won't get a goat."

"You don't know how much I appreciate that." Tim got up slowly, hanging on to the back of the chair for longer than he should have, then started for the living room.

"But I am fixing the fence tomorrow."

She stopped at the doorway and waited for her father, who stood by his recliner, to answer.

"I can help you when I come in for lunch."

"I'll be done by then. My horse is using the pasture, I can fix the fence."

"You shouldn't have to do that."

Liv's eyebrows shot up. "We worked on the fence all the time when I stayed with you." It was a spring ritual to check and tighten fence, replace the corner braces, tighten the gates.

"Taking care of this place is my job. If you want to help that's one thing—"

"I am helping, Dad. I'm fixing the fence tomorrow."

MATT WALKED OUT of the Bozeman physical therapist's office in a much worse mood than when he'd gone in, but his determination to come back from his injury hadn't diminished one iota. He'd been doing his exercises and his range of movement was increasing, while the amount of pain he endured during the half-hour-long sessions was decreasing, so the obvious conclusion was that he was on the mend. And the therapist agreed with him, right up until Matt said he was about to start riding again.

That was when the lecture about lateral motion and collapsing knees began and when Matt had begun to tune out. He'd forced himself to listen under the time-honored premise of knowing your enemy—or in this case, your infirmity—however he was not taking the gloomy prognosis as gospel. People had come back from worse injuries than his.

Pessimistic bastard...

Matt wasn't going to accept the therapist's blithe opinion that his career was over, because it wasn't.

He'd step up his exercise program, continue eating protein, take his supplements, work at building the muscles around the joints and only wear the brace for extra support when he was roping or riding.

Matt yanked open the truck door and got inside, banging his knee on the steering wheel and letting out a curse.

Shit. Was nothing going right today?

He hadn't heard from Willa, even though Craig's week was officially up as of yesterday, so it looked like he was going to have his roommate for an indeterminate amount of time. Not that he minded, but he wanted Willa to do him the courtesy of calling—not for his sake, but for Craig's.

Craig didn't seem all that put out by the deadline coming and going, but Matt knew all too well how kids could harbor resentment and not show it. He'd spent years bearing one hell of a grudge and as far as he knew, had hidden it like a champ.

Matt stopped at Safeway to pick up a prescription the Bozeman doctor had phoned in after his visit there, only to find that due to some glitch the order hadn't been filled. The excellent day continued. As he waited, reading the labels on the vitamin display and wondering if there were anything else he could be taking to build up his knee, he heard his name. Turning, he saw Pete Barnes walking toward him.

"I heard you were back. How's it going?" Pete glanced down at Matt's knee. "Making progress?"

"Some," Matt said. "You know how it is. Slow

going at first." Pete knew. Matt had seen him recover from almost the same injury in high school and he was still roping. Not professionally, but he burned up the local circuit and earned some decent money.

"Hey," Pete said, "I saw your horse at the arena two nights ago. That big sorrel."

"Was he wandering loose?" Matt asked.

"What? No. Liv was riding him with Susie's drill team. He was having a hell of a time keeping up with them. For some reason she kept turning him in the wrong direction."

Matt felt his jaw start to drop. His horse in a drill team.

The pharmacist's assistant dropped a bottle into a bag and raised it so that Matt could see that his order was ready. Matt pulled his wallet out of his back pocket before looking over his shoulder to ask Pete, "How often does the drill team practice?"

Pete shrugged. "A lot. Susie and I are trailing down together tonight. I'm roping and she's riding in the warm-up arena."

"Yeah? What time?"

"Seven."

"Thanks."

"Hey, uh…" Pete nodded at the pharmacy bag. "How do you like Dr. Fletcher?"

Matt frowned, wondering if Pete was looking for a referral. "He's okay."

"I thought he was too cautious, myself." Pete

stepped up to the counter and handed the assistant his prescription slip.

"Cautious how?" Matt asked.

Pete gave a soft snort. "Cautious like once you injure a knee, you're done for life." He gave his head a slow shake. "That isn't so."

"You seem to be walking pretty good," Matt said.

"Yeah. No thanks to Fletcher."

Matt was about to ask who he was seeing when Pete gave a slight shake of his head. "I'll catch up with you later."

"Yeah. Sure. Later."

As soon as he got into the truck, Matt tore open the bag, popped one of the anti-inflammatory pills into his mouth and washed it down with cold coffee. The best roping horse he'd ever owned on a drill team. He had to get him back.

He reached down for the ignition. Well, at least he now had a way to see Beckett, because Liv sure as hell wasn't going to let him lay eyes on him at her place. And it still fried him that she'd assumed he'd stolen Beckett—although *steal* wasn't quite the right word for getting back something that already belonged to you. What kind of a guy did Liv think he was?

The kind that wasn't above doing what he had to in order to get his way, according to Liv.

Whatever the hell that meant.

Matt put the truck into gear and carefully backed out of the parking place, ignoring his instinct to tear out of the lot.

THE HOUSE WAS SPOTLESS, Craig was on the sofa, reading as usual. He looked up when Matt came in and hung his hat on the hooks.

"Mom called. She gave me a number for you to call her tonight."

"Great."

Craig watched him carefully while pretending not to. Matt made an effort to keep his expression bland, unconcerned. The kid may act as if this situation were totally normal to him, but the still-packed suitcase told Matt otherwise. He was ready to leave, to put down some roots somewhere, have a stable life.

"I'm going down to the roping tonight. Want to come?"

"Actually, there's a movie I want to watch."

Matt didn't ask twice, although he did wonder how Craig stayed so thin when the kid never got off the sofa except for when he was cleaning. He must really work up a sweat with the vacuum.

He wasn't going to spend that much time down at the arena. Just get a look at Beckett under the guise of watching the roping. He needed to see his horse.

CHAPTER SEVEN

MOST OF LIV'S teammates were in the arena warming up when she pulled into the parking lot twenty minutes late. The small tractor had broken down before she'd gotten it out of the barn and she and Tim had lost track of the time as he tinkered with the engine and she'd handed him tools—just like old times. She didn't know if she'd been lost in some nostalgic time warp or what, but it'd felt good to be communicating with her father again, even if it was only over a tractor, and hoped that it might lead to discussing more important stuff—like his health.

When she pulled her trailer up to the end spot, she was relieved to see that Susie and Margo were still tacking up their horses. She'd be late, but not that far behind the others.

Liv jumped out of the truck and ran back to the trailer, unlatched the door and pulled it open. Beckett, who hadn't been tied, obligingly stepped out. She caught the lead rope draped over his back as he walked by and then tied him to the trailer next to the tack compartment.

"Hey, Liv," Susie said as she passed.

"Hi," Liv replied as she ran a quick brush over

Beckett's back to get the road dust off. "Will you tell Linda I'll be there in a few?" *Late, late, late.*

"Will do," Susie called over her shoulder.

Liv tossed the brush into the grooming bucket and yanked out her pad and saddle. She carefully settled the pad in place and then turned to pick up the saddle. A shadow fell over her, startling her, and she looked over her shoulder just in time to see Matt yank the saddle pad off Beckett's back.

"What the hell happened to him?" he asked.

Liv slowly straightened back up, the saddle still lying at her feet, trying to make sense of what was happening as a very angry Matt Montoya ran his hand over the large white spots where the saddle sores had healed.

"How the hell did you manage to rub him this raw?" His gaze was deadly as it settled on her. "Didn't you notice that the saddle didn't fit?" He stepped closer. "How many times did you ride him with that saddle?"

"Never."

"Bullshit." He turned back to the horse, ran a hand down Beckett's legs as if checking for injury, then smoothed a hand over his neck and left it there. "Those spots didn't just appear."

"No. They healed after I got him," Liv said coldly. "They had maggots in them."

Matt's eyes darkened. "There's no way you got him in this condition."

"Well, I did." She folded her arms as she began

to get an idea of what was happening here. "And since Trena was afraid of horses, as far as I can tell, there's only one person who could have put those sores there."

If anything, Matt looked even more outraged. Oh, he was good. "You think *I* put them there?" he demanded.

"Who else?" Liv took a step forward, brought herself closer to him, determined to show him that she would not allow herself to be intimidated any more than she would allow herself to be charmed. She didn't know what his game was, but she wasn't going to let him get away with it. If he thought for one moment that he could get some leverage in this situation by accusing *her* of animal abuse...well, it wasn't going to work. "It had to be you." She stabbed a finger at him. "Don't try to do this, Matt."

"Try to what?"

"Accuse me of abuse so that you can get the horse back. There are people in Billings who saw Beckett when I first got him. My vet treated the sores. There are records. Dated records."

"What *kind* of a guy do you think I am?" Matt took a step away from Beckett—toward her—and without realizing what she was doing, Liv took a step back. She instantly stopped and drew herself up. She would not retreat, even if he were so close that she could practically feel the heat of his body. "I don't abuse animals and I'm not going to use underhanded tactics to get one back. Even one that should still be mine."

Liv simply raised her chin. "If you don't abuse animals, then explain those sores. And why did Beckett refuse to take a bit when I first got him? Why was he so head shy that it took me over a month to get to where I could rub his ears?"

Again the stunned and angry expression. "Why don't you tell me?"

"Because you might be so intent on winning that you don't realize the damage you're doing to the tools you use to win."

Cold anger froze his expression and Liv once again felt like taking a step back. Then Matt pulled his gaze away from Liv, focused on Beckett, his jawline pulled taut. He didn't seem to notice when Margo rode by, but Liv noticed. The woman had probably heard everything. Damn.

Finally, Matt shifted his attention back to her. He was angry. Confused...or trying to look that way. She wasn't going to let him work her again.

"You know me, Liv. How the hell could you think I could do something like that to a horse?"

"I don't know you, Matt."

The expression of confusion intensified. "We spent months together."

"Yeah, we did. But I don't know you." She dropped her arms to her sides, facing him squarely. "I only know what it's like to be used by you."

For a moment Matt simply stared at Liv. Just when he thought things couldn't get any stranger, she came up with this.

"Are you talking about studying together?" Her color crept up, telling him that yes, that was exactly what she was talking about. "I used you? I asked if you'd help. You agreed. I didn't twist your arm." In fact, he'd thought she'd kind of enjoyed tutoring him despite the fact that she barely said two words to him that weren't related to calculus—not unless he asked her a direct question. She'd practically been paralyzed by shyness until she got into the heat of an explanation.

Those days were obviously long gone.

"You really don't know?" she asked flatly.

"Would I be asking if I did?"

She glanced over at the riders gathering in the center of the arena without her, then back at him. "I stupidly thought that we were becoming…friends."

"We were friends." Kind of.

"More than friends," she said abruptly.

For a moment he simply stared at her. *More than friends. Like…*

"You flirted with me," she said before pressing her lips tightly together as if to keep more words from coming out.

"I flirted with everyone."

"How was I supposed to know that? I didn't get to hang in your circle. All I knew was that you joked with me, teased me and…sometimes you touched my shoulder or my hand and…yes, it was totally ridiculous, looking back, but I thought that once we were done studying together that maybe we could go out or something." Her voice became almost deadly as she said, "I was waiting for your call."

"I—"

"And you did call. But it wasn't me."

Shae. He'd called Shae and asked her out. They'd dated for…what? Maybe two or three months before she'd dumped his ass.

What was he supposed to say now?

Apparently nothing, because Liv wasn't done.

"That was a long time ago, and trust me, I'm well over the *disappointment*—" sarcasm dripped from the word "—however, it gave me vital insight into the way you work."

"I wasn't working you."

"You were getting what you wanted. When you were done, you just walked away. Didn't even bother to talk to me in the halls at school. Did you think I was tutoring you for purely academic reasons?"

"Yes. I thought you just liked studying."

"You're an idiot," she said, picking up Beckett's lead rope and then snatching back the saddle pad that Matt still held. She settled it on the horse's back. Matt put his hand over hers, stopping the motion, and she jerked it away, the pad slipping off again. He bent to pick it up, shook the dust off, but he didn't hand it back. "I didn't use you and I didn't abuse Beckett. I've never abused an animal in my life."

Liv's blue eyes narrowed. "Well, something happened to him, and there's no way Trena did it. She wouldn't even go out into the corral to catch him for me when I came to look at him the first time. *I* had to catch him."

Matt had to agree that didn't make sense—if it were true. What was going on here? A regular injury he could understand, but injuries due to use?

Liv held out her hand for the saddle pad, a challenge in her eyes. Matt let go and she once again settled it on Beckett's back and then turned to lift the saddle and settle it into place. She pointedly ignored him as she busied herself with cinches and the breast collar, checking for fit and tightness with quick automatic movements. When she bridled the horse, she held the bit and waited for him to take it, talking in a low voice as if Matt weren't there. He thought he heard the word *bastard.*

What he'd just witnessed was habit; the actions of a person who knew how to handle a horse. But if Liv had not abused Beckett, that left him with a mystery to solve.

"I want to see those vet records." It was a stab in the dark, a way to once and for all eliminate Liv as a suspect.

Liv's eyebrows rose disdainfully. "I don't have to prove anything to you," she said. "I'm late." She swung easily up into the saddle—a saddle that was too small to have made the marks on Beckett's back. "Stay away from me, Matt."

She urged Beckett forward, riding past him, her jaw set. Matt stepped back, then strode toward the parking lot, all thought of catching up with Pete and asking about his knee treatment long gone. He was going to find out what had happened to his horse, ask some questions about what Liv had seen at Trena's. And if Willa ever called, he had questions for her, too.

ONCE PRACTICE STARTED, Liv had no choice but to pay attention to her riding—it was either that or possibly be smashed by an oncoming horse—but she couldn't push Matt's accusations out of her mind. She'd abused the horse. Right.

Fortunately, Beckett was learning the routine and anticipating moves, so Liv got away with being less than totally focused and the practice went far more smoothly than it should have, considering.

"Is everything all right?" Andie asked in a low voice during a brief break between runs.

"Fine," Liv lied. Just as fine as things could be. Yeah.

"I thought I saw Matt over by your trailer."

Linda called for attention, so Liv merely said, "No biggie."

Andie frowned as she turned her horse to get into position, and Liv realized that she wasn't ready to discuss her encounter with Matt. Not yet—not until she'd had a chance to work through it. There were so many questions. *Who* had abused the horse? Had she been wrong about Matt or was he a very, very good actor? And why, why oh, why, had she felt compelled to tell him about the crush?

As soon as practice ended, Liv rode back to her

trailer at a trot, dismounted and started untacking the horse. She'd barely flipped the stirrup up over the seat of the saddle when she heard someone walking along the other side of her trailer. Great.

She turned, cinch strap in hand, ready to tell Andie that they'd talk tomorrow, but it was Margo, leading her horse by the reins.

"I want to apologize for eavesdropping earlier," the older woman said matter-of-factly. "It wasn't my intention."

"I don't see how you could have helped but hear us," Liv said as she began undoing the cinch, grateful Margo hadn't also heard the confession of her high school crush. Although, come to think of it, high school crushes were nothing to be embarrassed about. Being accused of abusing a horse? Now, *that* was embarrassing.

"I want you to know that I don't for one minute believe that a daughter of Tim Bailey would ever mistreat an animal."

Liv momentarily stopped pulling the latigo out of the cinch ring. "You know my dad?"

"We graduated high school together."

Something in the way she said it told Liv that they were more than classmates, that they may also have been friends, so she asked, "Have you seen him lately?"

"I just moved back to Dillon a few months ago." A small ironic smile formed on her lips. "And your dad tends to keep to himself."

"Definitely not a social butterfly," Liv agreed, pulling the heavy saddle off Beckett's damp back. The white hair of the healed sores stood out against the sweat-slicked dark hair. Damn. If Matt wasn't responsible...

Margo laughed. "Understatement of the year."

Liv stopped, still holding the saddle. Margo really did know her father. Curiosity piqued, Liv said, "You know, if you ever wanted to stop by and say hello, Dad would probably enjoy catching up."

An odd look crossed Margo's face. "I'm not much for popping in to visit people." She folded the reins she held into an accordion before saying, "Although I wouldn't mind talking to him at some time."

There was a note in her voice that Liv didn't quite understand, making her wonder if perhaps she shouldn't have been so hasty with her invitation. Perhaps Tim didn't like Margo. Or vice versa. "Well, maybe we can work something out," she said noncommittally.

Margo laughed softly. "Yes. Maybe." Her horse nudged her shoulder and she reached up to run a hand over his nose. "I need to get going. I just wanted to make sure you weren't embarrassed at me overhearing your conversation and tell you that it will go no further than me."

"Thanks," Liv said.

"And...well...just so you know, Ronnie and Becca and I meet down here in the morning to practice the drills at a slower speed."

"You do?"

"Sometimes we just practice ground work and equitation, but most of the time we do the drills. If you're interested, the next time we meet is this coming Saturday at eight. Just show up. It's a lot more... relaxed."

"Thanks. I might do that."

Margo smiled and disappeared back around the trailer just as Andie rode up.

"So, no problem with Matt?" Andie said.

"Nothing I can't handle," Liv replied as she pulled the saddle off Beckett's sweaty back. "Just...horse stuff."

"All right..." Andie did not sound convinced, but she didn't push, either. "Ready for your first day of work?"

"Totally," Liv said. She was looking forward to something to think about besides Tim, Matt and Beckett. She'd tell Andie about Matt's accusation in a day or two, but right now she wanted time to think and work through a few issues, such as who was lying about Beckett. Trena? Or Matt?

MATT DROVE HOME on autopilot, his mind more focused on his horse than the road. One mystery had been solved and another more disturbing mystery had taken its place.

What the hell had happened to Beckett since the last time he'd seen him? His gut kept twisting in knots as he thought about his horse being hurt.

It was now obvious why Liv was treating him like crap; she thought he was responsible—that he'd used the horse to the point of abuse and then dear Trena had taken advantage of his absence to sell Beckett in order to save him.

A grim smile formed on his lips. Oh, yeah. Trena was truly a champion of animals, which was why Beckett was all scarred up.

But his ex hadn't caused Beckett's injuries. He was positively certain of that, because she was nervous around any animal larger than a cat. The few times he'd tried to get her to ride had been disastrous. She'd ridden to please him, clinging to the saddle horn and smiling bravely. He'd thought she'd eventually relax, as most people do, but Trena was truly uncomfortable on horseback.

Therefore, the only logical conclusion he could come up with was that she'd allowed someone else access to Beckett. And he had a very strong feeling that the someone was a he, not a she.

So who had Trena loaned Beckett to? And where had the guy ridden Matt's horse to the point that he'd caused serious sores without any of the locals seeing him?

Easy answer. Not here.

Beckett had pulled a tendon at the very beginning of the Texas circuit and he'd brought him home to heal. It should have been a matter of weeks, but Matt hadn't bothered driving the thousand miles back home again to pick up the horse. He was doing okay in Texas on Ready, his other horse. He figured he'd give Beckett a good rest, then start using him again on the Montana circuit, which started in July.

Almost four months passed before he'd returned home again—earlier than intended thanks to Willa's tip—to find Trena and Beckett long gone. She'd remained in the area until just before he'd returned. But had Beckett? That was the question.

The answer was almost certainly no.

The only way he knew to get the answers he wanted was to hunt Trena down and demand them. But even if he did that, would the answers be truthful?

Knowing what had happened would allow him to beat the shit out of whoever had hurt his horse, but it wouldn't solve anything and it wouldn't erase the pain Beckett had suffered.

Matt slowed as he approached the Y where the pavement turned to gravel. In the distance he could see the lights of the Bailey Ranch, two miles down the right fork. Did Tim also think he was an asshole animal abuser? Had Liv told other people that he'd hurt his horse?

No. It would have gotten back to him, but then again...*would* people tell him? Or just assume he had a dark secret and not call him on it?

Matt's jaw tightened as he realized just how possible that might be.

How in the hell could Liv have ever believed that he'd injure his best rodeo horse? And apparently *still* believed it, even after he told her he had nothing to do with Beckett's injuries. Okay, so maybe he'd missed that she'd had a crush on him in high school—which was understandable, since she'd never shown a sign of having any feelings that way—but that didn't make him a horse abuser.

Shit.

Five minutes later, he parked the truck in its usual spot by the barn and sat for a moment. It was a night where he would have preferred to be alone, primarily so that he didn't have to make an effort to be civil when he was feeling anything but. But he wasn't alone, so he needed to suck it up, go inside, be friendly.

"Hey," Craig called from where he was sitting at the kitchen table typing on his laptop when Matt walked in the door.

"Hey," Matt said, hanging his hat and then pushing his fingers through his hair. He needed a haircut. "Something wrong with the sofa?"

"What?" Craig's eyebrows went up behind his glasses, then he caught on. "Ha. Funny one." He went back to his typing.

Matt smiled a little in spite of himself and debated. Disappear into his room and stew, or have a beer and pretend not to stew here in the kitchen? He hated being cooped up in his room.

"What are you doing?"

"Researching. Getting a feel for your profession."

"You're researching calf roping?"

"*Tie-down* roping. The name of the event has changed." Craig looked over his glasses. "You knew that, right?"

"I'm aware," Matt said, wondering again how Willa had ever produced a kid like this.

"I was just wondering how someone can make money roping a calf when my mom can't make ends meet doing hair and training horses." Craig pushed his glasses up as he stared at the screen. "Criminal," he said. "I think my mom needs to brush up on her roping skills."

"It's not all it's cracked up to be." And not many people made enough money at it to live. Most, like him, had additional income or a spouse with a decent job.

"Seems like you've made some bucks," Craig said.

"You're researching me?"

"Oh, yeah." Craig leaned back so Matt could see the screen with his smiling face on it. "You have a fan club."

"Unofficial," Matt muttered. "It's, like, three people."

"Not according to this," Craig said, pointing to the member box. "Looks like a good part of them are women." Craig looped an arm over the back of the chair. "So this roping gig is a good way to meet chicks."

Matt fought the urge to reach out and turn off the computer.

Craig started typing again. "It looks like your knee is going to hold you back. There's some question as to whether you'll even compete."

"I'll compete." Matt's decision was made. Beer. He opened it behind the fridge door and poured it into an opaque glass, not wanting to set a bad example.

"On the Montana circuit?" Craig asked without looking at him. "Because according to this article in the *Montana Standard*, you won't make it."

"They don't know jack."

"Read what this Madison guy says about you."

Matt set down the glass with a clunk and crossed the small kitchen to read over Craig's shoulder, trying not to focus too closely on his half brother's smirking face. He knew why Ryan trash-talked him—it was, in fact, his own fault—but that didn't make it any easier to take.

After he'd discovered his father's infidelity, he'd wanted to rage and hammer on the old man, but couldn't because of his mother. So he'd drawn into himself and took out his frustrations the only way he could—by competing with his brother and beating him as often as possible. He was the better son and he made no secret of his disdain for Ryan Madison. A little over a year after Matt had made his gut-wrenching discovery, Ryan had cornered him at a rodeo and asked what the hell the deal was—why Matt seemed to hate him so much.

Matt couldn't recall exactly what he'd said, but he'd gauged it to hurt as much as possible. He'd been successful, too, because a split second later, Ryan had punched him square in the jaw. A couple of their roping buddies had seen the action and rushed in to drag them apart before their coaches saw them fighting and, after that, it was game on. Ryan became an ever fiercer competitor and he also lost no opportunity to get a dig in at Matt. Usually subtle, something that those who were familiar with their rivalry would understand, never anything that made Ryan look like a jerk, more's the pity. It was easier to contend with a jerk.

In this particular article Ryan expressed his sincere concern for Matt—that it didn't seem fair to compete against Montoya when he was less than one hundred percent—especially after him not making it to the finals last year.

"How are you going to feel when I beat you and I'm not one hundred percent?" Matt muttered under his breath. He leaned closer to see the bottom part of the page, then barely suppressed a curse when he read the quote toward the end of the article, an answer to a question about opposing philosophies. "Matt's a champion," Ryan was quoted as saying, "but he's hard on himself, hard on his horses. My approach is more laid-back. I think that's why I'm in better shape physically."

Hard on his horses?

How far had Liv's story spread?

Matt straightened up and automatically reached for the beer.

It may not have spread at all. Ryan may have been making a point. But still… It behooved him to find out just what Liv had been saying and, if she'd done damage to his reputation, then she was damned well going to figure out some way to undo it.

And he had to figure out the best way to approach this matter, since the Liv he'd once known was not the Liv he was dealing with now.

"SEE YOU TOMORROW," Etta Sinclair, the clinic receptionist and one of Liv's former classmates, called as Liv let herself out the side door, tote bag full of files in one hand and her keys in the other.

"See you," Liv called back as the door shut behind her. It'd been a long, trying day, as first days often were. She'd worked with seven patients, had follow up appointments for all of them later that week and consulted with three more. Andie had already referred her two more cases that day that she would see tomorrow.

She was almost to her car, ready to go home and saddle up Beckett for a short mind-clearing ride before cooking dinner, when someone called her name from behind.

She turned to find Matt walking toward her from his truck, parked in the side lot.

What now? Was he going to accuse her of abuse again? Make another offer for the horse? Just generally make her crazy?

Did he not know better than to tangle with a woman

after a very long first day of work? She waited where she stood, although she would have preferred to get into her car and leave.

"Liv," he said after he'd stopped a few feet away, but not so far away that she couldn't see the color of his eyes. If anything, remembering how mesmerizing she used to find them during their study sessions strengthened her.

"Matt." And then she waited for whatever was coming next.

"I owe you an apology."

Not what she'd been expecting. Not even close. Liv took care not to let her surprise show. Or her suspicion. Instead, she simply raised her eyebrows. An apology. Hmm.

"And you owe *me* one."

"Excuse me?" she said, her eyebrows rising even higher. "Why do I owe you an apology?"

"For telling people I abused a horse." Liv clicked the keys to unlock her car door. She didn't need this. "Who'd you tell?" Matt asked.

"Andie and my father."

"And who did Andie tell?"

"I have no idea who Andie told. Maybe you should be more concerned about who Trena told. She's the one who had it in for you."

Which made her wonder what kind of guy Matt was to live with. The Trena she'd bought the horse from was not the Trena she'd been in awe of in high school. The woman was still beautiful, maybe even more beautiful, but she'd also been withdrawn and sullen. Not a woman happy in her marriage.

And the reason for that was standing right there in front of her, looking sexy as hell. Shae had once said that Matt wore sexy the way other guys wore clothes and Liv hated that she had to agree with that assessment. What a waste.

"I don't know where Trena is, but I know where you are."

"I didn't try to destroy your reputation, Matt. I have no reason to do that. I bought a horse that had obviously been used roughly. Tell me who you would have thought was responsible, given the circumstances."

She could see from the way he shifted his weight that he not only understood her point, but he'd also probably come to the same conclusion himself.

"Will you do me the courtesy of telling Andie and your father that you were wrong?"

Liv almost said that she didn't know that she was wrong, but something in his expression stopped her.

"I don't know who Trena lent Beckett to," he said seriously, "but she lent him to someone who used him hard, then she sold him to get rid of the evidence before I got home."

Liv listened to excuses all day long. And lies. People pretending that they'd done their exercises when she knew that they hadn't. She was pretty good at reading the signs...and she didn't read anything in Matt's face except harsh sincerity. And it made her feel uncomfortable. As if she'd done something wrong.

"Maybe that's so," she finally said. "I have no way of knowing."

"I'm telling you I didn't abuse the horse…and back in high school I didn't mean to behave in a way that made you feel like you'd been used."

The unexpected shift in topic brought heat to her cheeks, which irritated her.

"That's what you're sorry for?" She'd forgotten he'd started out saying that he owed her an apology.

"It's a crime I actually did commit."

"Not exactly a crime," Liv said. She adjusted her shoulder bag, keeping a hand on the strap. "Just unrealistic expectations on my part."

He didn't deny it, which she hated to say, stung a little. Instead, he looked her up and down with half-hooded eyes, eyes that made her wonder just how good he was in bed. No one should have this much sex appeal.

"I need to go, Matt."

"I am sorry."

"Yeah." Liv swallowed. "Me, too—but I'm not ready to apologize about the horse thing, because I still don't know what happened there."

"What do I have to do to convince you?" he asked.

"Nothing, Matt. Nothing at all. Just leave me and Beckett alone and I'll tell Andie and my dad that you didn't hurt the horse." She turned and started walking to her car. "I'll tell them to spread the news," she muttered.

Right now, it didn't matter if he hurt the horse because he was never getting him back.

CHAPTER EIGHT

LIV WENT STRAIGHT to the barn when she got home. Beckett often spent the afternoons in his stall, avoiding the heat, before venturing out to the pasture again in the early evening. The fence still wasn't fixed properly, but thankfully he hadn't shown any inclination to wander to the neighbors' again. Liv had done what she could after the tractor broke down and told Tim she was satisfied with the job, even though she wasn't. There was still time to do it right before winter.

"Totally spoiled," Liv said as the horse nosed for treats.

"I'll be back," she said. "So don't go rolling in the dirt or anything." She patted his neck and then headed back to the house, where Tim was waiting on the porch.

She gave her father a once-over as she approached, thinking he looked as peaked as ever, despite his assertion that he was feeling *so-o-o* much better. Right. Every time she looked at her father her stomach made a knot.

"Hey, Dad," she said as she mounted the steps, doing her best to hide her concern.

"Home late."

"Yeah. Well, I had a meeting I wasn't expecting." She was such a bad liar, but she didn't want him to know she and Matt had tangled again.

Tim merely grunted a reply and held the screen door open for her. Liv went straight to her bedroom, where she took off her shoes and started changing into her riding clothes. She figured she had time to make the loop around the fields and be home in plenty of time to put dinner on the table.

Tim was off the tractor early and the fields were full of bales waiting to be loaded into the retriever, but he had a set schedule and he stuck to it. Dinner at six. Liv was happy to oblige because it gave her some time to deal with the Matt situation, get a few things straight in her mind.

Bend Beckett's ear a little.

Her boots clunked across the hardwood floor as she headed for the front door. Tim looked up from his paper. "Just going for a short ride," she said. "I'll be back in time to make dinner, so don't do anything."

Tim let out an eloquent sigh and went back to reading.

FOR ONE GLORIOUS hour Liv managed to avoid thinking about Matt or her father—for the most part anyway—focusing instead on Beckett, the feel of his solid body beneath her, the wind blowing back the hair that had escaped from her ponytail, the feeling of total freedom she always got when she rode. It was as if Beckett's strength flowed into her through some magical connection that she was too logical to believe in but felt all the same. Once her feet were back on the ground, the mystical power evaporated and thoughts of Matt began crowding in.

Liv resolutely shook them off. She'd handled Greg—which had not been easy, because Greg could be damned persuasive when he put his mind to it— and now she'd handle Matt. At least he wasn't trying to buy her off with flowers and jewelry. Yet. Right now she was more concerned about dealing with Tim. Last night he'd looked like he was ready to keel over when he'd come in off the tractor and tonight he'd looked no better.

He wasn't in his chair when she walked into the living room, but he hadn't cooked dinner, either, so they were making some progress. She slapped together a meal of frozen ravioli and canned sauce.

He wandered into the kitchen from the direction of his bedroom at six o'clock sharp, took a chair without meeting her eyes.

"Not very fancy," she said as she set the pot on the table. "I need to start planning a little more in advance, I think."

Tim merely nodded and filled his plate.

They ate in silence. Tim was no talker, but usually they exchanged a few remarks during dinner— or they used to before Tim had started clamming up about whatever was making him feel so bad.

Liv pushed her food around her plate, having no

appetite herself, and finally gave up and scraped most of what she had taken into the trash.

"What's wrong?" Tim asked.

Liv frowned over her shoulder at him, then opened the dishwasher and started unloading it. She'd only put two plates in the cupboard when he said, "Well, something's wrong," before setting his fork down on his still half-full plate. Between the two of them, they'd barely eaten a single serving.

Liv stopped putting away the dishes and turned to face him, one hand propped on her hip. "And if it is?"

"I'm just wondering if that guy is bothering you again."

"Matt?" Liv asked, wondering who had seen them wrangling in the parking lot and reported back to Tim.

"No. The other guy. The one you were engaged to."

"Greg?"

"Yeah."

"I haven't heard from Greg in two months."

"But he was harassing you."

"How do you know?"

"I'm not stupid, Liv. After you broke the engagement, you changed. You got more, I don't know, stressed."

"And from that you knew he was harassing me?"

"I wondered." Tim took his plate to the trash and scraped out most of the ravioli. "You just confirmed my suspicions. You should have told me about him."

"Oh, yeah," she said, setting a plate in the rack

with exaggerated control. "Just like you've been so open with me."

"There's nothing I haven't told you that you need to know."

"I guess I can say the same."

She wondered if her father knew how much his appearance had changed just over the past few months, how his face was pinched with pain, his shoulders slightly stooped. "Do you have cancer?" she asked, tired of playing nice.

Genuine shock registered on his face. "Cancer?"

"You don't know, do you?"

His mouth went tight.

"Because you won't go to a doctor."

"I don't have cancer."

Liv gave him a tired look. "Why don't we make sure?"

"I have a stomach problem. I've had one for my entire life. It wasn't cancer when I last saw a doctor, and it isn't cancer now."

"Maybe it's an ulcer. Those are treatable."

"I will go to the doctor when I feel like I need to. Right now I'm fine. I had a few bad weeks and maybe I should have seen someone, but I'm on the mend and I don't need help making decisions as to my health care."

The conversation was going exactly as she'd known it would, making her feel like she should just beat her head on the counter rather than try to talk to him. It would be just as effective.

But getting angry with Tim wasn't going to help. He would only clam up more.

THE NEXT MORNING Tim came into the kitchen where Liv was sitting at the table, eating a bowl of cereal before going to work. Usually he was out on the tractor by this time, but today, for some reason, he was still in the house. Could it be that he was ready to talk? That he'd come to his senses last night and realized that she was right?

Apparently not. He poured cereal and sat at the table in his usual place. The two of them ate without speaking, the noise of their spoons in the bowls ridiculously loud in the stony silence. Finally, Tim dropped his spoon into his bowl, but instead of saying, "You're right, I need to seek medical advice," he said, "Are you ready for your first drill performance?"

Liv snorted—both because her dad was so freaking stubborn and because she was *not* ready for the first performance. "Not even close. My stomach hurts just thinking about it. I'm going down to the arena to practice with a couple of my teammates on Saturday."

"Andie?"

"No. Becca and Margo."

Tim's eyes came up slowly. *Ah.* "You might know Margo."

"I only know one Margo. Margo Beloit."

"That's the one. Nice lady."

Tim gave a quick nod, then got to his feet and

carried his dish to the sink. Conversation over, and Liv was done pushing for the day.

She was almost to her bedroom when she heard her cell phone ringing. Her mother's ring. Quickly, she went into her room and snagged the phone out of her bag, wondering what kind of wedding induced emergency she was about to contend with.

Please, not more shopping. "Hi, Mom."

"Liv. Thank goodness you're there."

"Did you call before?"

"Three times."

Liv sat on her bed and started prying the boots off her feet. "I left my phone in my bedroom during breakfast." Because she was still breaking the habit of being available to everyone whenever they needed her.

"It's Shae," her mother said. "This wedding is getting out of hand."

"Are you surprised?"

"David wants it perfect for her." And so, of course, that's what Vivian wanted, too. Liv was surprised that Vivian was actually voicing concern instead of silently bearing the stress, as she always did when her own needs conflicted with her husband's.

"How's it getting out of hand, Mom?" Liv asked gently.

"We can't afford it," her mother instantly replied.

"I thought that Reed and Shae were footing the bill."

"So did I, but David will have none of it. It's a mat-

ter of pride, I think, but he's determined to pay for
this wedding. And Shae is determined to make it a
splashy affair."

"What happened to the small wedding idea?" Liv
was truly curious about that. "Did Reed finally agree
to give Shae carte blanche?"

"He must have, because Shae's motto seems to be
full speed ahead, take no prisoners."

Liv laughed. Rarely did her mother say what she
was really thinking.

"So talk to her."

"David won't let me."

"Excuse me?"

"He said that I am to keep my concerns to myself.
But it's hard when it's eating into our retirement."

"Mom, you can't let that happen."

"What choice do I have?"

Vivian didn't want a solution. She just wanted
some empathy. And Liv wasn't feeling empathetic,
because doing what David wanted was going to hurt
her mother financially, and give her an ulcer worrying about the matter when she could be doing something to fix it.

"Mom…you're a partner in this relationship, you
know. You can tell David your feelings."

"I have. He said he was paying for the wedding."
Her mother hesitated briefly before saying, "There's
nothing I can do. I probably shouldn't have called,
but I thought that maybe, when Shae is planning, if
you could suggest some lower budget ideas…"

"I'm happy to do that, Mom. And you should consider having another serious talk with David. It isn't like he'll kick you out of the house. You've been married for how many years?"

"He'll go into one of his moods, Liv. And I don't think I can handle that on top of the wedding plans."

"You can't let him control you with black moods, Mom." The words shot out of Liv's mouth and were followed by a very long silence. "Mom?"

"I am not controlled," Vivian finally said.

Then what would you call it when you're afraid to negotiate with your husband?

Liv should know. She was guilty of doing the exact same thing for too many years. Was it even possible to have a close relationship with someone without giving up control of your own life? For Shae maybe—but that didn't count because she was the controller.

Not that Liv didn't have sympathy for her mother. She did confront problems now, instead of working around them or hoping they'd go away, but no matter how many affirmations she muttered, direct conflict was still difficult for her. How could she expect her mother to be any different? Especially when Vivian didn't see acquiescing to everything as being controlled but rather as a survival technique?

"I will try to talk Shae down," Liv said.

"You can't tell her I talked to you."

"I won't." She smiled grimly. "I kind of set the

stage with the bridesmaid dresses, so I'll just continue like that."

"She did budge a little there," Vivian said with a note of optimism in her voice.

"Yes, she did," Liv replied reassuringly. Almost two hundred dollars worth of budge, which was huge. "Don't worry, Mom. We'll get the wedding pared down to a reasonable amount of money."

"Thank you, sweetheart—" She heard a male voice in the background and then Vivian said, "Just Liv, honey, with some questions about the dresses. I'll be right there." Liv put her palm on her forehead and closed her eyes. Oy. To live like that.

You almost did.

"I have to go, sweetie. Thank you so much."

"No problem. Relax. I'm in your corner. *Silently* in your corner," she added before saying goodbye. The line went dead almost before the last word was out of her mouth.

For a moment Liv simply stayed where she was, phone loosely held in one hand as she stared off across the room.

Her mother was happy with David. He made her feel secure, but the cost seemed steep. Why was the balance of power in successful relationships often so one-sided?

Because that was what made those relationships successful.

Shae was probably going to have a very successful marriage.

"That Madison guy is talking smack about you," Craig said when Matt came into the house after more than an hour of straight dummy roping. His shoulder hurt and he headed for the cupboard to get a hit of ibuprofen.

"How would you know?" he asked as he made his way across the shining kitchen floor to where Craig sat at his computer.

"That research I told you about. I've been keeping tabs on your career on the internet."

Craig leaned back in his chair. "Look at this."

Matt knew better, but he looked anyway. More of the same. Ryan was getting pretty damned good at twisting the knife just a little while maintaining a facade of classiness.

"Well, what now?" Craig demanded.

"I either live with it or do something about it," Matt muttered.

Craig gave a satisfied nod, obviously figuring living with it wasn't a viable option. The kid was correct. "What's the plan?"

Matt poured a glass of water. "I guess I'd better get on a horse and see what I can do." He'd been advised not to, of course, but the doc was probably thinking he wanted to rope and dally. Instead, he'd break away—rope the calf and then release the lariat rather than dismounting and tying—which should be easy enough on his knee, and he could start tuning up Ready for the competition. He'd rather be tuning up Beckett, but that wasn't going to happen. No. Instead, the best rope horse he'd ever ridden was doing patterns in an arena and his lawyer had been adamant that there wasn't one damned thing he could do about it. The sale was legal. Bogus, but legal.

"Want me to help you mount?" Craig asked with a cackle.

"Maybe," Matt said, smiling when the grin faded off the kid's face and thinking it was kind of good to have Craig around, keep him from dwelling on maddening matters beyond his control. "But I think it'd be better if you ran the chute for me."

"What does that entail?"

"Pulling a lever."

"I'm your man," Craig said, closing out his screen with a stab of his index finger.

Matt got on the phone and made some calls to see if anyone he trusted, as in someone he didn't mind seeing him at his worst, was available to help out. There were only a few people he could call—Wes, who immediately opted out, saying that he didn't think Matt should be roping so soon, Pete, who wasn't answering his phone and Jed, whose father had once worked for his father.

Jed happened to be free—for the night anyway, since his wife was about fifteen months pregnant from the way he was talking—and was more than happy to spend the evening roping. So he had someone to chase the calves back and a guy on the chute. He was good. Now if his knee would just cooperate.

Jed arrived a little more than an hour after Matt's call, minutes after the horses had been saddled.

"Corrie's okay with this?" Matt asked as Jed got out of the truck.

"She said it may well be my last hurrah, so to enjoy myself."

Jed unloaded his horse and he and Matt, riding Freckles, his most dependable practice animal, pushed the calves into the corral on the other side of the chute. Ready stood in a holding pen where he would stay until Matt's last few runs. If he was going to be rough, he didn't want it to be on his rodeo horse.

"Let me show you what to do," Jed said to Craig, dismounting and crossing over to where the kid stood regarding the apparatus with a perplexed frown. "Just throw this lever when we nod at you."

"Just a nod," Craig said.

"Yep."

As Matt got into position, Craig kept his gaze zeroed in on Jed, one hand on the lever, waiting for the nod.

"Uh...Matt is nodding," Jed finally said with a tolerant smile.

"Oh, right." Craig flushed as he threw the lever and the chute opened. The calf raced to what he thought was freedom on the other side of the arena.

A few seconds later, Matt charged after the calf, swinging his loop. The calf rounded the far end of the arena as the loop settled over his neck and Matt released the rope.

"Good one," Craig called.

Not really. He'd be in the stratosphere time-wise if he'd had to tie the beast. He lifted his hand to acknowledge the kid's comment, then went to collect his rope off the calf and then Jed got into the box.

An hour later, his knee was killing him, but his time was improving. Riding put its own unique stress on the joint, and although Matt was well aware from past experience that it was going to hurt, he hadn't expected it to hurt this much.

Not that he couldn't take the pain.

"You about done?" Craig asked.

"Yeah," Jed said before Matt could answer. "We're done."

Matt loosened his rope and pulled it off the calf that was trying to escape out the far gate, and then coiled it as Ready trotted across the arena. "Done for now," he said.

"Not too bad," Jed said after he'd loaded his horse.

Matt handed him a beer without asking, then twisted the top off his own. Jed reached in his pocket, pulled out his phone, checked the screen, then opened his beer.

"All clear?" Matt asked.

"Is what all clear?" Craig wanted to know.

Jed smiled at Craig, a weary dadlike smile. "Am I all clear to stay and enjoy a beer before going home," he explained as he leaned against his trailer before turning his attention back to Matt. "So far, so good.

Last time Corrie was two weeks late, so she's determined to have this baby on time."

"Good luck with that," Matt said. He'd once thought that he and Trena would have a kid by now. They'd agreed to wait two years and then try, but nothing had come of it. Now Matt was glad because he'd hate to have some poor kid caught between them. He absently leaned down to test the area around his knee, doing his best to keep the pain from registering on his face.

"You okay?" Jed asked quietly.

Craig appeared very interested in the answer and Matt did not want the kid trying to take care of him—although he wouldn't mind if he tried to cook for him.

"I've been worse," he said honestly. "Hey, Craig, go get that bag of chips, would you? And something that's not a beer for you to drink."

"Sure." Craig headed off for the house and Matt flexed his knee a couple of times.

"Hurts like hell," he said. "But I figured this first time would be bad."

"You going back on the circuit?"

"Going to try. Pete has a guy who helped him get back in the game. Some local guy. I'm going to try to see him."

"Local guy?" Jed asked with a perplexed frown. He pushed back his hat with the lip of his beer bottle. "I wonder if he's talking about McElroy?"

"Don't know."

"If he is…well, all I can tell you is that the guy has a shaky reputation."

"How so?"

Jed shrugged. "Used to do some stuff for some local football players. Nothing technically illegal, but let's just say they played pain-free."

Which wasn't sounding that bad right now as his knee was threatening to explode on him. Matt ran a hand over the back of his neck, surprised at how taut the muscles were. His entire body was seizing up from the pain in his joint. "You don't happen to know of anyone else offhand?"

"No, but I hear Liv Bailey is back in town doing physical therapy."

"Trena sold her my best roping horse," Matt said before taking a long draw as if trying to wash away bitterness.

"I know."

Who didn't? Matt smiled tightly. "Don't get divorced."

"Don't plan on it," Jed said with a certainty that stirred a whisper of jealousy inside of Matt. Must be nice to be that sure. So was Jed going to be blindsided like Matt was?

Unlikely, since Jed seemed to be staying at home with his bride in a way that Matt never had.

"As far as roping practice goes, I imagine you're going to be busy for the next several years?" Matt asked with a half smile.

"I'll let you know. I can probably get away for a

night or two every now and then, but since I hear that two kids feel more like four, no promises."

"None asked." Craig came out of the house carrying a bag of chips and a liter bottle of Mountain Dew.

"You never told me where you picked up a kid," Jed said before Craig got into earshot, and from his expression, Matt realized that Jed probably thought Craig was his kid.

"Willa's boy. She's working on a dude ranch and I agreed to keep him for a while."

"Ah," Jed said, looking faintly embarrassed.

"Hey," Craig said, plopping down on the trailer wheel cover and handing Matt the chips. Matt dutifully took a handful as did Jed. He wasn't particularly interested in chips, but it had been the only thing he could think of to get rid of Craig long enough to ask Jed about knee doctors. The last thing he wanted was for Craig to start in-depth internet research on the subject.

"I'd better get going," Jed said after he'd emptied his beer. He checked his phone again, then got into his truck. "If I get any names I'll let you know," he said through the open window.

"I'd appreciate it," Matt said.

"What kind of names?" Craig asked.

"Baby names," Jed replied with a crooked smile.

Craig's mouth twisted. "Well, whatever you do, steer clear of Crag."

CHAPTER NINE

ACCORDING TO THE phone book, Dr. Randall McElroy rented an office at Andie Ballentine's clinic, which meant that if Matt went to see the guy, he'd probably run into Liv. After that last encounter, he wasn't sure if that was a good idea.

At least he'd finally gotten it through his head that he hadn't really known Liv—and she hadn't known him—especially if she believed that he'd hurt Beckett.

Matt waited until Craig went out to feed the calves before dialing the clinic. "Uh, yeah. This is Matt Montoya," he said when the receptionist answered. "I'd like to make an appointment to see Dr. McElroy."

"Oh, hi, Matt. This is Etta. How are you?"

Etta. Great. "In need of an appointment."

"Well—" she dragged the word out "—Dr. McElroy is no longer with the clinic."

That was a positive. Now he wouldn't have to run into Liv. "Do you know where I can find him?"

"Are you a patient?"

"Not yet."

"Then I suggest you make an appointment with Andie."

"Uh, no. I don't think that will work."

"Because…?"

"Etta, are you supposed to ask questions like that?"

"Well, it isn't like we don't know each other."

And had slept together a few times. "I'd rather see a male doctor."

"Then I'm afraid we can't help you."

"I don't want you to help me, Etta. I want you to tell me where to find Dr. McElroy."

"You know what? I wouldn't tell you if I knew."

"What?"

"He's bad news, Matt. I can give you some other names. Hang on." He heard the shuffle of papers, then Etta said, "There's L. M. Reynolds in Butte, Bob Murphy in Butte, Lyle Crenshaw in Anaconda—"

"Thanks," Matt said. "I'll try one of them." He hung up before Etta could answer and found Craig standing behind him.

"We have a problem."

Another one? "What now?"

"Your horse has bad scrapes on his back legs. The spotted horse."

"What?" Matt headed out the door, Craig hot on his heels. Sure enough, Ready had dried blood covering most of one hind leg.

Matt clamped his mouth shut to keep from uttering the curses that were lining up on his tongue. The smooth wire fence was sagging from where the horse had somehow caught his leg—probably trying to kick through it at the horse on the other side.

"Shit," he said as he opened the gate. He glanced at Craig, who shrugged.

"Mom's favorite word."

He put a hand on Ready's rump as he leaned closer to assess the damage. The skin and hair were burned off the leg. Son of a bitch. He hoped there was no muscle damage. Matt went back out the gate, barely getting it closed when Craig handed him the phone.

Matt looked up the vet's number and dialed. In all his years of having horses in smooth wire, this was his first injury. And even if there was no muscle damage, it was going to be a while until he was riding Ready again. The horse needed time to heal.

The vet's assistant answered almost immediately and Matt described the problem as he wearily studied the practice horses in the next pasture over. Clancy, the horse Ready had probably tried to kick when he'd injured himself, was a nice horse. Lots of potential. But too green to be used for his comeback bid.

Damn.

He'd been counting on Ready, hoping that the horse would make it through the season unscathed while Matt worked at bringing Clancy up to speed for the next year.

So what now? Did he lease a finished horse? Try to get Beckett back?

He snorted. At best Liv would laugh in his face. At worst she'd publically accuse him of injuring another horse through carelessness.

Matt was in a world of hurt.

"Guess who called looking for McElroy," Etta said as Andie walked into the office.

Liv flipped open the chart of her first after-lunch patient, skimming it quickly as Andie said, "Who?"

"Matt." Etta paused, then added, "Montoya." Liv looked up. She couldn't help herself. "I tried to book him with you," Etta said to her, "but he said he wants a male doctor." She smirked a little. "So I gave him some names. My guess is that he doesn't care if they're male or not. He wants someone who's good with a needle."

"You don't know that," Andie said, flipping the file closed. "And you probably shouldn't say it."

Etta shrugged carelessly. "I dated him. I know his hierarchy. Roping, women, partying."

"How long ago was that?" Liv asked, somehow pushing the words out of her throat in a conversational tone and ignoring the sharp look Andie sent her.

"Oh, let's see…I was the one right before the one he married." She smiled as she shrugged philosophically. "I had no illusions where I fit into the scheme of his life, but boy howdy, it was hard to walk away. He is hot. *H-O-T*—"

"We get it," Andie said. "Have you made the appointment reminder calls today?"

"Getting right on that," Etta said, reaching for the phone. Andie shook her head and went into her office, taking care not to look at Liv.

Why? Did she feel sorry for her?

Liv knocked on the open door frame and then walked inside, closing the door after her. Andie looked up from the lab report she was reading. "I don't want to encourage her. Etta is good with the patients, but she gossips too much and I don't like it."

"Right," Liv said. "And now I have a question for you. Most of McElroy's patients were jocks or athletes of some kind, right?"

"They were people who were more interested in numbing pain than dealing with the cause." Andie set down the report. "And he does this—" she gestured with one hand as she made a disgusted face "—growth hormone stuff that's supposed to regenerate cartilage. Nothing proven or even approved by the FDA. I don't like it."

"Great."

"Yeah. And honestly? He creeped me out. So-o-o smarmy." The phone rang, and Andie automatically reached for it. "Give me a minute, then send him in," she said. Liv headed for the door. She didn't like this one bit, even though it was so not her business what Matt Montoya did to himself.

"Hey," Andie called and Liv turned back. "Can I bum a ride to practice tonight? My trailer has a flat."

"I'll pick you up at six."

"Thanks."

DON'T DO THIS.

After a near paralyzing moment of indecision, Liv blew off her cautious inner voice and, instead of turning right at the Y, turned left and began traveling toward where Matt's place should be. He'd said he was only two miles away and surely she'd be able to see his truck—unless, of course, he parked it in a garage.

He didn't. She'd traveled for less than a mile when she spotted the silver-and-black truck near a house that was dwarfed by the indoor arena next to it. Liv slowed as she regarded the canvas-covered building.

An arena of his own.

Apparently, world titles paid well.

There was a white utility truck parked next to Matt's Dodge, and as Liv slowed to pull into the driveway, her heart beating harder than it should have been, Matt and another man came out of the barn followed by a teenage kid.

She hadn't planned on a crowd. Definitely bad timing on her part, but it was too late to drive on—especially since all three of them were now staring at her.

She parked on the opposite side of Matt's Dodge and got out of the car as if stopping by his house were the most natural thing in the world.

"Liv," Matt said as she approached, his expression less than welcoming. "This is a surprise."

"Matt."

The guy standing beside Matt had to be a vet, judging from the bright yellow Betadine stains on his shirt and the kit in his hand.

"Dr. Hoss," Matt nodded at the vet. "Liv Bailey, Tim's daughter."

The vet stuck out his free hand, which was only

slightly bloody. Liv took it. "Good to meet you," he said as her fingers were swallowed up in his large hand.

"Are you a horse vet?" she asked.

"Hoss for hosses. That's me." The vet smiled congenially, released her hand, then turned back to Matt. "Everything should be fine, but give me a call if there're any problems. I've got another call, so..."

"Yeah, well, thanks for coming." Matt walked the vet to his truck, the two of them continuing to talk in low voices, the kid, who Matt had never introduced, trailing along behind them. Liv shoved her hands in her back pockets, feeling awkward. This time her cautious voice had been correct. In a few seconds they were going to be alone and some of the steam had gone out of her—the steam that was supposed to get her through this before sanity set in.

Dr. Hoss opened the truck door and got inside. Liv waited for the teen to jump in the passenger side, but instead he continued to stand beside Matt. The truck started up, and with a quick wave, the vet pulled away.

Yeah. Definitely a bad time for a semiprofessional visit.

"This is Willa's boy, Craig," Matt said after the vet's truck crossed the culvert on the other side of the house. "You remember Willa, right?"

Who could forget the girl who'd beaten up the freshman quarterback when he'd teased her about her name? "Uh, yes. I do," Liv said. "I can see the resemblance." Craig did have his mother's piercing blue eyes, but their similarities ended there. Willa's hair was pale blond and Craig's was reddish-brown, her face round and his narrow and angular.

Craig gave her a candid once-over. "You and my mom must have gotten along okay," he said.

"I think so," she said cautiously, cutting a quick look at Matt, who was studying her intently, his expression hard and unwelcoming. Why? Because she'd dared to tread on his turf? Because he knew why she was there and didn't want to hear her lecture him?

"Just saying, because sometimes people get this weird look when they find out who my mom is." He smiled as if quite comfortable with that circumstance, perhaps even a little proud.

"We didn't know each other well, but yes, we got along okay."

"Glad to hear it," Craig said. He bounced a look between Matt and Liv then said, "I have a computer game I need to get back to."

"Nice meeting you," Liv called. Craig lifted a hand in acknowledgment as he headed for the house.

"Seems like a nice kid," Liv said, turning back to Matt, wondering why she couldn't have just gone home. Going home would have made her life so much easier. Why make it harder by doing this?

Because she had some things to say and she was no longer the kind of person who avoided unpleasantness in order to keep other people happy.

Because she hated to see anyone give a guy like

"Dr." McElroy money. Or destroy their joints by numbing them with painkillers so they could compete—not that she knew for a fact that Matt was going to do any of those things, but from what she understood from Andie, toward the end of his practice, people only saw McElroy for one reason.

And because part of her wanted to tell Matt that she knew what he was doing and that it was wrong. Just plain wrong.

"Word travels fast," Matt said.

Liv frowned. "What are you talking about?"

"My horse."

"I'm not here about a horse," Liv said. "I'm here about a quack."

OH, YEAH. This was turning out to be one fine day.

"McElroy?" Matt asked wearily. This was why she was here all fired up? He was glad it wasn't about the horse, but still…

"Got it in one," she replied with the same quiet intensity she'd had when she was trying to explain a math concept that he just wasn't getting. "I don't know if anyone else is going to tell you that seeing McElroy is stupid and unethical, so I am."

"Really."

She nodded.

"Well, first of all, you don't know what I'm going to do. Second, it's none of your business and third, why do you care?"

Her color rose on the third point, in a rather fascinating way, actually. Anger or self-consciousness?

"Fourth," he continued in a low voice, refusing to let himself be fascinated by the woman who wouldn't return his horse, "how do you know I'm going to see McElroy?"

"Our receptionist was concerned about you."

Matt snorted. "I think your receptionist wouldn't mind seeing me in hell."

"She did mention something about heat," Liv muttered.

"You know, Liv, you may have helped me through calculus, but you really don't have much say in what I do."

"But I know what's ethical and what people should and shouldn't do to their body. And who they should and shouldn't give money to. You're supporting a quasicriminal if you go to this guy."

He moved a step closer, not much liking her point about supporting a quasicriminal because he had a feeling she was probably right. "Just what is it you think I'm going to do to my body?"

From the way her lips parted then closed, Matt once again got the feeling that she was more aware of him, in a man-woman sense, than she wanted to be. Which would have been an interesting circumstance in another time or place.

"I think you're going to numb the pain in your knee so that you can compete. And then I think you're going to destroy the joint."

"But you aren't a doctor. McElroy is."

"Allegedly."

"I need to get back into the game before it's too late," he finally said. "I can only be competitive for so long and the clock's ticking."

"Maybe it's ticked past midnight."

"Thanks, Liv."

"It's possible."

"And it's also possible that the guys I've seen about my knee have approached the matter with a closed mind. They know the norm. They don't know *me*."

"How many therapists and doctors have you seen with closed minds?"

"Two. One doctor. One therapist."

"Don't make McElroy number three."

"So maybe I should come to you? Would you approach things with an open mind?"

"I would tell you the truth."

"Yeah?" He tilted his hat back slightly so that he could see her face better. "Seems to me that you went a long time without telling me the truth."

It took a moment for his meaning to sink in. "That doesn't count," she snapped, blushing again. "I shouldn't have come. You just go ahead and do what you have to do." Liv turned to walk back to her truck, but Matt reached out and took her arm, his hand sliding down to her wrist to stop her.

She jerked back at his touch and he instantly let go. "Don't go, Liv."

"Why?"

"We have things to settle." Before she could respond, he said, "Things other than doctors, alleged or otherwise, and old crushes."

"What things?" Liv asked, her expression dead. He was touching too many nerves, but it worked both ways. If she could come here and shove health advice at him, then he could settle another matter.

"What do you think?"

"Beckett is mine," she said.

"Do you think I hurt him?" he asked. It was very important to him that she know he hadn't hurt the horse. She hadn't given him a straight answer last time and he needed one.

She appeared to fight with herself for a moment before she confessed in a low voice, "I no longer believe you hurt him." She let out a breath, as if the admission had hurt, then once again met his gaze. "So, if that's settled, I need to get home and cook for Dad."

"Yeah. I wanted to ask about that, too."

"What?" Her eyes widened, making him wonder how back in the day he'd managed to miss the fact that she had gorgeous eyes. Probably because he'd been a self-centered jerk. "Cooking?"

"Your dad. The ranch is a wreck, Liv."

"I'm aware," she said stiffly, making it pretty easy to follow her thoughts. *The ranch...none of his business.* Just like McElroy was really none of hers. "I need to get going," she said again.

"Yeah. You go on home. But we have more to talk about. In the future."

"I don't think so."

Matt didn't say another word so she walked to her truck, her back stiff. No "goodbye" or "see you later." But he would see her later—and not entirely because of Beckett.

Liv put the truck into Reverse and swung it around. Matt stood at the edge of the gravel drive, and he couldn't help but notice that she gave him one last long look in the rearview mirror before putting the rig into a forward gear and pulling away.

As Liv PULLED out onto the county road, she glanced toward the house one last time. Willa's boy came out to meet Matt on the deck and Matt shook his head at something the kid said.

What was the boy doing there? Matt did not look like the babysitting type.

And what was that about a horse?

Liv had been so flustered before she hadn't asked why on earth Matt had thought she was there about a horse. Something to do with the vet, no doubt. What had he thought? That she'd heard another of his horses had gotten injured and come swooping down on him like a vigilante posse of one?

He gave her more credit than she deserved, although she had kind of swooped down on him, but for a different reason. And rightly so. Guys like McElroy preyed on other people's needs and dreams. The football player trying to advance his career, the coach who needed that player. The rodeo rider who needs just a couple more wins to move up in the world standings. McElroy could help them do just that—for a price, both physical and financial.

Liv gritted her teeth. She really hated slimy doctors.

And she was trying hard not to think about how Matt had jangled her nerves. If she hadn't been driving, she would have thunked her head on the steering wheel. She'd delivered her message and felt a sense of satisfaction there, but she'd also received a message that left her feeling edgy and uncertain.

They had more to talk about.

What?

It had to be Beckett.

In that case, she was fine.

Except for that part where she'd kept noticing all the little things about Matt that had distracted her back when she'd been trying to teach him calculus. Things she didn't want to notice again.

CHAPTER TEN

MATT WAS STILL mulling over Liv's visit the next morning when he pulled into the parking lot of Murdoch's Western supply store to pick up some vet wrap to doctor Ready's leg. She'd come on a mission, but he wasn't exactly sure if it had been to save him from the dangers of the needle or to keep McElroy from getting more business. Or maybe just to beat him up some more.

Regardless of why she came, he knew why she'd left. Because he'd rattled her. Which felt satisfying and he wasn't certain why. He smiled a little, watching the ground as he crossed the parking lot, when a familiar voice said, "Careful where you're going."

The smile instantly evaporated as Matt found himself facing his father. And as always, even after all these years, he felt a prickle of betrayal. Betrayal wasn't compatible with warm fuzzy feelings, and Matt had never tried to pretend. If Charles Montoya wondered what had happened between himself and his son, he never said anything, but at times that Matt could sense his frustration. There wasn't much he could do about it. There was no way in hell Matt was going to say, "I know your dirty secret."

Well, actually he'd love to say those words, but feared repercussions. What if his father felt compelled to do something about it once confronted with the knowledge that Matt knew? What if he confessed to his wife? Matt couldn't handle hurting his mom.

"How're you feeling?" Charles asked in his gruff way, which meant he felt self-conscious. He shoved his big hands into his denim jacket as he waited for Matt's response.

Matt gave a careless shrug. "Fine." His dad was nearly two inches taller than him, his hair now almost entirely silver, but looking at his dad was like seeing himself in the future. He was practically a clone of his old man…which bugged the hell out of him sometimes.

"The knee?"

"I'm working on it."

"Meaning?"

"I'm working on it," Matt said with a spurt of impatience.

"That doesn't tell me a damned thing."

"I'm doing exercises to strengthen it and wearing a brace. It's getting better. I'm roping."

"Maybe you should give it a rest this year."

"I don't think so," Matt said.

"What would it hurt?"

"Well, for one thing it'd hurt my pocketbook."

"You still have cows."

Matt narrowed his eyes. When they had these conversations, part of Matt instantly assumed his father was trying to make things easier for Ryan. It wasn't logical, but the thought always sneaked in, accompanied by the ghost of a devastated fifteen-year-old boy who should have been where he'd said he'd be.

"I'm roping. I'm competing. It's what I do."

"Maybe it's time you did something else," his father said.

"Why?"

"Why?" Charles echoed incredulously. "Because you're beat to hell and it's the sane thing to do. You could come to work on the ranch. Your ma's been after me to draw up papers, make you a partner."

"I don't think so." Like he was going to put himself through that.

Charles just shook his head. "What are you going to do for a living then? Sell cars?"

"I've got to go, Dad. Say hi to Mom."

"You could come by and tell her yourself."

"Yeah. I'll do that."

"I'll tell her to expect your call."

"Thanks."

Charles turned and walked into the store without another word. Matt watched the door close behind him.

Sell cars. Shit. Thanks for the slap in the face, Dad.

Matt started after his dad, wondering how many times they'd bump into each other inside the store, when he was hailed from behind by a familiar voice. He turned to see Pedro Garcia, his father's foreman, jogging across the parking lot toward him. Pedro never walked when he could run.

"Matt! Long time!"

"Pedro. Good to see you."

"Hey, you, too." The older man slapped Matt's arm. "What are you up to? Are you getting better? When will you compete next?"

"The Bitterroot Challenge."

"Really?" Pedro scrunched his face up. "You're going up against Madison, you know. That kid can do no wrong."

"So I hear."

"Your dad and I went and watched him a couple times last summer. You got your work cut out for you, Matt. He's getting better and better." Pedro beamed congenially at him. "But I know you can beat him."

The old man's words sounded more like just a platitude, but Matt barely registered the fact. His father had made special trips to watch his half brother rope?

Why did it still piss him off so much? It wasn't like he was vying for his father's affection.

Because it was dishonest. And not fair to his mother.

Plus, he hated thinking he wasn't as good as his half brother and the sad truth was that right now, he wasn't.

"Hey," Pedro said, still smiling. "You haven't seen your dad, have you? I'm supposed to meet him here."

"Yeah, I did. He went inside."

"Great. Thanks, man. See you in Butte!" Pedro

clapped Matt's arm again, and then started jogging to the store entrance.

Oh, yeah. He'd see Matt in Butte.

"GUESS WHO CHANGED his mind about an appointment?" Etta asked in a coy voice, telling Liv exactly who had changed his mind.

"Matt Montoya?" She felt her pulse rate bump up as Etta nodded, which in turn ticked her off.

"The same," Etta said. "Called this morning. I put him in that three o'clock that Mr. Jones canceled. I hope that's okay?"

Actually, Liv had planned on leaving early that day and dealing with some issues around the ranch, but nothing she could do about it now.

"Fine." Just fine. No problem at all.

Four hours later, Matt came into the examining room wearing a plain white T-shirt and a pair of athletic shorts. And, heaven help her, Liv's first thought was that he had terrific legs.

Which he did. Perfectly muscled. Not too bulky. Just…perfect, except for the scars from too many surgeries on one knee and the fresh scars on the other.

She frowned slightly before meeting his eyes. "It looks like both your knees have been through a lot."

"The right one, yeah. The left? This is the first time it's gone out, which is why I don't buy what the other PT told me."

"Who are you seeing?"

"Rich Nygaard."

"I don't know him."

"Just moved into the state. Supposed to be good according to my doctor."

"But he's not making you better fast enough."

"How'd you know?"

"It's a common complaint."

Matt just shrugged. "So I'm impatient. I want to start practicing."

She gestured for him to take a seat, then reached out for the envelope he held in one hand. He gave it to her without a word and she took a few minutes studying the images inside. Wow.

Turning back to Matt she knelt in front of him and put her hand on top of his knee, forcing herself to think of him just as she'd thought of her previous patient, old Mr. Zachary. Except that Mr. Zachary's skin hadn't felt so warm beneath her hand, and she'd had no difficulty at all meeting his eyes.

"Tell me what you've been doing for both passive and active treatment."

"The usual stuff. Anti-inflammatory medication. Ice when it swells. Knee brace when I might stress the knee."

"Not that you'd ever do that."

"Of course not." He smiled crookedly, momentarily turning on the Montoya charm. "I have a suite of exercises I do nightly."

She tested the joint, focusing on the knee rather than on Matt's face, or his hands, which were clasped loosely in his lap. She was way too aware of him, which would never do in a patient/therapist situation.

"What is it exactly that you want to know?" she asked.

"I want your opinion."

"You want to know when you can start roping calves again."

He nodded.

"Never," she said, letting go of his leg and sitting back on her heels. "At least not at a professional level. Not with this kind of injury."

Matt exhaled, his mouth tightening as he focused across the room.

"I can't change the facts," she said.

He met her eyes fiercely. "I've seen people come back from more serious injuries than this. Broken backs, broken necks—"

"I'm giving you my professional opinion, Matt." One she had no doubt he'd heard before. "I can give you some exercises to help strengthen the area around your knee, which will help support it, but it's never going to be one hundred percent and at some point you'll probably be looking at a knee replacement."

"I don't need one hundred percent. I can make up for the lost time with quicker catches."

For a moment Liv simply stared at him. "Why?"

"What do you mean why?" he asked impatiently.

"Why do you have to keep roping? You've had a great career, but you knew it had to end sometime."

"Not now," he said stiffly.

"Do you need the money?"

"I need to rope."

"So, it's like your…identity?" Liv asked softly, wondering why that bothered her so much.

"It's what I do," Matt said, gripping the table on either side of his thighs. "And it's what I plan to keep doing. I'm not buying what you say."

"What did the other PT say?" Liv pushed the hair back from the side of her face. "What did your doctor say?" *And why won't you listen to us, Matt! We're all saying the same thing.*

Matt got off the table, bracing his hands on his hips as he stood in front of her. Liv slowly rose to her feet, her gaze locked on his. "It doesn't matter. What matters is what I can do with some willpower and determination."

"You'll destroy the joint."

"And then what? I'll never rope again? According to you guys, that's where I am right now, so what do I have to lose?"

"Matt…you could end up with a permanent limp—at least until you get a knee replacement—and you want to hold off on that as long as possible, so you don't have to do it twice in your lifetime."

He nodded in a way that made her think he'd heard all this before. "Noted."

He spoke sharply, then tightened one corner of his mouth as he rubbed a hand over the back of his neck, squeezing the tight muscles there. "I know you believe what you're saying and I asked for your opinion. Sorry to snap."

"It's understandable," Liv said. "I mean, an injury like this is life-changing."

"If you allow it to be."

Talk about stubborn. But Liv knew better than to say those words. She'd lived with her father for too long not to recognize the futility of arguing with a person in this mood.

"I can give you some exercises, but I imagine they're similar if not identical to the suite that you're doing now."

"Yeah, but I wouldn't mind a few more."

"Show me your routine."

Matt went through the exercises and then Liv said, "Those are the same I would recommend." She reached out to touch his upper arm, as she would any of her patients…except that this didn't feel anything like her other patients. She had wondered for so long before and during their study sessions what it would feel like to touch Matt, to be touched by him, and some primitive part of her brain was still interested in the exploration—which wouldn't do at all.

Even if he wanted to be her patient, she wouldn't take him on—not when he was so intent on destroying the joint.

Oh, yeah, and that's the only reason…

It wasn't. Liv knew it, but that didn't mean she wanted to dwell on it.

"Thanks for your time, Liv."

"No problem." She smiled weakly. "Sorry I couldn't give you a better prognosis."

"Yeah."

"Just one more thing…"

"What's that?"

"Don't do the injections."

Matt kept his mouth shut, obviously not about to make a promise he might not keep.

"I should have lied to you," she muttered as she wrote on his chart. She jerked in surprise when his fingers touched her chin, her eyes flashing up to his, which were so warm, so dark.

"You told me you'd tell me the truth and I guess that I appreciate that you did. It seems that we simply have different opinions about what's possible."

What could she say to that? For one long moment she stared up at him, wishing that circumstances were different. That they could be friends. But there was too much awareness between them for that and she simply didn't trust herself. It would be so easy to fall back into her old habits with Matt, become a pleaser. She wasn't going to do that for anyone.

"Fine," she said. "Just don't numb that knee." She made a note on his chart and handed it back to him. "Please give this to Etta and you're good to go."

"NC?" he asked. "No charge?"

She shrugged. "You wouldn't have come if I hadn't shown up at your place and told you not to go to McElroy."

"And you're sure of that."

"Damned sure of that," she said with a half smile, feeling like she was edging toward safer ground now.

"I pay my debts."

"I can't do anything for you the other guy isn't doing, and I practically dared you to see me—" *which was a mistake* "—so I'm comping the consultation."

Matt shrugged. "Have it your way."

"ARE YOU OKAY?" Andie asked after Liv came out of the office to see her next patient, another that Etta had squeezed in on a day when she'd wanted to go home early.

"Why wouldn't I be?" Liv asked.

"Matt?"

Liv let out a soft snort. "The consultation went fine. He didn't like what I had to say and he's not coming back."

"Well, I'll give him credit for at least coming in," Andie said, her gaze traveling over Liv in a way she didn't like at all. Andie was too damned observant. "Here's guess number two as to why you look so stressed," she said. "Tim?"

Liv blew out a huff of breath. "Yes." Better for Andie to think it was Tim and only Tim raising her blood pressure. "He says he's better. I don't believe him."

"We may have to kidnap him," Andie said, sounding as if she weren't kidding one bit.

"If we do, we'll have to take him to a male doctor. My father has strict notions concerning gender."

"Nothing like dealing with a stubborn man."

"Amen to that." Liv gestured at the waiting room. "In fact, I have another one waiting for me. Won't do his back exercises because they hurt."

"Which means they hurt even more when he does do them." Andie pulled a chart out of the holder on the door closest to her, then smiled. "Well, good luck with that."

"Do you need a ride to practice tonight?" Liv asked before Andie could open the door to the examination room.

"Not unless you want to give me one."

"I like the company," Liv said. And Beckett had made friends with Andie's horse, Mike.

"Sure. Pick me up at six? No…better make it five-thirty. We get our uniforms tonight."

"I'll be there," Liv said. Five-thirty wouldn't leave her much time to get home after this last patient, but it also didn't give her too much time to think. She liked that last part because she was still thinking about Matt. It seemed pretty damned impossible not to.

MATT DIDN'T GO home immediately because he didn't want Craig to key into his mood. The kid was remarkably astute and right now, Matt would just as soon keep his frustrations to himself.

What if the experts were right? He'd had three opinions and they all agreed that his career was over.

Could he deal with that?

Not now. He'd always figured he'd choose the time

to retire, not have it forced upon him. Damn it, he wasn't ready to stop competing.

He tossed a rock into the river, watched the ripples. He couldn't remember a time when rodeo competition wasn't important to him. It'd been how he and his father had bonded when he'd been very young, and later it had been the only way he could deal with his feelings after discovering his father's betrayal.

Another rock broke the surface of the water. He quickly threw a third rock, destroying the ripples from the second, and felt an odd satisfaction.

The fish were rising and for a moment he stopped tossing pebbles and watched as the bubbles came closer.

He and the old man had fished, too. They'd done a lot of things, but finding out about Ryan had pretty much ruined everything—his hero worship, his respect. Pretty much everything in his relationship with his dad had gone sideways.

And the old man had no one to blame but himself.

He wondered, as always, if his father knew he knew. Matt didn't know how his dad would have found out, but he had to wonder.

So let him.

Matt got to his feet and headed for the truck. Craig was probably polishing the silver by now, or he would be if Matt had any.

Maybe he should show the kid how to clean and polish bits, spurs and conchos. Keep Craig busy while keeping his gear nice. Something to think about.

Something else to think about was why Liv had comped his visit. There'd been a healthy vibe humming between them as she'd examined him and there'd even been a point while she'd been running those small hands of hers over his lower thigh when he'd been pretty damned certain that he was going to embarrass himself. And her.

She was still nervous about him taking Beckett back, yet she'd come to warn him off McElroy. Challenged him to come see her. So he'd gone. Out of curiosity, really, and a vague hope that maybe she could help.

Instead, she'd given him her blunt opinion, comped the visit, wished him good luck, sent him on his way. She could just as easily have lied to him and told him she could help him get better. Strung him along, taken his insurance money, more importantly, kept him from seeking help from the doctor whose practices she so deeply disapproved of. But she hadn't.

Again, why? It didn't add up.

And why did it matter to him?

TIM WAS SITTING on the porch when Matt parked in his usual spot under the elm tree. Amazing that he'd been here so often that he had a usual spot.

Tim stood as soon as Matt started toward him, moving carefully since he wasn't wearing his brace. "Liv's not here. And neither is *her* horse." Tim wiped his hands on the sides of his pants, as if preparing to settle a score. Next thing he'd be spitting on his fists and getting ready to fight.

"That's why I'm here."

That got the older man's attention—and maybe not in a good way, judging from the scowl on his face. But then Tim had never been a big smiler.

Matt shoved his hands into his back pockets and looked around, assessing the damage, before focusing once again on Tim. It was pretty obvious from the way Tim's scowl deepened that he was aware of Matt's train of thought, so Matt didn't waste any time outlining the situation. Instead, he simply said, "I can help."

"Help with what?"

"Help you get this place back into shape." If anything, Tim's expression darkened even more. "I don't know what happened," Matt continued, "and it isn't my business. But if you need a hand getting things set right again, I have some time I can give you."

"Must be nice."

"Oh, yeah. It's swell," Matt said in a voice edged in bitter irony. "But a guy can only rope a dummy for so long every day."

Tim was studying him closely now, looking for the catch, and Matt knew better than to try to play innocent. It might work on some guys, but not Tim Bailey.

"Why?"

"It's not to get the horse back," Matt said. "Although I want that horse back more than you'll ever know." This was harder than he'd thought it'd be, facing off with Tim like this. The guy was stubborn and proud, as was his daughter—although Matt hadn't figured that out until recently.

He shifted his weight, rocking back slightly. "I want to help Liv. Like she helped me."

"That was a long time ago."

"Yeah. I know. Feels like a century."

"Feels like yesterday to me."

Matt cocked his head at the man's unguarded admission, spoken so softly he almost didn't hear it. But now the walls were back up, as if the admission had slipped out of the older man without permission and Tim was going to make damned certain it never happened again.

"Liv took a look at my knee today. Professionally," Matt added. "She comped the visit. When I tried to write a check, Etta tore it up."

Tim's lips twitched slightly, so Matt knew he'd amused him. Hell, it had been kind of funny, but as a guy who didn't like being indebted, it hadn't seemed funny at the time.

"So I owe her for more than calculus. It looks like her hands are full now with a job, so she can't help you out. I can."

Tim would have loved to have said he didn't need anyone's help—Matt knew, because it was exactly what he would have wanted to say under the same circumstances—but the condition of the ranch made it impossible to tell that particular lie.

"Your parents have a fine ranch you could be helping on."

"They don't need help."

Tim let out a breath. Matt wanted to say there was nothing wrong with needing help, but kept his mouth shut. Finally, Tim gave one short nod.

"That back fence needs tightening."

"I can do that." Matt tipped his hat back slightly. "I can do it tomorrow morning." Tim still didn't appear thrilled, but for some reason he'd caved. "I have a kid staying with me. Willa's boy. Do you care if he comes along?"

"Why would I?"

Matt shrugged. "Just thought I'd clear it with you."

CHAPTER ELEVEN

AFTER HER LAST cranky patient, who'd actually managed to take her mind off from Matt for a few minutes, Liv was running late. She'd finally convinced the guy that the pain was inevitable and would only get worse if he didn't endure it now, but it had taken fifteen minutes longer than he'd been scheduled for.

Even though she'd hated to bother him, Liv called Tim as she headed out and asked him to hook up the trailer and load Beckett so that all she had to do was to change clothes and hit the road.

Sure enough, the truck and trailer were ready when she got there, Beckett saddled and loaded. She dashed into the house to find it filled with the rich scent of pasta sauce.

"I thawed one of the casseroles Walter's wife sent over last year when I sprained my wrist. Do you have time to eat?"

Liv shook her head. "I'll grab an energy bar and eat when I get home."

She pulled into Andie's yard at 5:35, loaded Beckett's good buddy Mike, and the four of them headed off for the arena, arriving just as the other team members were gathering at Linda's truck.

"Oh. My," Liv said, staring at the group as she pulled the keys out of the ignition. "What is that thing she's holding up?"

"One of our new shirts," Andie said mildly. "Rhinestone Rough Riders like spangles, thus the name."

"And fringe."

"Yes, indeed," Andie said, getting out of the truck.

A few minutes later Liv had a neatly folded bundle of clothing—a red glittery shirt with *long* white fringe, sparkly black pants, a giant rhinestone belt buckle to go on the belt of her choice, a rhinestone tiara for her hat and white fringed gloves. A smile quivered on her lips, but she didn't dare let it break out. Her teammates appeared all agog over the new outfits, even Margo, whom she'd thought was more of a wool-and-corduroy type person.

"How often do you get a chance to indulge a dress-up fantasy in public?" Andie asked as they carried their bundles back to the truck.

"Halloween?" Liv said.

"What did the Billings gals wear?"

"Dark jeans, white shirts and red neckerchiefs."

"Pfft." Andie smirked as she stowed her clothes in the rear seat of the truck. "No fringe?"

"Not a strand." Liv started for the trailer, but Andie stopped her.

"We're not done."

"No?"

"Got to go back for our horse gear."

The horse gear consisted of a saddle pad cover, bridle, breast collar, leggings and various beribboned tail barrettes—all sparkly red.

"This clashes with Beckett's coloring," Liv said as they made their second trip back to the truck.

"Don't think that hasn't been brought up. Next year they're talking turquoise or blue to complement all the horses."

"Where does the money come from?"

"Various fund-raisers. And we have a few sponsors. Like me."

"You're responsible?"

Andie hunched a shoulder. "I *like* to live my childhood dress-up fantasies in public. What can I say?"

The practice was a long one. Linda was stressed since their first performance was only a week away and the team kept messing up the pattern. There was no slowing to a trot, though, so Liv spent the evening flying around the arena, hoping for the best... and kind of enjoying herself. She'd finally come to terms with the fact that she was no longer part of a sedate parade team. She was now a Rhinestone Rough Rider with the spangles to prove it.

On Linda's whistle, Liv pulled Beckett to a sliding halt, performed a rollback in perfect sync with Andie and then thundered off in the opposite direction.

"Way to go!" Margo called as she passed.

"Thanks," Liv yelled back, even though she was now too far away for Margo to hear. Shae, who'd always called her a chicken on horseback, would have been amazed at how far Liv had come.

Shae... Now, there was something to think about besides Matt and her father. Liv had to keep her promise to her mom and try to rein in her stepsister the next time they had a wedding meeting. Linda blew the whistle and Liv reversed course again.

She'd think about Shae later.

THE NEXT MORNING was Liv's first day off from the clinic, and she slept in—if one could count staying in bed until six-thirty as sleeping in. She heard Tim moving around in the kitchen as she crossed the hall to the bathroom and was glad that he was no longer heading out to the tractor at the crack of dawn. The weather had cooled over the past several days as a stormy weather pattern approached and he no longer had to try and beat the heat.

"Beautiful," Liv murmured as she caught her first glimpse of herself in the mirror. She'd showered off the arena dust the night before and had gone to bed with her hair wet. Now she was paying the price. Bent, alien hair. She reached into the drawer for an elastic and pulled her hair into a ponytail, then doubled it over and caught it again, making a messy bun that would have had her mother sending her back to the bathroom to fix it had she seen it.

Well, she couldn't see it. No one could see it because Liv was spending the day at the back fence.

Tim was gone by the time she got to the kitchen.

The carafe was full of coffee, though, and scrambled eggs were waiting in the warming oven. Maybe he really did feel better. Maybe it just took a while at his age to totally recover from whatever had knocked him for a loop.

Damn, she hoped so anyway.

She made toast, ate her eggs, did the dishes, then filled a travel cup with coffee and headed out the door toward the barn where the small tractor was parked. Tim finally had it running and she could use it to fix that fence.

Humming a little as she walked out, she stopped dead, almost dropping her cup, when she saw Matt's truck parked under the elm tree.

Not right.

The passenger door was open and Matt was dropping tools into a bucket. Liv started marching toward him. He closed the truck door and hefted the bucket just as she came to a halt a few feet away from him.

"What are you doing here?" she demanded, looking him up and down.

"Helping Tim."

For a moment, she simply stared. "I don't understand."

"It's pretty simple, Liv. I'm going to tighten the back fence so that Beckett doesn't go visiting the neighbors again."

"I'm going to do that."

"You're free to help. We'll get done twice as fast that way."

He walked toward his tractor, putting on his gloves. Liv hesitated a moment, then jogged after him. He stopped abruptly and turned toward her. Liv skidded to a stop, ending up closer to him than she'd intended. "I want to know what you're up to."

"I'm paying a debt."

"To whom?"

"To you."

Outrage boiled up inside of her. "You owe me no debt. I looked at your knee because I wanted to. No strings."

His mouth curved slightly. "Maybe that isn't the debt."

She felt the stupid color start to rise in her face. "There is no other debt."

"I took a lot of your time once. And apparently missed a lot of cues because I was pretty damned self-centered. Trust me, you dodged a bullet—"

"I know I dodged a bullet," Liv said from between her teeth. "I'm relieved, which is why there is no debt. Your payment to me was being too obtuse to realize that I was head over heels for you at that time." Her mouth tightened briefly before she repeated slowly and distinctly, in order to get it into his male brain, "At. That. Time."

He smiled again. A maddening ghost of a smile. "I've only got a couple hours to spare today. Are you coming or not?"

"No, I'm not coming."

He shrugged and started for the tractor again. Liv

fought the impulse to pull off her shoe and chuck it at his head. Instead, she headed back to the house. Out in the field, Tim puttered along on the big tractor, oblivious to the upheaval he was causing.

Although Matt didn't seem that concerned. All of the upheaval appeared to be on her part, which seemed wrong.

Well, damn.

Behind her the usually cranky tractor started up first try, and a few seconds later, the engine roared as Matt put it into gear.

Matt Montoya on her ranch. What had Tim been thinking?

She was damned well going to find out at dinner and put an end to this Matt-the-helper nonsense. The thing that bothered her was the why. Why was he doing this? Shouldn't he be roping or something? Why help Tim? Was it truly because she'd poured her guts out to him and he felt guilty? Well, if so, a better way to pay the debt would be to stay off the place. Away from her and away from Beckett.

Liv waited for all of half an hour before she walked the half mile out to where her father was working. He stopped the tractor when he saw her coming, turning off the engine as she strode across the field, his expression one of concern.

"Why is Matt Montoya stretching the fence?" she asked.

"It's sagging."

Liv kicked a clump of dirt. "You know what I mean."

"He offered. I said yes."

"Dad—"

"I felt for the kid, all right?"

"You...*what?*" Felt for the kid? Matt was no kid and why Tim would "feel" for him, she had no idea. Tim wasn't a feely type of guy.

"He's not in a good place," Tim explained, sounding more like Andie than himself.

Oh, this was great. "So the answer is to let him stretch fence."

"He offered."

For a moment Liv thought her head might explode. She pressed the palms of both hands to her temples. Then she simply turned and started walking across the field.

She'd made it all of five yards when he put the tractor back into gear. So now she had two men running tractors, which was one man too many. Liv had had enough.

She pulled the cell phone out of her pocket and dialed her mother. If someone had told Liv that she would purposely put herself in the line of fire and get involved in Shae's wedding preparations, she would have laughed, but right now it seemed like a great idea. Unfortunately, her mother wasn't answering the phone.

Liv sucked it up and dialed Shae.

"Liv, what a surprise," Shae said when she answered.

"Just checking in," Liv said. "How's it going?"

"Things are hectic. Very hectic. I got this great idea about using origami flowers instead of the real thing, but the time involved is crazy and hiring someone to do it is not going to be cheap."

"How does the cost compare to real flowers?"

"A little less than the lilies," Shae said. "But the origami would be so cool and since I'm wearing a simple column dress, the overall effect would be incredible."

A simple column dress that cost more than Liv made in a month.

"Oh, and bad news," Shae continued. "I ordered the bridesmaid dresses a week too late. The sale was no longer in effect, so they're twenty percent more than expected."

"It's only money," Liv said, hoping the irony in her words hit Shae square in the face.

It didn't.

"Yeah. I know. Hey—how are you at folding paper?"

"I—"

"Just kidding." She let out a sigh. A happy kind of sigh that told Liv that although her stepsister's life was hectic, she was enjoying her wedding preparations. "I may give up on that idea, but if I do, then I'd have to go with lilies and they are mucho expensive."

"It has to be the lilies? Why not white roses? Or carnations? Carnations smell so good."

"Oh, come on," Shae said. "First of all the symbolism is all wrong and roses are so passé. And carnations? Boutonniere fodder."

"They're pretty and they are a lot less expensive. Besides that," Liv said, thinking of her mother's call, "do you really need to break the bank on this wedding? I know it's important, but in a year or two, will it matter?"

"This will be my *one* wedding," Shae said. "I want it to be right."

"But what about mom and dad and finances?"

"I offered to pay. Dad said no, but don't worry. Reed and I will strong-arm him into taking at least half of the money."

"Are you sure you'll be able to do that?"

Shae laughed. "When haven't I been able to get Dad to do what I wanted?"

No one should be that sure of themselves and somehow it depressed Liv, who couldn't get her own father to admit that he was feeling ill.

"By the way, did you get the email about shoes?"

"Our shoes don't show, Shae."

"They're not that much."

"They're satin and pretty much one use." A total waste of seventy-nine dollars.

"Order before your size goes out of stock."

"Aye, aye," Liv said. "Well, I've got to run. Say hi to Mom for me."

"Uh, all right. Thanks for calling."

Liv hung up and shoved the phone into her pocket.

Shae drove her crazy. But she hadn't thought about Matt for a whole five aggravating minutes.

And she wasn't going to think about him. She was getting out of there. She could see the tractor at the far end of the pasture so felt safe hooking up the trailer and loading Beckett. She and her favorite confidant were going to the mountains, where she was going to put all her cares aside and enjoy a day in the saddle.

THE TRUCK AND TRAILER disappeared down the driveway in a cloud of dust. Matt opened his water bottle and took a long drink. He'd kind of hoped that he and Liv might "talk" again before he left, but it looked like she wasn't up for that.

He capped the water bottle and put it away. Another half hour and he'd have the fence done, then maybe he could talk to Tim about some other stuff he could do around the place. Just an hour or two for a few days—enough to make the point to Liv that he did pay his debts, past and present, and to maybe see if he could light her up again.

Had she been like this all along? Hiding her feistiness behind the facade of shy braininess?

The crush had probably only added to her shyness. Well, she wasn't shy now, and Matt found himself more than a little intrigued by that fact. What had made her break free?

Once the fence was finished, Matt walked out across the field Tim was working. The big tractor rolled to a stop and Tim took it out of gear and climbed down out of the cab. From the way he winced when his feet hit the ground, Matt wished he hadn't.

"All done," he said, pulling off his gloves.

Tim nodded.

"I, uh, could come back and do some other stuff." He was roping in the afternoons, but his mornings were wide-open.

"Like what?"

"What did you let slide while you were sick?"

"The grain sheds need to be scraped and painted. Screws need tightened on the plank fences. Need new gravel in the driveway, have a couple gate posts that need reset."

Okay, he hadn't expected a list, but apparently Tim had had some time to think while driving in circles around the field.

He sucked in a breath. "All right. What needs to be done first?"

"Gravel, then posts, then planks and if Liv hasn't kicked you off the property or you're not sick of paying your debt, you can tackle the sheds."

"You think she will? Try to kick me off the property?"

"I think it's a good possibility."

"Then why are you letting me help?"

"I got no beef with you." Tim pushed back the Zimmatic emblazoned ball cap he wore. "But if she kicks you off the property, then you should probably go."

"As in gives me a direct order as opposed to just hinting she doesn't want me around?"

"Yeah. Direct order."

WHEN LIV GOT BACK from work on Friday, the driveway was freshly graveled.

"Hey," she said to her father as she came into the house. "Did Walter finally get his dump truck fixed? The driveway is nice."

"Matt did it. Borrowed the truck off his dad's ranch."

Liv sat down on the arm of the sofa. "Dad, why are you letting Matt help around the place?"

"I think I answered that already."

She let out a sigh. "Fine." As long as she wasn't here when he was, she didn't care. It was a help to her father—although it irked her that he'd let Matt do stuff he wouldn't let her do. "But if he's just looking for a time to steal Beckett, I'll never forgive you."

Tim snorted. "I think he'd have done it by now."

"He still wants him," Liv said.

"So he's said."

"He has?" Liv's stomach instantly knotted.

"Yeah."

"He has other horses." One of them injured, but hey, he shouldn't be roping anyway.

"Some horses are special."

"You don't even like horses."

"But I once knew a woman that did."

Liv felt her mouth start to fall open, but caught

it before any uncensored questions popped out and caused her father to clam up. "Beckett is one of the special ones," she agreed. "I'd hate to lose him."

The thought made her feel a little sick inside.

Which might well be what Matt had felt upon losing the horse himself.

Liv didn't want to think about it. Instead, she went to her room to get ready for practice. She brushed Beckett before saddling him and loading him in the trailer.

Once upon a time Tim had known a woman who'd loved horses.

Was that woman Margo Beloit?

THE NEXT MORNING—Saturday—Liv slept in and once again she found Matt's truck parked under the elm when she walked out onto the porch with her coffee.

She was simply going to have to stop sleeping in. It was too unnerving having him on the place. Where was he this morning?

A clatter near the shed answered her question and a second later she heard the distinct sound of an aluminum ladder being put into place, followed by scraping.

Painting? Really? She could paint.

Both Tim and Matt were beginning to piss her off.

She walked around the shed to where Matt was halfway up the ladder.

"How long are you going to be doing this?" He opened his mouth and she added, "And don't give me a time estimate on the shed. How long are you going to keep coming here to 'help' my father?"

"A couple more days." He was wearing a ball cap and with the sun behind him, she couldn't see his face. But she thought he might be smiling. "Why does it bother you so much that I'm here?"

"Because Tim never lets anyone help him and it unnerves me that he's letting you," she said in a low voice, since she didn't know where her father was. The tractor wasn't running, so he could be anywhere. "Finish whatever it is you're here to do and then leave. Just…don't play games."

"I'm not here to play games, Liv." He started down the ladder and Liv had to force herself to hold her position until he got to the ground. "I'm here to pay a debt."

"Screw the debt!" Liv sucked in a breath through her teeth and once again did a surreptitious check for Tim. "I don't trust you," she said.

"No!"

"I'm not sure what your agenda is, but know this… I'm not giving up my horse."

"I'm not here for your horse, even if I want him back. There. How's that for honesty. I admitted that I'd like to have the horse. But I probably won't get him."

"Probably," Liv said, jabbing a finger at him. "You said probably. That means you're going to try."

One corner of his mouth tilted up. "Maybe it means that you'll someday see the light and sell him back."

"Ha. Fat chance."

"A guy can always hope."

"Don't waste your energy," she snapped.

"This isn't about the horse, Liv. Tim needs the help. I have a few hours I can give him in the morning before I practice. Maybe he's more comfortable with me helping him than with making his daughter do manual labor. Has that ever occurred to you?"

"I happen to like manual labor."

"But does Tim like having you do it?"

No, he did not. Which was an outdated notion, but one he'd never successfully shaken.

"Liv, I'm not here to make you miserable."

"Well, you are."

"Sorry."

"Ha," she said again before turning and stalking toward the house.

"ARE YOU STILL working here?" Tim asked as he sauntered around the corner of the barn. Together they watched Liv march off toward the house, sloshing coffee out of her cup as she went.

"She didn't give a direct order to leave," Matt said. "Just wanted to know how much longer I was going to be here."

"And you told her...?"

"A couple more days."

"Then your debt will be paid?"

"In a way."

Tim was silent for a moment. He reached out with the toe of his ancient boot to nudge a dirt clod. Then he cocked his head as he looked up at Matt. "Why don't you just ask her to dinner or something?"

Matt wasn't going to hedge. If the old man had figured out part of his motive—to get a bead on Liv—then so be it. "Don't think she'd go with me."

Tim once again fixed his attention on the clod. "Probably not." And that was that. Tim was not going to elaborate on why she probably wouldn't go out with Matt and Matt wasn't going to ask questions. Nope. Better to leave things as they were.

"Well, if you could tighten up those gate posts before your debt is paid, I'd appreciate it."

Matt grinned. "You got it. And, Tim? If you ever need help again, give me a call."

"If you're here."

Matt snorted. "Actually, I hope I'm not." He hoped he was back on the road pursuing his title. "If I am, though, I'd be glad to lend a hand."

Matt spent a good two hours on the sheds, prepping them for painting. He figured tomorrow he'd get that job done, the next day he'd reset the three gate posts and then his time here was through. Debt paid.

And no more excuses for running into Liv.

CRAIG HAD DINNER—two frozen entrées—in the oven when Matt got home from roping practice with Jed. Clancy had not done well and Jed's wife, who'd run the chute for them, still hadn't had her baby. Everyone was antsy, so it wasn't the best practice ever, but it was practice. Matt's swollen knee was proof.

"You're late," Craig said before Matt got in the door. "Off seeing that lady friend of yours again?"

"I have no lady friend and no. I was roping. Like I told you." Matt pulled his hat off and hung it, now well trained in the put-your-stuff-away department.

"Right. No lady friend. Then why do you keep hanging around her ranch?"

"I'm not— Never mind."

"I talked to my mom," Craig said, unfazed, "and she thinks she knows of a horse you can lease up in Belgrade."

"Great." Clancy was coming along, but Matt needed something more reliable during the weeks while Ready healed. "By the way," Matt said as he washed his hands at the kitchen sink, "did she say how the job is going?" Translation: Will you be starting school here? Not that Matt minded having the kid around. As time passed he discovered that he appreciated not being alone all the time.

"The job's going good." He swung the monitor around. "Here's the horse email."

Matt leaned over and quickly scanned the message. Yes, she was doing well—or at least that was what she was telling her son—and planned to come and see him on her first free day.

"She hasn't had a day off?"

"She's been volunteering to work extra days. There are only a couple of full-time positions and she wants one."

"I understand. And next time you write, tell her you can stay as long as you want."

"Really?"

"What can I say?" Matt asked, straightening up again. "You're good company." And his cleaning lady would be quite happy if Craig stayed on for a while. He could probably tell her to stop coming, since all she did was to vacuum the already clean carpet and wash down the already clean kitchen. But once Craig left, he was going to need her, so he let her enjoy her easy days and paid her full price.

Matt jotted down the number of the horse owner— a guy whose name he recognized—then went outside to call while he checked Ready's bandage.

"Yeah, hi," he said when the man answered the phone. "This is Matt Montoya from Dillon and I'm looking for a rope horse to lease. I heard that you might have something available."

"Matt Montoya?"

"Yes," he said with a smile in his voice. There were some perks to being known.

"Um. Well, unfortunately, the horse is no longer available for lease."

"You've already placed him?"

"No."

"Then…" Suddenly Matt knew why the horse was

no longer available, and why the guy was speaking in such a clipped, no-nonsense tone. The story about Beckett. How far had it spread?

I have people who will vouch for me....

But Matt wasn't going to beg. "Thanks," he said before abruptly ending the call.

"Already gone, eh?" Craig asked.

"Yeah." Matt set down the phone.

"I'll have Mom keep an eye out."

"Thanks," Matt said just as the timer went off. Craig jumped up from the computer and put on two oven mitts before taking the aluminum trays out of the oven.

"Go wash up," he directed. "I'll set the table."

"Thanks." Matt walked down the hall to the bathroom, closed the door and stared at himself in the mirror for a moment. He had dirt on his face from the arena. Automatically, he reached for a washcloth, dampened it and rubbed it over his face.

He was irked, but wasn't able to bring himself to fully blame Liv anymore. Trena had done this to him, to make him pay for crimes he may or may not have committed.

No. He'd committed some crimes. He'd left her alone for too long. He could tell himself all he wanted that she'd agreed to the deal, but when she found she hated the road, he hadn't tried to make any concessions. Her revenge seemed over the top, but maybe that was just how bitter he'd made her. He'd probably never know because they'd probably never cross paths again.

So what now?

He didn't want to sink thirty thousand dollars, at the minimum, into a new horse, but he needed something that would put him in the money until Ready was, well, ready.

All he could do was put the word out that he needed a horse temporarily—at least until the Bitterroot Challenge was over. The problem was that most of the guys he knew who owned horses of the caliber he was looking for were using those horses and were also his strongest competition.

Maybe he could ask Liv to borrow Beckett. Not to take him back permanently. Just to borrow him. Or lease him.

Would she agree?

Maybe he shouldn't have been pushing things with her the way he'd been recently. It didn't strengthen his position, but he hadn't realized just what kind of position he was going to be in.

CHAPTER TWELVE

SINCE MATT HAD STARTED working around the place, Tim had become distant in a way that Liv couldn't quite define, but still felt. He was preoccupied rather than defensive. As if he were thinking deep thoughts, coming to important decisions.

Did it have to do with his health? With other issues? What other issues could he have?

The crazy thing was that he'd also become more open in some ways. He occasionally asked her questions about work and the people she saw there, about drill practice and her teammates. He didn't ask specific questions, but instead set the stage and then let her rattle on, encouraging her with a nod or a word or two. Strange for a guy who'd never been much of a conversationalist. Not that he was conversing, but he was listening and not retreating behind a book or newspaper. It was odd, almost as if he were trying to get some quality fathering in at the last minute—a thought that totally froze her up. Tonight, however, would not be one of the new chitchat-at-dinner nights.

"I have an unscheduled practice this evening," Liv said when she came in the door after work. "A dress rehearsal. If it's okay with you, maybe we could just reheat the rest of the spaghetti from yesterday?"

"Fine," Tim called as Liv headed past him to her bedroom. "But why do you need a dress rehearsal? It's going to rain tomorrow. Surely they'll cancel the performance."

Liv shook her head. "From what I hear, the show goes on even if the arena is a giant bog."

Tim lowered his book to his lap. "Should be interesting."

Liv sincerely hoped that the performance didn't go beyond interesting. "Will you be coming to see us?" she asked. "I'm sure you'll run into some of your buddies there." And she really wanted Tim to spend some time with other people instead of keeping himself holed up on the ranch.

"I don't think so. Not this time anyway."

Liv felt a pang of disappointment, but she smiled. "I guess I can understand wanting to stay home warm and dry."

It DIDN'T TAKE long for Liv to understand the need for a dress rehearsal. It took time to deck out the horses. The manes and tails were braided in a certain way that Gretchen demonstrated to the newer folk, and Linda wanted to make certain all the equipment was on right.

After the equipment check, they went through the drill once slowly, mimicking the speed they'd have to travel in a muddy arena if it did indeed rain the next day.

"Now, ladies," Linda bellowed after the run through, "do it that way tomorrow."

"Shall we do it again?" Ronnie called.

"Good heavens, no." Linda looked horrified. "We don't want to risk jinxing ourselves." Linda smiled tightly, then dismissed the team.

Once at her trailer, Liv removed Beckett's bridle, put on his halter and tied him before heading off to use the facilities before the drive home. A few minutes later Susie breezed by her, going into the restroom as Liv came out.

"You have a visitor at your trailer," she said brightly. "Matt Montoya."

Liv's first instinct was to race back to reclaim her horse, but instead she walked. Rapidly. She slowed her pace as she rounded Margo's trailer, which had up until that point blocked her view. Sure enough, Matt was standing next to her trailer, rubbing Beckett's ears and talking low as the big sorrel leaned into him. She instantly sensed a familiarity between man and horse, a bond, and she didn't like it one bit.

"What are you doing?" She spoke calmly, considering the fact that she wanted to order Matt away from Beckett.

Matt simply smiled at her. That crooked, make-the-knees-go-weak smile he used so well. Well, it wasn't going to work. "I'm early for the roping."

Liv put a hand on Beckett's neck without conscious

thought. It was only when she felt his solid muscles beneath her palm that she realized she was in essence claiming him.

Matt, taking the hint, stepped away from the horse and then gave Liv an exaggerated once-over, taking in the red silk shirt with the long white fringe, shimmering jeans, giant sparkly belt buckle. He smiled slightly but didn't make a comment. She was glad she wasn't wearing the hat with the tiara—only because she'd forgotten the tiara in the truck, much to Linda's displeasure.

"So the big day is tomorrow."

"Yes. And I'm nervous, which probably seems stupid to someone like you who's spent so much time in front of crowds." There. She was making conversation. She was in control.

"I'm always nervous."

"You have more at stake."

"Yeah…" Matt fell silent, but he had more to say. Liv waited, acutely aware of the now familiar stirring inside of her. He was hot, as Etta said, and that hotness was a threat—mainly because she didn't know how to handle it. If he came on to her, she had to say no.

She didn't want to.

People rode by, someone knocked against the far side of Liv's trailer, but she barely noticed. She needed to move, get out of there. Instead, she said, "How's the knee?"

"I'm doing my exercises."

"Are you roping?"

"I am."

"Ill effects?"

"None so far."

"Try to keep it that way. Don't push things."

"Is that the professional talking?"

"Of course," she said with a cool half smile. She could do this, hold her own against Matt.

"Tim asked me to take you to dinner the other night."

The smile instantly evaporated, as did her cool demeanor. "My father asked you to take me to dinner?" Matt nodded and even though it seemed improbable, she believed him. "But you didn't take me to dinner," she pointed out, struggling to regain her composure.

"Would you have gone?"

"Maybe."

"Want to go to dinner, Liv?"

"No."

He laughed and all Liv could think was "Please do not ask why," because she didn't have an answer. Not one she could articulate, anyway, so instead she changed the subject—back to his knee.

"Have you gone to see McElroy?"

"No." The laughter faded from Matt's eyes. Liv wanted more, like a cross-your-heart promise not to support a drug-dealing charlatan, but it wasn't her business and the last time she'd poked her nose into his affairs, she'd caused herself trouble.

"I need to unsaddle my horse," she said.

"Is that a hint for me to leave?" Again he gave her the smile that made her feel as if…something…was about to happen between them.

No, it wasn't.

Matt reached out to rub Beckett's ears before she could say anything.

"I'll see you around, old son," he murmured to the horse. "You, too," he said to Liv, who stood planted to the spot, unable to move without taking an awkward side step.

"Looking forward to it," she said, trying for casual, managing husky.

Matt had barely walked away when Andie came out from around the trailer.

"I didn't want to interrupt."

"Nothing to interrupt," Liv said. She pulled the cinch loose and started unsaddling her horse, very much aware of the look her friend was giving her and choosing to pretend she was not.

HE HADN'T BEEN able to bring himself to ask to borrow Beckett. Liv didn't trust him. The look on her face when she'd seen him standing there with the horse had been telling. She was afraid he was going to take "her" horse and he wasn't going to risk a flat-out "no" with zero possibility for negotiation.

Not that he was giving up, but he was going to wait a day or two. Figure out the best way to ask. Mentioning Tim's dinner plans hadn't been the smartest thing to do, but he'd half hoped she'd say yes and then maybe they could discuss the matter in a more relaxed environment. So much for half hopes.

And if he was telling himself he only wanted to go out with Liv because of Beckett, well, he was a liar. He was curious about her and it didn't help that every time they met, every time she faced him down, he became more and more aware of her as an attractive woman. Liv had changed, he had changed, and maybe it was time to discover what possibilities—if any—lay between them.

He went home and, after feeding Craig a pizza since it was his turn to cook, he saddled up Clancy and rode in small circles around the round pen. Back in the early days of his career, Matt trained his own horses. Now he sent them off to trainers. Clancy had been set to leave in July, but now…

Now nothing. He needed a rope horse and he was fooling himself if he thought Clancy could do the job while Ready healed. He was going to have to try to pull in some favors.

And he needed his knee to stop throbbing.

Take the season off. Let Ryan have his victory. It didn't matter.

If only.

It was more than Ryan. He wasn't ready to retire yet; wasn't ready to risk having to go to work for his dad just to support himself. He didn't have many marketable skills, so he needed to milk this roping gig for as long as he could. Come up with some skills.

Such as…

Go back to school? He hadn't graduated with his first degree. In fact, he'd let his classes slide to the point that he'd been put on academic probation and that was when he'd quit instead of getting another tutor. The old man had thrown a fit, but he seemed all right with the decision after Matt started inching his way up the world standings.

For now, he needed a decent horse. Not a lease, but a purchase, which was going to take research and time—which he didn't have. But what was his other choice?

Beckett.

Liv, SUFFERING FROM A massive case of performance anxiety, did not sleep well the night before the performance, and when she did sleep, she dreamed that she and Beckett ran the drill backwards while Linda fiercely tooted her whistle at them and screamed for them to stop! Turn around! Do it right!

It was almost a relief to ride into the muddy arena the next afternoon and perform the drill in the misting rain. She'd made one small mistake, probably unnoticeable to the casual observer, caught herself, corrected and other than that performed a flawless routine.

"Well done, ladies," Linda said after they'd left the arena and gathered just outside the gate. "We'll meet at my trailer in ten minutes. Just a couple notes about tomorrow's performances, then you're free to go."

The group chattered happily as they dismounted

and led their horses toward their trailers, the spangles on their pant legs glittering through the mud splatters.

"One down," Andie said before she and Liv parted ways.

"Nine to go," Liv said, thinking that now that she'd survived the first performance and knew what to expect, she could do this in front of an audience and enjoy it. She was relieved, satisfied, and...hallucinating? Because the guy walking down the bleacher stairs and stepping out into the rain looked very familiar.

Tim?

He disappeared behind a concession stand and Liv decided she had to be mistaken, but as she started for the parking lot, she saw her father's distinctive truck parked under the eaves behind the arena—almost as if he'd been hiding it.

What on earth? She led Beckett in the direction of the truck just as Tim reappeared from behind the stand and pulled his keys out of his pocket.

"Dad?" she called before he opened the door. He gave a jerk, almost dropping the keys, and then, when he turned to face her he wore an expression she'd never seen before—a you-caught-me look.

"Liv. I was on my way home from the parts store and thought I'd stop and see you ride," he said. But from the way he was looking past her, Liv had a feeling it was more than that.

"Are you...feeling okay?" she asked.

"Fine. Fine. Like I said, I thought I'd stop and make sure you don't have any trouble getting home."

"I thought you were here to watch me ride."

"That, too."

"I have to talk to Linda for a few minutes about the logistics of tomorrow's performance." She held up the reins. "You want to take Beckett back to the trailer and load him? I'm sure he'd like to get out of the weather."

"Uh, yeah. Sure."

Liv watched him lead the horse away, wondering if it was a good or bad sign that he was down here. Was he terminal? Or trying to be more of a traditional father? A little late for the latter and she refused to think about the former.

Linda waited near her trailer until everyone was gathered around her, some still mounted, others on foot. "We did great!" she said. "And I think we'll do just as well tomorrow. The rain is supposed to let up, so make an effort to get the mud stains off your gear before tomorrow's performance."

Liv looked down at her spattered pants. Oh, yeah. She had some work ahead of her.

"Be sure to get here early. If you have a flat tire, call…"

Liv tuned out as Linda went through her list. Why was her father there and acting so oddly? Once Linda had finished, Liv walked with Andie as far as her trailer.

"Your dad is here," Andie said. "I saw him leaving the stands."

"Yeah. He said he wanted to make sure I got home

okay what with the mud and all." Andie gave Liv a quizzical look. "Yeah. I know," Liv said. "Worries me. But," she continued in a lighter tone, "no matter why he's here, I'd better see that he gets home."

"Maybe I could…I don't know…talk to him before you guys leave? Try to see if he'd come in for a physical?"

"I'm afraid it'll just make him more stubborn if he thinks I orchestrated something like that."

"You're probably right." Andie shrugged. "Keep at him."

"Will do." Liv started for her trailer, her boots nearly coming off her feet in the mud as she walked. She could see Tim standing at the rear, looking off at something she couldn't see. She walked down the opposite side of the trailer to tell him she was ready to go, when she heard Margo say, "Long time, Tim."

Liv stopped dead. There was something in Margo's steely tone that made Liv quite certain she did not want the older woman to know she was there. Tim didn't answer, which was no big surprise, but Margo had more to say.

"I've seen you here a couple of times."

Really? Her dad had been at practice and Liv hadn't known it? This was getting strange. And it got even stranger when Margo said, "You look like hell, Tim."

"You don't." Tim's voice was flat. Matter-of-fact.

Margo snorted. "Thanks." There was a long moment of silence during which Liv held totally still, embarrassed to be where she was and knowing if she didn't say something soon, it would be too late. Then Margo ensured her continued silence by saying, "I've never forgiven you, you know."

"I figured as much." Liv held her breath. It was wrong to eavesdrop, but she didn't know how to extricate herself from her hiding spot gracefully. "How long have you been back?" he finally asked.

"Does it matter?" Margo replied. Tim did not answer and a few seconds later she said softly, "As I thought. You're such a coward, Tim. You tore me to pieces in the name of doing *what's right,* and I think you should rot because of it."

"Margo—"

"What, Tim? I've been waiting a long time to tell you that to your face."

"I never meant to hurt you."

"Bullshit. You meant to save yourself being beholden and if I got hurt in the process, that was secondary to your freedom."

"That's not true."

"It's true from where I stand." Margo slapped her hand on the side of the trailer, startling Liv. "If you could have bent a little, just a little, Tim, I think we could have been happy."

Margo's voice broke slightly, but she cleared her throat and continued, "Back then, anyway. Before I knew how a real partnership worked."

Liv felt heat start to creep into her cheeks. What had happened between her father and Margo?

"And just so you know, I never touched that money you sent me back."

"It was your money."

"It was our money, Tim. *Ours!*" Margo let out a disgusted snort, then said, "I'm done." A few seconds later she appeared at the rear of the trailer, thankfully marching directly toward her trailer without looking back.

For a moment Liv stood frozen where she was, uncertain as to how to handle the next few dicey moments. If she just appeared, would Tim realize that she'd heard everything?

Not if she were noisy. When she heard Tim start to move, she walked to the back of the trailer where he was just closing the door, her boots making suction noises in the deep mud.

"I can't wait to get out of these wet clothes," she said in an overly loud voice, stepping up onto the running board to run her hand over Beckett's nose. "Ready to go home, big guy?"

She turned back to her father, who looked about as tense as she could ever remember, which was something, since Tim was one of the most tightly wound individuals she knew. "Thanks for loading him. Let's get home and I'll make us some tea."

"I think I'd prefer bourbon."

No doubt. "Whatever it takes," Liv said.

Tim insisted on parking the trailer and unhooking it in the rain while Liv put Beckett away. He was slightly stooped as they headed across the yard and into the house.

"Did you hear?" he finally asked, putting Liv in the position of having to choose between lying to her father and embarrassing him. It took almost half a second to decide. She met his eyes blandly, a slight frown drawing her eyebrows together.

"What?"

He studied her for a moment and Liv hung on to her innocent expression for all she was worth. She didn't want to know about Tim and Margo, didn't want to know what her father had done that made Margo call him a coward. Tim was the least cowardly person she knew, but Margo obviously didn't share her opinion. And the money. Their money.

Worlds were colliding, and Liv felt like she was smack in the middle.

"I, uh…" He let out a breath and started to the porch. After a slight hesitation, Liv followed. Once inside, they took off their dripping rain gear and then Liv headed straight to the kitchen to put on the kettle, ignoring the fact that her wet clothes were uncomfortably plastered to her skin.

"Do we even have bourbon?" she called into the living room.

"Cancel the bourbon," Tim said.

"Tea?"

"Nothing. I think I'll take a shower and go to bed."

Liv waited in the kitchen while the kettle boiled, going over the conversation in her head for about the hundredth time. She liked Margo, who seemed like a down-to-earth, genuinely nice person. But what did she really know about her? She certainly hadn't suspected that she and Tim had a history—and a very intimate one if they were sharing money and ripping each other apart.

The big question was, when had all this happened? Before her mother? After? During?

Liv pressed a hand to her forehead. She hoped it wasn't during. As it was, drill team had just become a whole lot more complicated.

MATT SPENT THE morning with Craig, helping him decide whether to buy a netbook or a tablet with the money Willa had just sent to Matt for Craig's keep. Matt was not taking a cent for having someone to talk to. Even if that someone was a kid, it beat staring at the walls. After Trena had left, Matt had kept himself very busy on the road; before she'd left, he'd had someone around when he was home. It struck him that he was beginning to hate spending so much time alone.

Craig eventually decided on a tablet. Matt placed the order, then they celebrated with a trip to the feed store for grain followed by dinner at the drive-in.

"What if I have to start school here?" Craig asked, finally airing the issue that had kept him quiet for most of the trip. "Mom said that she may not get an answer on her job until the end of the season. If school starts before she knows, then what am I going to do?"

Unpack? The kid was still living out of his suitcase. He did laundry, then folded it and put it back in the suitcase, even though Matt had emptied the bureau in the guest room for Craig's stuff.

"I guess you start school here," Matt said. "We'll probably have to see about getting you registered eventually. Shouldn't be a big deal transferring once your mom gets the job."

"Great." Craig smiled and started to put in his headphones. He had them halfway to his ears when he glanced at Matt and then wadded them back up and pocketed them. "Bad habit," he said.

"It's good to be available to the people around you," Matt said. Something he'd failed at with Trena. He'd been too tired to provide decent company half the time. It didn't have to be that way, though. Matt had made it that way.

Once home, they unloaded the grain, Craig dragging the bags to the edge of the pickup bed and Matt tossing them into the grain shed. They'd just finished when a big red Dodge pulled into the driveway, and Matt's stomach tightened.

Why was the old man here? This couldn't be good.

Then he saw his mother, small, blonde and smiling, and realized exactly what this was. A frontal mother assault. He hadn't called enough lately, so she was coming to visit.

Feeling vaguely ashamed of himself—when was he

going to get this relationship stuff right?—he walked over and waited for his parents to get out of the vehicle.

"Good to see you, Mom." He reached out to hug her, then awkwardly clapped his father's shoulder.

"And this must be Crag," she said as Craig stepped out of the house to stand next to Matt.

"Craig, ma'am." Craig extended his hand for a formal handshake, but his mother was having none of that.

"Crag, Craig, all the same," she said as she hugged him.

"Not if your name is Crag," the kid said. Nina laughed. Matt had always loved his mom's laugh. It came from the heart, because his mom was a genuinely happy person and he was going to do his best to keep her that way.

"We're just here for a minute or two, dear," she said to Matt. "Your father said you were going to call and when you didn't, well, you know the saying about Mohammed and the mountain."

"Yeah." Matt shoved his hands into his back pockets. Nina glanced up at her husband then back at Craig. "I'd love to have a glass of something. What have you got?"

"Mountain Dew," Craig said promptly.

"Sounds lovely." She smiled at Matt and followed Craig into the house, leaving Matt where he didn't want to be. Alone with his father.

"Word had it your horse got injured," Charles said.

"Scraped up. He's getting better fast." Just not fast enough.

"Maybe this is some kind of a sign," his father said.

"And since when are you a big believer in signs?"

"Since I decided I didn't want to see you get hurt."

Matt scowled. What the hell? "Not get hurt or not compete?"

"Same thing, really."

"I've never seen you get all concerned before. I've had other injuries."

"You're getting older."

"Bullshit, Dad. This is about something else."

"Meaning?"

"Meaning that sometimes I think you want Ryan Madison to walk away with the Bitterroot Challenge purse." His heart did a quick thud against his ribs as the words he'd kept from saying for so long came out.

Charles turned red, but his voice was only slightly strained when he said, "Why? You're my son."

All Matt did was hold his gaze, but there must have been something in his face that clued in the old man to what Matt knew. Charles Montoya clamped his jaw tighter, to the point that his lips began to show white against his reddened skin.

"I'm competing, Dad."

"I hope you win," Charles said. "And that you come out whole."

"And I hope that my mother continues to be a very happy woman." He gave his father the dead eye. "Do we understand one another?"

"Hey, Matt," Craig yelled out the door. "The Mountain Dew is poured."

"Thanks," he said, instantly turning toward the house, leaving his father to do whatever the hell he wanted.

By the time his parents left, his head was aching from stress. His dad had actually done an excellent job of appearing normal, so he hoped his mother didn't catch on that something was wrong between the two of them—or something more wrong than usual.

"You okay?" Craig asked after loading the dishwasher.

"Fine. Just tired."

"You want to get some practice in?"

They worked out a system where Matt roped and turned back alone and Craig moved the animals through the chute, then released him. It took time, but Clancy got practice, as did Matt.

"Not tonight. I think I'll do some work on the computer, then call it a night."

TWO DAYS AFTER the encounter with his father, Matt ended up with a temporary horse. He had no idea if his dad was involved, if it was some kind of peace offering, but Alvie Maynard, one of Matt's early roping mentors and an old friend of his father's, called and offered a mare for lease with an option to buy. Matt jumped on the deal, asking no questions that he didn't want the answers to.

His new mount, Snigs, was in good shape and fast. Not as fast as Ready or Beckett, but definitely competitive and she had good calf sense. She was also rough as hell on the stops. On the second catch, Matt jumped off early and almost went down. He limped to the calf and threw the animal, pain tearing through his joint.

"You okay?" Craig hollered across the arena.

"Stitch in my side," Matt yelled back.

Something had to give.

That night he fell asleep while checking standings with an ice bag on his swollen knee. He woke up with a Ziploc bag of water on the floor next to his feet and his laptop about to slide down to join it. Matt caught the computer and dragged it back into position and then reached down to cautiously touch the ruined joint, gritting his teeth at the pain.

He needed stronger anti-inflammatory medication and he needed something for pain. He was tired of piddling around, practicing less intensely than he should.

It was time to do something about it.

CHAPTER THIRTEEN

"I HAVE GOSSIP," Etta said.

Liv was not surprised. Etta not only had acute hearing, but she also haunted Facebook and had a huge network of friends. "Is it good gossip?"

Etta shook her head. "Disturbing."

"Yeah?" Liv had a bad feeling.

"Well, maybe not disturbing, but troubling…"

"Etta?"

"Matt Montoya was calf roping down at the arena with the other ropers."

"So?" Liv knew he was doing breakaway at home with the help of Craig. She'd learned that from Etta earlier that week.

"He's throwing calves and tying. And he's not limping afterward." Liv stopped going through her files. "Not even a little," the receptionist added significantly.

"Did you see him?"

"As a matter of fact, I did. Not only that, I asked him if he had any trouble finding Dr. McElroy. He just smiled."

That didn't mean he was using McElroy, but Liv didn't like the sound of it.

"Was he wearing his brace?"

"Yes, but—" Etta pressed her magenta-tinted lips together "—go see for yourself. You practice tomorrow, right? Just wander over to the roping arena and take a look. I bet he's there and you'll see what I mean."

"It's Matt's life," Liv said as she headed for the PT room. Matt's life, Matt's leg, and even if she hated the thought of him shooting himself up with painkillers, it was none of her business.

MATT WAS LOADING the dishwasher. It was his turn since Craig had put the frozen lasagna into the oven and poured dressing over the lettuce.

"I know your mom doesn't want you going to your friend Benny's house," Matt said as he scraped left-over lettuce into the trash, "but maybe he could come over here. Do you think she'd be okay with that?" Matt was becoming concerned about the kid spending all his time either with him or alone.

Craig shook his head from where he sat at the computer. "Benny's off seeing his real dad for six weeks."

"Where's his dad?"

"Dakota oil fields. I guess Benny gets to stay in his dad's trailer and play video games all day. He doesn't miss his sisters one bit."

"Or so he says."

"I guess, but come on…six little sisters? Pfft."

"Yeah. That does seem like a lot."

"And since he's the only boy and the only step-kid in the family, he feels kind of weird sometimes, you know?"

"I can imagine."

Matt wondered if Craig knew who his father was. Willa hadn't ever told anyone, but there'd been quite a bit of speculation at the Montoya dinner table whenever Matt had mustered up the strength to go to Sunday dinners.

And that in turn made him wonder if Ryan knew that Charles was his father. Surely he would have rubbed it into Matt's face by now if he did know.

"I thought practice went pretty good tonight," Craig said. "And I liked the part where Jed almost fell off his horse when he got the phone call."

Matt laughed. Looking back it'd been comical, but at the time he'd been concerned. Jed hadn't wanted to rope that night, but Corrie had forced him, telling him that he was driving her crazy. Before he'd made his first catch, she'd called and said she thought the baby was coming. Fast. Less than an hour later Jed had called Matt to tell him that little Eva Corrina had made a safe entrance into the world shortly after he'd raced into the delivery room and mother and child were doing well. The father needed a stiff drink.

"Your times are getting better," Craig said, studying the list he'd made during practice before entering the numbers into a spreadsheet he'd made. "But Madison is still consistently faster." Craig was starting to take the Montoya-Madison rivalry personally. "Probably because he has both knees."

"My knee is getting better," Matt said automatically. It was definitely hurting less, thanks to the pain injections. He only planned to take them twice a week, so he could practice dismounting, throwing and tying, and Dr. McElroy was happy to comply. And since it was his knee, his future, and he'd researched the possible consequences, Matt didn't feel one bit guilty. In fact, it felt good to have a few hours without pain.

"Good thing," Craig said, typing away. "Just don't push it. You still have a couple weeks before the Bitterroot."

"Thanks, coach," Matt said with a smile as he closed the dishwasher. He was going to miss Craig when Willa got that job.

LIV KNEW BETTER—knew that she didn't want to face the truth—but in spite of that, she stayed after drill practice to watch the ropers. Matt was there, on a horse she didn't recognize, which wasn't surprising because he had so many practice horses.

He flew out of the chute, caught in less than five seconds and was off the horse without any sign of pain or favoring the leg. None of her business. No reason she should feel cold inside.

But she did.

Go home...

She turned on her heel and walked back to the warm-up arena where she spotted Matt dismounting the red roan next to a fancy trailer with living quarters.

"Nice job," she said coldly. His head whipped around at the sound of her voice.

"Thanks." He pulled the saddle off the horse and carried it to the tack room with only the barest trace of a limp.

"I thought you weren't going to see McElroy."

He didn't play innocent. She'd give him credit for that.

"It's really none of your business, Liv."

Funny. She'd told herself that, but here she was. "What you're doing is stupid."

"Still none of your business."

"I know, but..."

"But what, Liv?"

"Maybe I hate to see you doing this to yourself."

"Why?"

How to fight the truth? "We've known each other a long time. Maybe I've come to kind of care what happens to you." She felt her cheeks go warm at the half-baked admission.

"Kind of care?" Matt asked, raising an eyebrow.

"Never mind."

She turned away, but before she took a step one of his hands settled onto her shoulder, stopping her. She could feel the strength in his fingers, even though his touch was light.

Just keep going.

His hand slid down to her upper arm, and gently, he turned her to face him.

"You're making a mistake with your knees," she said stubbornly.

"A lot of other guys have made this mistake and lived to tell the tale."

"Why is roping so damned—" The rest of the sentence was lost as he pulled her closer, startling her, and his mouth settled over hers.

Liv stiffened at the unexpected contact, her hands automatically coming up to flatten against the front of his shirt, putting up a barrier even as a small part of her whispered, *About time.*

His lips were warm, his chest hard as his heart beat steadily beneath her palms, and Liv found herself leaning into the kiss, breathing in the scent of man and arena dust and thinking it was one heady combination. The familiar and the unfamiliar. The unfamiliar was definitely the better of the two.

Matt ended the kiss seconds later, his point—whatever that may be—made, and Liv simply stared up at him, stunned at what had just happened. *Really? He thought he could just kiss her?*

Apparently so, because he gave her an odd look, as if surprised at the heat that had flared between them, then lowered his head to kiss her again. This time, though, Liv was ready and when his lips touched hers, she took the sides of his face in her hands and kissed him back. Kissed him deeply, touching her tongue to his, tentatively at first, then more boldly, to show him just who could kiss whom…and to see once and for all if what she'd wanted so desperately in high school had been worth all the sleepless nights.

Oh, yes. Worth every one.

Matt wrapped his arms around her, pulling her against him as he kissed her back, setting her senses ablaze, and then, while she could still think straight—or relatively straight—Liv pulled away, out of his embrace, touching her fingertips to her swollen lips.

This time it was Matt who looked stunned as his hands dropped back to his sides and through an onslaught of conflicting emotions, Liv felt a distinct sense of satisfaction. And a need to escape. Too much to process in a short period of time.

"I have to go," she said.

Matt shoved his hands into his pockets and it was all she could do not to follow the motion with her eyes. She wanted to look at what she'd felt pressing against her during that last kiss, but decided it might not be the best move.

"Because…"

"Because this is not what I want."

"You seemed to want it a few seconds ago."

"Changed my mind," Liv said as she started toward her trailer.

"You seek me out, claim to 'kind of' care, then this. What the hell, Liv?"

She rounded on him, found him only a few feet away from her. How had he managed to get so close?

"What the hell? I'll tell you what the hell. Don't kiss me, okay? Don't touch me."

Matt raised his hands, very much as he did when he'd finished tying a calf's legs together. Only this was a gesture of surrender, not victory. "Whatever," he muttered. He turned on his heel and walked back to his horse, leaving Liv staring after him before she stalked to her truck and trailer, where she unlocked the door with shaking fingers.

She hated confrontation. Hated being tongue-tied. Hated being kissed when she wasn't ready.

You are no longer that tongue-tied, confrontation-hating person. You are able stand up for yourself.

That might be so, but Liv also wished she didn't know that kissing Matt was every bit as good as she'd once thought it would be.

"Liv!"

Her head snapped up and she saw Matt heading back toward her, a serious expression on his face.

Why couldn't he have just let her drive away? Be done with him? "What?" she asked.

"You're right." He stopped a few feet away from her, allowing her some much-needed distance. "I shouldn't have kissed you."

"Yeah" was all she could come up with. An uncomfortable silence followed as she studied the dusty ground near his scuffed-up boots.

"Liv?" She slowly raised her gaze to his, telling herself she couldn't pretend this wasn't happening. "What's going on?"

More than she was comfortable with, that was for sure, which was why she was in high retreat mode. She cleared her throat, which suddenly seemed to be closing on her. Panic perhaps. "I don't know," she said softly.

"Bull." The word was equally soft, surprisingly gentle. Not what she expected from him after...well, after.

"This is not the place to discuss it," she said as a couple of ropers rode by, nodding at Matt who gave an unsmiling nod to each in return.

"If not here, then where? When?" he asked once the riders had passed.

"Is there anything to discuss?" Discussing meant acknowledging and Liv felt much more comfortable in denial right now. If she denied and kept her distance, then she wasn't going to have to deal with Matt. Matt, who kissed so well. Matt, who was standing in front of her right now, waiting for a response she didn't want to give.

Matt, who took a slow step forward, as if afraid of spooking her. Liv's breath caught. Truthfully, she had no clue how to handle her attraction to him. It just didn't fit into her master plan—the one where she controlled her own destiny.

If she hooked up with a strong-willed guy like Matt, a guy who had one hell of a time taking no for an answer, then she was basically digging the grave for her independence.

And she would not do that.

So she took the coward's way out. "I need to go, Matt."

"When?"

She pressed her lips together briefly. Take control. Do what you want to do. "I'm not seeing any time clear in the near future."

Matt's expression hardened. "Because I kissed you?"

"Partly."

"And because of McElroy's knee treatments?"

"Partly."

"And the rest?"

"The rest is all me."

SHAE HAD SEEMED oddly subdued during the cake tasting and the lunch that Vivian treated them to afterward, and Liv felt exactly the same way. Quiet. Preoccupied, which made it difficult to focus on her mission of keeping Shae's spending under control. They decided on the spice cake—Reed having given Shae his blessing to choose without him since he was on a business trip—with buttercream frosting instead of fondant. There would, of course, be tasteful layers and supports and cascading flowers.

Vivian had noticed Shae's mood also and suggested, when her stepdaughter had excused herself to take a phone call, that it was prewedding jitters. Liv thought instead that Shae's mood might be because she couldn't think of anything else to spend money on now that she'd signed a contract on the most expensive cake in the western part of the state.

Yes, the wedding was going to be tasteful and beautiful—an event that could be featured as a spread in a magazine, which was probably why it was being covered by a regional publication. A fairy-tale Montana wedding. Oh, joy.

Shae came back from her phone call beaming. Reed had agreed with the spice cake. She'd been concerned during the tasting, since she'd promised to try to keep the cost to a minimum, but with the magazine spread and all, it was important to have the right cake.

Vivian beamed back at Shae and reached out to pat her hand. "The spice cake is perfect," she said.

Liv also smiled. Perfect cake. Perfect groom. Perfect wedding. Perfect life.

Must be nice.

The rest of the day with Shae went well. Now that she and Reed were on the same page cake-wise, she was her old self, which made Liv think that perhaps he was a good match for her if she was concerned with what he thought instead of just riding roughshod over him. Finally, at close to 4:00 p.m. she hugged her mother goodbye, got an air kiss from Shae and started the long drive home.

Liv pulled into the town of White Hall for gas, thankful that there was no practice that night. She filled the tank, then started to pull out of the station when her phone rang.

It was a number she didn't recognize, but she answered anyway. The drill team had a phone tree to inform each other of practice changes and if tomorrow's practice had been moved, she wanted to know since it affected how long she stayed at work.

"Liv, it's Matt."

A small surge of adrenaline shot through her. There was something in his tone that put her senses on alert. And for once, not good alert. "Yes?"

"Are you driving?"

"Not yet."

"Don't start. Your dad had some kind of attack—"

Liv heard herself gasp. The sound startled her, since she wasn't conscious of making any sound at all. "What kind of attack?"

"I don't have any details. They won't give them to me since I'm not family. He called me to take him to the hospital about half an hour ago. I did and now he's being examined."

"Andie—"

"Is on her way. I can come and get you, Liv, if you tell me where you are."

"No!" Liv swallowed, then pulled in a deep breath. "No," she repeated in a calmer voice. "I can drive. I'm not that far away. White Hall."

"You're sure."

"Positive," she said. "Why didn't you call sooner?"

"Tim called and asked me to come over. I had no

idea why, then when I got there all I could think about was getting him medical care."

Liv's stomach went into free fall. "Tell me the symptoms he showed."

"He, uh…well he was in pain and doubled over. Said his gut hurt. And his arm."

"Left?"

"Right. And he was jaundiced. It was one of the first things the nurse that admitted him keyed into."

Then it probably wasn't a heart attack. "Was he communicating all right?"

"Yeah. When he wasn't doubled over."

Probably not a stroke. But that didn't mean it wasn't cancer or any one of a number of other nasty things. "Thanks, Matt."

"Is there anything I can do?"

"No. I just need to stop talking and get on the road."

"Drive carefully, Liv. I mean it," he said sternly.

"I will. Promise." She clicked off, then punched in Andie's number.

"Liv, I don't know anything, but I am on my way. Matt called me."

"I'm just leaving White Hall."

"I'll let you know as soon as I'm there."

"Thanks." Liv once again clicked the end button and then set the phone on the seat beside her, within easy reach.

Well, it had happened. Whatever Tim had been

silently battling had finally won. Now she knew for certain that he hadn't been getting better—she only hoped it wasn't too late. She knew there was nothing she could do, except to trust Andie and whichever doctor was on emergency call.

That and be thankful that Matt had been available to help.

Liv swallowed as she felt tears starting to build up.

Nope. Was not going to cry. She was going to calmly drive to the hospital and if by heaven's mercy her father recovered, well, she might just have to hurt him for being so damned stubborn.

Matt's truck wasn't in the lot when Liv drove in. She parked in the first spot she found and entered the hospital. Andie came through the emergency room doors just as Liv walked inside, her expression grim. She immediately went to Liv and looped an arm around her, steering her to the plastic chairs in the waiting area. Liv refused to sit.

"What is it?" she demanded.

"Acute cholecystitis."

"A gallbladder attack?"

"That's not the big problem. The real danger is that he's got a pretty major infection because apparently he's been muscling his way through the attacks and because of that he's developed abscesses, which created the infection."

"I'll kill him," Liv muttered, then put her fingers to her lips when she realized what she'd just said.

"Yes, you'll most probably get the chance to do that," Andie said.

Liv's heart knocked against her ribs. "Most probably?"

"There's always a risk with surgery. You know that. We have him on Demerol for the pain and intravenous antibiotics. Once his fever goes down, we'll operate."

Now Liv did sit. "When?"

"Within the next twenty-four to forty-eight hours. The sooner the better. Dr. Bates will do the surgery."

"Can I see him? Dad, I mean?"

"He's a bit confused and out of it." Andie sat down beside her. "You can see him, talk to the doctor, but then you should probably just go home."

"But—"

"I'll make certain you're called if there's any change."

"I'll stay for a while."

Andie smiled wearily, touched Liv's hand. "You'd be better off going home rather than sitting in these chairs until your legs go numb."

"I'll stay."

CHAPTER FOURTEEN

THE DRIVE HOME was lonely and dark, made lonelier by the fact that Liv had no one waiting for her when she got there. Not that long ago, when she'd lived in Billings, arriving home to an empty house was a normal occurrence, but not at the ranch. Tim had always been there. Now he wasn't.

He'd be back.

She hoped. While waiting for a chance to see him, she'd done research on her phone about acute cholecystitis, which was usually only life-threatening once infection set in. Good job, Dad. Way to take something treatable and turn it into a crisis.

Why? Why not just go to a doctor? Get treated. He'd obviously been in pain for a long time.

As soon as he was no longer loopy from medication she'd get her answer. Because he was in good hands and he was not going to take a turn for the worse. Oh, no, he was not.

Liv wiped moisture from under her eyes with the back of her hand. Stubborn old—

An owl swooped from out of nowhere into the headlights, startling her. Heart thumping, she slowed the truck to a crawl, took a deep breath. At least now

she knew what was going on with her father and that
was a blessing. Better than wondering if he had cancer.

Liv pulled into the driveway fifteen minutes later
and bumped over the cattle guard. Her eyes felt swollen, as if she'd cried rivers, when in actuality she'd
only allowed a few tears to spill over before regain-
ing control. Crying wasn't going to help her. Wanting to throttle her stubborn father wasn't going to
help, either.

The problem was that nothing felt like it was going
to help.

Time. That would help. As long as her father survived, that is. She needed Tim to get through this
operation and on the mend. Then she could relax.
Maybe even let herself cry. Right now all she could
do was to feed the blasted steers and go to bed. Trust
her father to be on death's door, confused and out of
it, and be worried about the cattle.

She rounded the corner of the barn and then immediately slowed to a stop. Matt's pickup was parked
under the elm.

She wasn't ready for this. Not on top of everything
else, but she owed Matt a huge debt of gratitude.

Slowly, she eased her car forward and drove past
the barn, where light shone through the windows.
She'd barely taken the car out of gear when the door
opened and Matt came out, turning off the light before he closed the door behind him.

Liv got out of her car, and for a moment they

faced off. "Thanks for taking Dad to the hospital," Liv finally said. Inadequate words, but the best she could do right now.

Matt hooked a thumb in his pocket. "I fed the steers."

"Thank you."

"You okay?"

A brief shake of her head. No, she was not okay. She felt angry and inadequate.

"How's Tim?"

"He's on antibiotics and painkillers. He's going to have his gallbladder removed and they think he'll be fine." *Stop there. Let Matt go home.* But for some reason she couldn't. "I didn't want to leave the hospital, but Andie insisted." Liv rubbed a hand over her forehead. "I feel so stupid and angry. I should have realized..."

"You did," Matt said. "But there was no way you could have strong-armed Tim into going to the hospital."

"I don't know—"

"Yeah, you do. This is Tim Bailey we're talking about." He gently took her face in his hands, tilting it up so he could look into her eyes, his expression very serious. "You know that's true. Right?"

"Don't kiss me," she said.

He smiled. A real smile with real warmth, not a smile calculated to charm her into doing what he wanted. "Wouldn't think of it." But his hands stayed where they were, making her feel connected to him—a connection she didn't know if she wanted. "But how about I make you some tea or pour you a bourbon or something? Just as a friend? Not someone trying to kiss you."

"We don't have bourbon," Liv said, remembering when Tim had wanted bourbon after his Margo trauma.

"I do," he said. "In the truck." He dropped his hands as he spoke. Connection broken. Liv felt both relieved and disappointed. The more logical part of her was saying she needed to handle this on her own.

"That's disturbing," she said. "Keeping bourbon in the truck."

"Not really. I'd just finished grocery shopping when Tim called. I dropped Craig at the house, but didn't take time to unload."

"Craig. Should he be alone?"

"He's fourteen, Liv. I think he's all right. Probably dusting up a storm, but fine."

"Dusting…?"

"I'll explain later. Tea? Bourbon?"

Since he was giving her the choice and not forcing the issue, Liv said, "Both."

"Atta girl."

Liv went into the house ahead of him, snapping on lights then automatically picking up the crossword puzzle book and pencil that lay on the floor next to Tim's chair. Was that what he'd been doing when he'd had the attack?

She went into the kitchen to put on the kettle. Matt

came into the house and then followed her over to the sink. He took the kettle from her hand. "I'm making the tea."

"I need to move."

"Fine. You make the tea, I'll pour the shots."

Liv looked over her shoulder, startled. "I thought I'd have the bourbon in the tea."

"A shot before and a shot in the tea."

Liv let out a breath. "Sounds good." And it did. She needed something warm inside of her, something to dim the jangling thoughts bumping up against one another in her head.

Matt had no trouble finding shot glasses. He set down a large one that read What Happens in Vegas… next to a smaller one with a smiley face on it.

"Nice barware," he said, making Liv feel the inane urge to laugh.

"Only the best."

He poured the bourbon, waiting to hand Liv her glass until after she'd turned the kettle on. Then he lightly touched her glass with his and said, "To Tim's speedy recovery."

The corners of Liv's mouth quivered oh so slightly before she nodded and sipped, and Matt, she could see, had noticed, so she worked up a weak smile. Then she sat in her usual spot at the table and Matt unknowingly sat in Tim's. It seemed odd. Wrong. But she was glad he was there. Maybe a little too glad.

Be careful…

Liv took another sip, studying Matt as he in turn

studied the glass in his hand as if trying to think of something to say. Under the circumstances it probably wasn't right for her to notice that he was one hell of a specimen of manhood, from his black hair down to his scuffed-up boots, so she shoved the thought out of her mind. Although dwelling on gut-wrenching concerns about her father didn't seem like a great alternative.

The kettle whistled, making her jump. She automatically pulled two mugs out of the cupboard when Matt said, "None for me. I'm driving."

She shook her head, amused in spite of herself, then dropped a tea bag into her mug and poured the water. When she sat at the table again, Matt uncorked the bottle and poured a glug of amber liquid into the brewing tea.

And then again they sat. In silence. And again, even though she didn't have much to say, Liv was glad he was there. For the moment. Soon she'd have to ask him to leave. Thank him and tell him she needed to be alone—even though she did not want to be alone.

She sipped the tea, the hot water and bourbon warming her in a way that the bourbon alone hadn't.

When she was half-done, she reached back and pulled the elastic out of her hair, running her fingers through the strands before letting them fall over her shoulders. An evening ritual. Come home, let her hair down. Literally.

"I always wanted to touch your hair when we were studying."

Liv met Matt's eyes, startled at his out-of-the-blue revelation. "You did not."

"Yeah, I did." He turned the almost empty shot glass in his fingers. "It was so shiny and smooth and I liked the way it fell down your back."

Okay. Liv took a minute to digest that bit of new information. He'd liked her hair. He'd dated Shae.

"But nice hair or not, you never really thought of me as a—" she shrugged "—possibility…did you?"

"I might have, had I gotten a hint," he said. "You were really, *really* closed off." He finished the shot, then set the empty glass on the table.

"Maybe I was waiting for you to scale my ivory tower."

"'Scale your ivory tower'?" Matt frowned slightly as he reached out and picked up the bourbon bottle, tilting it to check its level before he looked at her shot glass.

"No, honestly, I was waiting for you to make a move."

"Uh…"

Liv put her palms on the table on either side of her tea mug and leaned forward. "Would a hint really have mattered? Would the hot cowboy jock have dated the geek?"

Matt's mouth twisted sideways as he considered her question. "I thought you were pretty, but like I said, you were so contained…"

"As in afraid to put myself out there for fear of being rejected."

"Really?"

Liv made a face. "Yes," she said in a "duh" voice. Had Matt ever experienced the sting of rejection? Feared it as she had? "When you left after every session, I'd analyze everything we said and look for hints of how things were going…between us. I guess I never thought, until recently, just how subtle I probably was. I just expected you to know and to do something about it."

Liv's cell rang and she jerked at the sound, felt the blood drain out of her face, leaving her lips feeling number. Andie.

"Yes," she said as soon as the phone was to her ear. "How is he?"

"He's stable and the fever is going down. I'm calling to check on you," she said. "I take it you got home okay?"

"Just one startling encounter with a big owl."

"Well, get some rest so you are strong enough to help us handle Tim."

"Is he okay?" Matt asked when Liv ended the call.

"Yes. Andie just wanted me to get some sleep. She knows how I am."

"I should go," he said. "Are you going to be okay here alone?"

No. Liv did not want to be alone tonight. She wanted a distraction—but not if that distraction led to more complications in her life. A little comfort would be most welcome. A man she couldn't control would not. "I'll be fine."

"I could—" he shrugged one broad shoulder "—sleep in the truck."

Liv smiled at that, the corners of her mouth lifting almost of their own accord. "Yeah. That'd help," she said. "Go home to Craig. I'll be fine."

"All right. Maybe I can come back tomorrow and help out with the chores?"

"Tomorrow I'll probably be more myself and yell at you about your knee." Which still made her sick at heart. She hated that he was doing what he was doing to himself.

"I'll take the chance."

Liv smiled, then reached out to lightly smooth the shirt over his chest, before straightening the placket. Why? She didn't have a clue, but it'd been a long time since she'd touched a man. Greg had been well-built, but Matt's chest was harder, insanely well-muscled from throwing calves.

He watched the movement of her hands, his lips parting slightly as he inhaled, then met her eyes with an intense gaze. Liv stepped back, dropping her hands. Her breathing wasn't exactly normal, either.

"I'll, uh, see you tomorrow." He also took a step back, putting distance between them.

All she had to do was say the word and she'd have company for the night. Something to take her mind off Tim. So very tempting, and stupid.

"Thanks, Matt." Her voice was husky and sounded

way too needy. Not clinging needy, but woman-wants-a-man needy. "See you then."

"Yeah." A few seconds later she pushed the protesting front door shut, catching one last glimpse of Matt as he headed for his truck before it closed all the way and the latch clicked.

The house was still, so the sound of the truck engine sounded overly loud when it started. Liv listened as the Dodge swung past the house then bumped over the cattle guard.

Heaven help her, part of her truly wished she'd asked him to stay.

THE NEXT MORNING Liv was at the hospital early. Andie was not there, but Dr. Bates, the man who was handling Tim's case, was.

"I hope to operate later today," he said. "You father is responding to the antibiotics, the fever has dropped significantly, so yeah. Later today unless something happens."

"I have clients," Liv said. "Could you have someone give me a call when you make a final decision?"

"You bet." Dr. Bates touched her upper arm with his clipboard. "I think we're in good shape here. I'm just glad he didn't put off coming in any longer than he did."

If he could have, he would have.

Liv shook off the aggravating thought as she left the hospital for the short drive to Andie's clinic. As she pulled out of the hospital parking lot, a familiar truck pulled in.

Margo?

Liv hit the brakes, watching in her rearview mirror as Margo parked in the same spot she had just pulled out of, then got out of her truck and marched through the front doors of the hospital like a woman on a mission.

Liv felt an instant urge to turn around and try to protect her father, to demand to know what Margo was doing there.

It might not be related to Tim.

But it seemed reasonable that it was. Liv stayed where she was, blocking the entrance and debating, when the doors opened again and Margo came back out.

She stepped on the gas and continued out onto the street. Maybe it was time for her and Margo to have a talk. Maybe at the next practice. She would not have that woman upsetting her father while he was trying to recover.

LIV DIDN'T CALL, so Matt didn't go to her place to help with chores. He recognized her as a woman who would disappear from his life if he pushed too hard, and it startled him to realize how much he didn't want her to disappear.

"Hey, Matt!" Craig bellowed from the living room.

Matt poked his head out of his office, where he'd been reading the mail. "What?"

"Mom just sent a text. She got the job! Benefits and everything! She'll call later tonight, but I don't have to register for school here. She's taking care of all that up there!" Craig punched his fist in the air, grinned and said, "Ah, the joy of financial security."

Matt smiled. "Excellent."

Craig jumped to his feet. "Maybe I'd better pack."

"As in close your suitcase?"

"Something like that." He headed past Matt, down the hall to his bedroom. Matt watched him go, aware of an odd knot forming in his gut.

He was really going to miss the kid. Go figure.

"Hey, you want to go to roping practice tonight?" he called.

"Here?"

"No. In Dillon."

"I don't think so. The next season of *Star Crusher* starts tonight and I don't want to miss the first episode."

"All right." Matt went back into his office. Maybe all for the best. He was going to stop by McElroy's house, get an injection, continue on to the arena. He was going to have to see about doing the injections himself on the road, something that was not all that legal, but he figured he might be able to talk the good doctor into cooperating—for a fee, of course.

Tonight was Liv's drill practice, but she probably wouldn't be there.

Fine. It'd give him a good excuse to stop by on his way home. He'd proceed with caution, not push things. See where this journey took him, because frankly, this was a journey he was very interested in taking.

IN SOME REGARDS, Liv was glad she hadn't cleared her morning schedule—only the afternoon—because focusing on patients kept her from worrying about Tim. "He'll be fine" was her silent mantra through the three appointments she had before lunch. She continued the mantra as she drove down to the hospital, only to find that surgery had been delayed until the next morning as they worked to stabilize her father and bring his fever, which had spiked up again, down to a tolerable level.

This time she did get to see him, but he was heavily drugged with painkillers and the visit left her with a knot in her stomach. It didn't help that young Dr. Bates was not as chipper and confident during this consultation as he had been during the last.

"I hope to operate tomorrow morning," he said.

Liv listened as he explained his plans, what may or may not happen, the prognosis for recovery.

On the drive home, Liv called Etta, had the receptionist clear her schedule for the next day. Then she went home to do the chores, pace and stew. Yesterday, when Matt had been there, she'd believed that by this time Tim would have had his surgery. But he hadn't. Things had changed. Tim had taken a turn for the worse and she had no one to talk to. Vivian didn't need this stress on top of dealing with Shae and who else could she call?

Call Matt. Talk to him.

Are you crazy? Call Andie if you want to talk.

But Andie was at drill practice and Liv ended up calling no one. It was better that she was alone. Better that she dealt with this as she dealt with all major issues in her life. Alone.

Or so she thought until she heard the distinctive throb of a diesel engine.

CHAPTER FIFTEEN

LIV MET MATT at the door, looking pale but composed. Her reddish-brown hair was down, swinging past her shoulders, making him want to put his hands into it.

"Hey," he said, stopping a few feet away. "You weren't at practice, so I thought I'd stop by. See if you needed anyone to pour bourbon for you."

She smiled a little and stepped back so that he could come inside. "You left the bourbon," she said, "so I could have poured it myself."

"But isn't it so much nicer when someone pours it for you?"

She smiled, but once again it faded too soon. Something was very wrong. Matt reached out to gently run his hands over her upper arms before saying quietly, "Something happened."

Liv swallowed, then nodded.

"Bad?"

She nodded again and Matt suspected from the way she'd suddenly dropped her eyes that she was fighting tears.

"Come here." He opened his arms, offering what she couldn't, or wouldn't, ask for. Apparently, he'd done the right thing, because Liv barely hesitated before she stepped into his embrace, sliding her arms around his waist and pressing herself against him. His arms closed around her, but Matt held her loosely so that she could escape when she felt the need. He knew with a certainty she would soon feel that need.

Sure enough, a moment later Liv loosened her hold and eased back...but she didn't let go. Instead, her hands stayed at his waist, her thumbs lightly pressing into him.

"What happened?" He brushed back the hair at the side of her face and felt his body stir as the silky strands moved through his fingers. He liked the way Liv felt against him, wished the circumstances were much, much different.

"Tim's fever spiked and they couldn't operate."

"Damn. I'm sorry."

"Yeah." She pulled in a breath that made her shoulders rise and fall a good inch or two, then, as he'd known she would, she stepped back, breaking the contact, and Matt let his arms drop.

"They're supposed to operate tomorrow morning." She closed her mouth tightly, as if not wanting to say more, but lost the battle. "I didn't see this coming. No one did. It...worries me." She fought to keep her voice from breaking on the last words, making Matt feel helpless, since all he wanted to do was make things right. And he couldn't.

"Do you want tea?" she asked.

"Not really."

"Me, either. But I wouldn't mind a sip of whiskey."

"I'll pour," he said, moving past her and finding the bottle on the table, right where he'd left it the night before. He found the shot glasses back in the cupboard, set them up side by side and poured. Liv was still in the living room, her arms hugged around her as she stared into the blackened front windows.

"Not a lot of light out there."

"The yard light burned out last night," she said. "Just one thing after another, but at least Tim won't be climbing the pole."

"I can take care of that for you. If you like."

"It'll need to be done and I hate heights," Liv said, taking the glass from him. Their fingers touched briefly and she didn't jerk hers away as she had in the past, which reminded him of how she'd straightened his shirt the night before. And how he'd wanted to pull her into his arms afterward.

"Do you mind if I sit?" he asked, gesturing to the sofa, feeling a lot like a high school kid on a first date.

"No." He took a seat, stretching his free arm out along the back on the sofa, and pretended not to be surprised when Liv plopped down next to him. There was a good twelve inches of cushion between them, but she leaned her head back so it touched his arm and closed her eyes, holding her almost full shot glass at chest level. Matt let his hand drop down to her shoulder and Liv scooted closer, laying her head against his upper chest.

"I'm so damn worried," she whispered.

"I know."

She straightened then to take a small sip of the bourbon before she tossed back the shot. She met his eyes with a candid gaze, as if daring him to comment. He had nothing to say, and a few seconds later she settled her head against his shoulder and closed her eyes.

Matt held very still as her breathing became more even, her muscles less taut. Relaxed or asleep? He didn't know. Didn't care. He was just glad he was there. She gave a little sigh and his lips curved up. Sleeping. Cool. He lifted the shot glass, took a sip, then closed his own eyes.

LIV WOKE WITH a start, then, when she felt Matt's arm tighten around her shoulder, realized where she was. And with whom. Slowly, she pushed herself up into a sitting position, brushing her hair away from her face. Matt smiled down at her.

"Wow," she said. "I didn't mean to fall asleep. Just to…relax for a couple minutes."

He said nothing, which made her feel more self-conscious. How many times had she dreamed about snuggling on a sofa with Matt Montoya? Schoolgirl fantasy come true under rotten circumstances.

"What time is it?" she asked, moving his arm so that she could see his watch. "Eleven?" She jumped to her feet. "You shouldn't have stayed for so long. I bet Craig's worried."

Matt got to his feet slowly, stretched, then slid a hand around the back of her neck, where it stayed, warm and comforting...and making her want to invite him to step down the hall for a spell.

"Craig's fine and I wanted to make sure you were fine, too."

"Thank you." The words came out too fast. *Get a grip. You fell asleep. Big fat deal.* "I appreciate you staying. I feel...better."

"Do you want me to stay longer?"

What a loaded question. Liv cleared her throat. "I'm all right. Now. Thanks."

"Good." He picked up his hat and started for the door.

"Matt?"

Liv crossed the distance between them. "Thanks."

"No problem."

And then, just like the night before, he was gone. She was alone with only her worries about her father for company.

This sucked.

BY THE TIME Liv got to the hospital the next morning, her father was in the operating room.

"They had a window and they took it," Andie said. "He wasn't responding to the antibiotics as well as hoped, so they took a chance."

Took a chance were not the words Liv wanted to hear, but she nodded and put on her brave face as she took a seat on the hard plastic chairs. Andie perched beside her for a second.

"I have a lot of faith in Dr. Bates."

Liv couldn't bring herself to talk about faith in doctors. "How long?"

Andie shrugged. "Depends."

Liv didn't ask what it depended on. Instead, she leaned her head back against the wall, recalled how comforting it had felt curling into Matt last night. Why he kept coming by, she didn't know, but at this point, she wasn't going to analyze. She'd done enough of that in high school after their study sessions. She was going to accept comfort and not take it at anything except face value. She and Matt had known each other a long time. They were friends—their reunion may have been a bit rocky, but they'd worked it out. Yes. Friends. Friends didn't have to have a controlling influence on your life.

"How was practice last night?" Liv asked without looking at Andie.

"The usual. We were missing two—you and Margo."

Liv frowned over at Andie. She wanted to ask if she knew anything about Margo and Tim, or if maybe her father, who'd practiced law in the area forever, knew anything, but couldn't bring herself to do it. This was Tim's business. Not hers.

"What?" Andie asked.

"Nothing." Andie reached out and patted Liv's leg. "Don't you have patients?" Liv asked.

"Yes. The first is at ten o'clock. I have a little time."

"Thanks for being here."

"Thanks for letting me."

"What does that mean?"

"It means," Andie said patiently, "that you're not so good at accepting moral support."

"I'm getting better," Liv said, feeling the warmth rise in her cheeks as she thought about Matt and how she'd allowed herself to accept his help. "All part of the process."

The words were barely out of her mouth when the doors opened and Dr. Bates came out, wearing his scrubs. Liv jumped to her feet, thinking it was too soon, that there was only one reason he'd be out so quickly.

"The gallbladder is out," he said. "He's not out of the woods yet, but barring more infection, I'd say the prognosis is good."

"When will you be more certain?" Liv asked, holding her breath as she waited for the answer.

"I'd say if by tonight he has no fever, I'll feel optimistic. But I want to keep him for at least two more days."

The doctor disappeared back through the door and Liv turned to Andie. "Is he telling the truth?"

Andie laughed. "Yes. He's just being cautious. He hadn't expected Tim's infection to be so resistant to the antibiotics, so what had seemed like a slam dunk became…shall we say…troublesome?"

"Troublesome. Seems appropriate. So…I can relax?"

"I'd say we're dropping from a code orange to a code yellow."

"Code yellow. All right. I can deal with that."

AT THE END of Dr. Bates's shift, he gave Liv a cautious thumbs-up. Cautious because, as Andie had said, Tim's case had not been the slam dunk he expected, and he was candid about that. But now he felt confident that the worst was over. Tim was remaining in the hospital as a precaution and because he was already showing signs of becoming his usual self, the doctor told Liv he'd appreciate her help convincing him to stay put once the medications started wearing off. Liv promised to do the best she could.

Tim was fairly alert when she visited him one last time before going home, and she listened patiently as he listed all the chores that needed doing, when what she really wanted to do was to yell at him for scaring her.

She had exactly two blood relatives, since both of her parents were only children and her grandparents had passed on, and had just come too close to losing one of them. Stubbornness in the face of adversity wasn't all it was cracked up to be. It might have gotten her pioneer forefathers to Montana, but it'd also almost killed her dad. Life was short. One had to seize the day. Enjoy what they could.

Which was probably why she took the wrong fork at the Y and drove to Matt's house, hoping he was home and that there wasn't a crowd this time.

There wasn't. Just Matt in the yard roping a dummy calf head stuck on a straw bale.

And he was so damned good at it. Swing, toss, jerk, shake off the rope and coil. Swing, toss, jerk...

He stopped when he saw Liv's car slow at the driveway and began coiling his rope as he walked toward her.

She left the engine running as she rolled down the window. Matt hooked a hand on her mirror. "Is everything okay?"

"Yeah," Liv said, feeling all her former shyness come barreling back. She swallowed before saying, "Just thought I'd let you know that my dad is doing all right."

"Great," Matt said, breaking into a wide smile.

"And…if you wanted to stop by tonight…again… well…that would be okay."

There was a very long, very pregnant pause before Matt cocked his head and said, "Yeah?" And she could tell from his tone that he understood exactly what she was offering.

Escape. Now. With your pride.

Too late.

Liv shrugged. "Yeah," she echoed, impressed that her voice didn't sound at all as if her heart were halfway up her throat. "If you want. I thought I could fix something to eat. As a thank-you." Dinner, yes. Good save.

Matt nodded, the smile having turned to more of a cautious half smile. At least it wasn't a smirk. "Should I bring Craig?"

That hadn't been in her plans. "If you want to."

Matt's expression edged back toward amusement… and something more, which made Liv feel like swallowing again. "I think I may feed Craig and leave him here to watch his *Star* show."

"Great," she said, reaching for the ignition and turning it, even though the car was running. The nasty grinding sound startled her and color washed over her face. "Damn," she muttered.

Matt laughed. "I've done that," he said, and she liked him more because of it.

"I better go," she said. "Before I do something else to the car." Matt stepped away, and she put the car in gear, being careful that it was the correct gear, then turned a tight U-turn and headed back out of his driveway.

Okay, she wasn't smooth, but truthfully, she didn't regret the invitation. Dinner with a guy who'd been there when she needed a shoulder. That was all this was. She wouldn't let it be anything else.

MATT SHOWED UP for dinner with a bottle of wine and a deep curiosity as to how the evening was going to play out. Liv the aggressor was something he hadn't expected. Not that she was exactly aggressive once he arrived. No, she hid behind the ritual of cooking, stirring sauce, draining pasta, refusing all help.

Matt sat at the kitchen table, sipped wine and watched, letting her orchestrate the evening. She fed him an excellent but simple meal, complimented his wine and talked to him about her work.

They did not talk about roping, or Beckett or her

father—other than her brief announcement that all was still well and she was grateful.

Matt watched the one-woman show with a touch of amusement and a touch of awe. Liv wasted no movements. She glided from one task to another, making them look effortless. Liv would have made a decent calf roper.

Matt smiled a little and Liv cocked her head. "What?"

"Just...admiring."

"Yeah?" The reply was offhand, but her color rose.

They ate the dinner and Matt insisted on doing the dishes. Not helping, but doing. It didn't take long, since Liv had been cleaning as she went in a way that would have made Craig proud.

Then she turned off the kitchen lights and they went into the living room, where they sat side by side on the sofa staring at the opposite wall.

"Well, this is awkward," she said.

"How so?" Matt asked innocently.

Liv smirked at him. "Have you ever in your life felt awkward? Do you have a clue?"

He half turned toward her on the sofa. "You're talking to a man who's been knocked off his horse in public more times than I want to admit, has taken facers in the mud, been kicked in the nuts by a squirming calf in front of a woman he wanted to impress... need I go on?"

She laughed, hugging her arms around herself. "I

spent a good deal of my life feeling awkward. But I have never been kicked in the nuts by a calf."

"You don't know what you're missing." She leaned her head back against his arm, as she'd done the other night, and after a few silent, not totally uncomfortable minutes, he asked, "Why did you invite me over?"

"To say thanks."

"And?"

She met his eyes directly, though he had a feeling it cost her. "You have to ask?" she asked lowly. Her voice was husky, filled with meaning.

Matt felt himself begin to rise to the occasion.

She'd done it. For the first time ever she'd flat out told a guy what she wanted. Oh, she'd hedged a bit with the dinner and all, but she'd eventually taken the leap. And then for one long moment, nothing happened. All she could hear was her own breathing. And Matt's.

Then Matt slid his hand up under her hair and leaned over and kissed her. Only this wasn't like that first kiss, the one that had taken her by surprise. No, this one was slow and deliberate, a long, thorough kiss that made her want to start shucking off her clothes. But she wouldn't allow herself to react too soon. Her instinct for self-preservation was too strong. Yeah, she'd said what she wanted, but she needed to take her time, make certain she hadn't made a mistake.

She smoothed her palms over the planes of Matt's

cheeks, pulled his lips down for another kiss, this one even deeper and longer.

"This is what I wanted to do during the study sessions," she confessed, smiling against his mouth. Matt pushed his fingers back into her hair, then twisted the strands around his hand, holding her head as he spread his fingers over the small of her back, pressing her against him.

"This," he said in a low voice, "is what I would have wanted to do had I known you were interested in anything other than derivatives."

He was hard. Very hard. Liv's breath caught at the feel of his erection pressed against her and all her many insecurities came racing back. For an instant she was seventeen-year-old Liv, in awe of eighteen-year-old Matt, yet wanting this so badly.

Then he ran his mouth down the side of her neck to the sensitive area at the base of her throat and a tremor shot through her, making her gasp. If she responded like this when he touched her neck, then what was it going to be like when he explored other more sensitive areas of her body?

Sheer heaven.

Matt pulled her to her feet and took hold of the bottom of her shirt. Liv lifted her arms, allowing him to pull it up over her head before he dropped it on the floor. She unbuttoned his shirt, sliding it down his arms until it joined her T-shirt at their feet. She reached back to pop her bra open, let it slip off, then pressed against him, not quite ready for him to look at her.

Shyness. Did it never end?

"You're beautiful," he murmured, reading her reaction.

"Mmm," was all she said in reply. Maybe she was. Or maybe he just wanted to get laid, which was fair, because that was what she wanted, too. To have hot sex with a guy she trusted as a friend. To make her forget everything for a few hours.

Liv took a step back, allowing Matt's hand to slide down to her waist, then come up to caress her breasts before pulling her back against him and let his hands drop down to cup her ass.

"I can't believe we're doing this," she murmured, then cringed as she realized she'd said the words out loud.

"All your dreams come true?" he asked, making her want to smile. Who would have thought that Matt Montoya didn't take himself that seriously—as a guy anyway? As a roper...that was a different story.

She shook her hair back, feeling bolder as she pushed her pelvis against him, felt him push back.

"Just not something I saw coming a few weeks ago." She reached for his belt buckle, hoping she didn't fumble too much, since she had a history of being awful with buckles. This one slid open with no problem and then hung heavily on the end of the belt as she undid the top button of his jeans and then eased the fly down over his erection. It wasn't easy getting that zipper down, but Matt did nothing to help.

Liv bit her lip, finally got it to the point that she could push his pants down his hips and then…oh, yes, this was good.

But she didn't have much time to admire because Matt kicked his pants the rest of the way off and then went to work on hers, getting the job done in half the time. More practice? She didn't know, didn't care. Not one bit. His past? None of her concern. His future? Likewise.

She circled her arms around his neck, pressed into him and savored the feeling of skin against skin as she pulled his head down for a deep kiss.

"Where?" he asked softly, his breath warm against her lips.

She tilted her head toward the hall and they made their way to her bedroom, moving in tandem, kissing as they walked. She closed the door and then found herself trapped against it by a very hard, very insistent male body. He maneuvered his erection so that it was between her legs, making her more than a little crazy as he claimed her mouth.

"Matt…?"

"Door sex comes later," he said. He took a step back and easily swung her up into his arms. Seconds later, before she could protest about him possibly straining his knee, they were on the bed, Liv on the bottom, Matt very much on top. And she loved the way he felt there. Was there any part of him that wasn't toned and hard?

"Are you ready?" he asked, his voice little more than a husky whisper.

"Oh, yeah," she murmured, wrapping her legs around him as he pressed into her. So. Very. Ready. Yes, it hurt a little. She hadn't had sex in a very long time, and she could truthfully say she'd never had sex with a guy like Matt. He eased in slowly, taking his time, watching her face. Then, when he was all the way home, he kissed her, a soft kiss that became more intense as he started moving inside of her. Liv gasped against his mouth as he hit the sweet spot just right and he smiled.

"You like that?"

"It's okay," she said.

He laughed low in his throat and began to move, taking his time, making her crazy.

"Better than okay," she admitted, her words barely audible as sensations threatened to overpower her. She wasn't ready for this to end. Not yet. Not after waiting all this time.

"I should hope so," he said, but the teasing note in his voice was strained. And then the talking stopped and Liv lost track of everything except for Matt driving into her. He was so damned good and she did not want him to stop—

And then she exploded against him, long before she wanted to. Matt groaned against her neck as she arched beneath him, then he drove in deeply into her one last time.

What had she just done?

They were both still breathing hard as the questions began crowding into Liv's brain, but she was soon distracted by Matt kissing her. A sweet, gentle kiss that made her want to melt back into him.

They were two people who understood each other. He wouldn't tell her what to do, and she wouldn't tell him what to do....

Except for that knee thing. That still bothered her.

"I'd like to stay," he said, pulling her against him.

"Craig," she said.

"Yeah."

"That's okay," Liv said. "I think...I need some alone time."

"Regrets?" Matt asked softly.

"No." Liv hoped she wasn't lying.

Matt got out of bed and pulled on his pants, dragging the denim up over his wrecked knees, buckling the belt around his lean hips.

He looked like a hot cowboy who'd just stepped out of some kind of magazine advertisement. And she... Liv caught her reflection in the full-length mirror on her far wall—she looked pale and tousled and not at all magazine worthy, but she would never have known it from the expression Matt wore when he met her eyes in the mirror. Her heart stuttered at the intensity of his gaze.

He smiled a little as he shrugged into his shirt,

then he came to sit on the bed beside her and pulled on his boots.

"I'll come back to help you feed in the morning."

"Don't." The word came out so quickly that Liv was barely conscious of saying it.

Matt held her gaze for a moment, then exhaled. But he said nothing. A moment later he kissed her lightly on first the forehead, then the lips.

As he straightened, he smiled again and Liv couldn't help but notice that according to the evidence showing through his worn jeans, he was seconds away from crawling back into bed with her.

And she was seconds away from insisting on it, consequences be damned.

"Good night, Liv."

Liv rolled onto her back, pushed the hair back from her forehead as she stared up at the ceiling and listened to the sounds of the man she'd once thought she'd loved more than anything leaving her house.

What had she just done?

She'd done what had felt incredibly right. At the moment. And she'd enjoyed it, shutting off the warning voices in her head and simply experiencing what Matt had to offer.

When he'd started making love to her, his motions had felt practiced, automatic. But then...then things changed. She'd responded, and he'd done the same. By the end, Liv had the strong feeling that Matt was charting some unknown waters. Or at least waters he hadn't experienced in some time.

She rolled over onto her side, cushioning her head on one arm as she heard his pickup start up. She'd rung his bell. Her lips curved into a wearily sad smile. She had the power....

And she didn't want it.

Resolutely, she closed her eyes. She needed sleep if she was going to deal with her father in the morning. As if.

Her last thoughts, jumbled one on top of the other, were that there was no way she would ever be able to fall asleep and that Matt hadn't asked when he could see her again.

The last thought made her smile.

CHAPTER SIXTEEN

"WHY IN THE HELL didn't you come see me?" Andie demanded.

Tim rolled his head on the pillow to see her better. "I don't have insurance and I was waiting for Medicare to kick in."

"What happened to the insurance, Dad?" Liv asked, shocked at his admission. Her father had never been a fan of spending money needlessly, but foregoing insurance?

"I dropped down to just the ranch policy, which covers accidents, not illness. Since I've never been sick, I thought I could save some money."

"And then you got sick," Andie said. Tim said nothing, staring up at the ceiling. "We'll work something out."

"Like what?" he grumbled. "Medical bankruptcy?"

"Stop it, Dad."

"Had you seen me earlier," Andie said, "or Dr. Bates, or any health professional, then we could have solved this in a less dramatic way."

Tim continued to stare at the ceiling, as if he hadn't heard her, his face pinched with pain.

"You're staying a few more days, Dad."

Again no response.

"We have ways we can help you deal with this," Andie said.

But Liv knew her father would never agree to any of the "ways" she was speaking of, since they smacked of charity.

"I'll talk to the hospital about a payment plan. We'll get through this." Liv forced a smile. "If I started paying rent, then that could be your payment."

The thought didn't seem to cheer Tim any, but he reached out anyway to take Liv's hand. He squeezed her fingers, his hand rough from decades of hard work, then dropped his hand back to the sheet.

"How are the steers?"

"As fat as they were yesterday," Liv said.

"Good. We'll have to sell them early."

It was going to take more than the steers to settle the bill, as they both well knew, but if selling the cows made Tim feel better, Liv was all for indulging in the fantasy.

And speaking of fantasies, Liv was determined to stay firmly grounded in reality when it came to her new relationship with Matt. It was important that they understand one another. She was pretty certain they did, but no sense taking chances.

So how, and when, did she bring this up?

Or was it better to just see how things played out?

Maybe they'd had a one-night stand. Liv stepped out of the hospital into the bright morning sun as the happy thought occurred to her. She could live with that. Maybe. Parts of her were whispering, "Are you crazy? One time when you could have more?" and it was hard to shut them up.

Okay, she and Matt would talk. When?

Liv didn't have a lot of experience with morning afters, having only experienced two in her lifetime, spaced quite a distance apart. And she'd never before slept with anyone that she hadn't been in a relationship with.

New territory to go with a new life.

Part of her liked thinking that she could sleep with a hot guy and walk away. Another part of her thought that smacked of using the other person unless they were on the same page.

Of course they were on the same page. This was Matt Montoya she was dealing with, the guy who attracted hot babes like a magnet. He was used to one-nighters. He liked her and she liked him. They both had their own lives to live, so really, there shouldn't be a problem.

But they would talk all the same.

The day passed quickly since she was booked solid. She stopped to see Tim on the way home, promised again to take extra special care of the steers and told him in return he needed to do exactly what his doctors advised. He'd grunted in a semi-cooperative way and Liv accepted his answer as the best she was going to get. He was hurting and he was angry with himself and she couldn't do anything about it except to let time do its thing.

When she got home, the steers were already fed, but Matt was not there. For a moment she thought it might have been a guilt feeding, then realized it had to be a roping night. Of course. Nothing stood between Matt and roping practice.

Liv smiled as she headed to the house. She liked a guy with priorities, especially when she wasn't one of them. And she wasn't going to ask him to stop feeding the steers, because he was doing it for Tim and not for her.

When she drove into the rodeo grounds for practice that evening, the first thing she noticed was an absence of a big black and silver Dodge. The second thing she noticed was a pang of disappointment and she firmly told herself to get a grip.

Linda took Liv aside before the first drill to offer her condolences on her father's illness and inform her that the team had conferred and they were going to hold a fund-raiser to help with Tim's medical bills.

"I...uh...don't know," Liv said, thinking how much Tim would hate knowing that his private affairs had been the topic of a drill team meeting. "My dad is kind of funny about that kind of stuff."

"Your dad needs to accept the fact that neighbors take care of one another," Linda proclaimed.

"Probably," Liv said on a sigh, realizing that stopping Linda from doing what she thought was right was probably a lot like trying to stop Shae from choosing the most expensive dress on the rack. The conversation was apparently over, because Linda mounted her buckskin and headed for the arena gate, blowing her whistle to signal the rest of the team to follow.

Liv mounted Beckett, thinking that once Tim was strong enough, he could fend off those who wanted to help him. It might give him an incentive to take care of himself.

The practice was intense since they had a rodeo performance the next day and Liv was thankful to have something to focus on other than the men in her life. The rodeo was close to Dillon, so she could perform and still visit Tim before going home—if they managed to keep him in the hospital that long.

The difficulty there was driven home when she got a call early the next morning from Andie, asking her to stop by the hospital on her way to the rodeo. Tim, it seemed, was giving the staff grief. He wanted out and he wanted out now.

"Dr. Bates wants to keep him one more day than originally planned just to play it safe." Liv could hear the stress in her friend's voice and figured she'd probably already gone a couple rounds with Tim. One more day. Thousands more dollars. Her father was probably having a fit.

"Be right there."

Twenty minutes later she met Andie in the waiting area.

"Is there no way around this? I mean, he's going to be so stressed out calculating finances, wouldn't it be best to get him out of here ASAP?"

"Got to make sure there're no complications. Bates isn't taking any chances." Andie hugged her clipboard to her chest. "If he'd come in sooner..."

"Yeah. I know. But he didn't." And now he had consequences. "Okay. I'll talk to him."

"Try to explain to him that one extra day won't be that much what with the rest of the costs being covered."

Liv stopped in her tracks. "Covered by what? The ranch policy doesn't pay for this kind of stuff."

Andie's eyebrows inched up. "Covered by the person who paid his bill. In cash."

Liv swallowed drily, wondering if she was hearing correctly. "That's...that's not possible. Who would do that?"

Andie looked both directions then lifted her clipboard to shield her face as she whispered. "Margo Beloit. Didn't you know?"

"Didn't have a clue." Liv started down the hall toward Tim's room, her mind racing.

"Does he know?" Liv asked, pausing at the door.

"He does," Andie said. "I thought it would make him relax and stay another day without a fight. Should have known better."

Liv snorted as she reached for the door handle.

"Not that I'm chicken," Andie said, "but I think you two need to work this out alone."

"I agree," Liv said, giving her friend a weary smile before opening the door.

"I am not taking charity," Tim said through gritted teeth as soon as Liv walked into the room. He was wearing a hospital gown and was tethered to an IV, thinner and grayer than before, but he looked as fierce as Liv had ever seen him. "Margo can take her money and—"

"If you don't calm down, you won't be going home," Liv growled. "You'll have a stroke or a heart attack." She took a couple paces at the foot of his bed, then asked the question she didn't want to get the answer to. "Why did Margo pay your bill?"

"Damned if I know."

"Bull."

Apparently, Tim wasn't used to his daughter talking to him that way because his pulse rate jumped on the monitor. He rolled his head sideways, but Liv walked around the bed to make eye contact. "Trust me, Dad, I really don't want to know, but I can't help you if I don't know what's going on."

He closed his eyes briefly, clenching his jaw as he did so. When he opened them his expression was one of resignation.

"We almost married once. I walked out on her."

Liv did her best to look shocked since she wasn't supposed to know how close Tim and Margo had once been. Actually, it wasn't that difficult to appear stunned, since it was the first time her father had told her anything truly intimate about his life.

"So why would she pay the bill?" Liv asked.

"I don't know." His words carried a ring of truth. "But I won't accept it."

"I don't know what you can do about it right now, except to pay her back. Apparently, the account is settled except for this extra day." Liv bit her lip, knowing the next suggestion was going to go over like a lead balloon. "Maybe you can work out a payment schedule with her."

Tim exhaled, then winced, since Dr. Bates had dropped the level of pain medication and apparently every movement hurt. "I don't see where I have any choice."

Liv walked over to lay a hand on her father's shoulder. She couldn't help but feel for him—a proud, stubborn, self-sufficient man lying in a hospital bed, the recipient of unwanted charity. And he'd just shared intimate details of his life. Three of his worst nightmares come true.

She gave his shoulder a squeeze. "We'll work this thing out, Dad. Pay Margo interest and the whole nine yards."

"Yeah. I will," he agreed. "It's the only thing I can do."

Liv shook her head. "Any chance that you could take it easy for the next day so that they let you out of here?"

"I'll do my best," he said grimly. "Because I want out like nobody's business."

"Then behave yourself and I'll pick you up Sunday morning."

LIV AND BECKETT had their best performance ever at the Twin Bridges rodeo—which wasn't saying a lot, since it was only her third performance and the first dry one. The only strange part was dealing with Margo. Or not dealing with her. The woman, who'd been friendly up until Liv had overheard her conversation with Tim—making Liv wonder if Margo had known she was there—now kept her distance. She didn't make eye contact and only spoke if absolutely necessary.

But she had paid a gigantic hospital bill in cash. She was a widow, yes, but how well off was she? And why pay Tim's bill?

Did she dare ask?

Margo's demeanor did not invite confidences or questions.

This was Tim's problem. It was not Liv's job to smooth the waters and make everything all better for him, in spite of her old instincts rearing up and threatening to take hold again.

"Who's a good boy?" she asked Beckett to distract herself as she took off his bridle and haltered him. As usual she pulled a treat out of her pocket and offered it to him before unsaddling.

"You're spoiling him."

Liv stilled at the unexpected sound of Matt's voice from behind her, anticipation quickening her pulse. *Oh, man.*

"He doesn't bum," she said as she turned to face him, keeping one hand on Beckett's neck as if to ground herself. The heat unfurling deep inside of her intensified as she met Matt's dark eyes, saw the answering heat there.

How could he possibly look better than he had before? Because she now knew what he looked like naked…and wouldn't mind seeing him that way again.

"That's because he's a gentleman," Matt said, patting the horse's rump. Liv forced herself to move, folding the stirrup over the seat of the saddle and pulling the latigo from the cinch ring. A few seconds later she dragged the saddle off, the cinch hitting the ground because she hadn't tied it up as usual.

"Want me to do that?" he asked as she started lugging the saddle to the tack room.

"No, no." She stepped up into the small room at the front of the trailer, slid the saddle on the holder. *Breathe. You need to breathe.*

She felt Matt follow her in, once again forgot to breathe, then turned to tell him not to close the door, somehow sensing he would. He, of course, closed the trailer door before she could get a word out and the space immediately got very, very small. Liv was aware of the scents of the leather, horse sweat, grain. And Matt. That wonderfully masculine scent made her even more aware of him.

"That sometimes locks itself," she said, raising an eyebrow in the direction of the door.

"In that case we'll call for help."

"Perhaps you'd like to check it now."

Matt turned toward the door, but instead of checking to see if it was open, he clicked the sliding lock sideways.

"Now you've done it," she said.

"I certainly hope so." His mouth came slowly down onto hers as she backed against the trailer wall. The kiss was possessive, deep. Knee-buckling. Liv realized that her hands had somehow come up to clutch his shoulders.

"Being locked in wouldn't be that bad," he murmured against her mouth before gently nipping her lower lip.

Liv pulled his mouth back against hers, wrapping her arms around his neck as she kissed him, shoving aside her plan to discuss expectations, parameters and limitations. She'd get to it. In time.

Matt's hands settled at her waist when he raised his head again, his grip possessive, his fingers warm through the satin of her shirt. He smiled slightly, making Liv wonder what he was thinking, then he boosted her up onto the platform formed by the nose of the trailer. Liv landed with an *oof* and a laugh. She popped a hand over her mouth, hoping no one had heard her.

And then she didn't make a sound as Matt slowly unsnapped her shirt with one hand, watching her face as he did so, his eyebrows going up in a silent question as he reached snap number four.

She really needed to say "Stop."

After the last snap popped open, he pushed the

fabric aside and then leaned in to kiss her breasts, now at perfect mouth level, where they spilled out of the top of her simple demi-bra.

He traced his tongue under the edge of the fabric and Liv swallowed a groan. Then she buried her fingers in his hair as he went lower, his mouth trailing down her stomach to the waistband of her jeans, his tongue warm and deliciously wet against her skin. Liv's eyes drifted shut as her head fell back. Her fingers left his hair, found his shoulders, dug in.

Not since her high school crush on him could she remember wanting something so badly that she simply couldn't have. Not with all the people walking by. Not with the very tiny lock, the lock that undoubtedly wouldn't stick when she wanted it to, between her and Matt and the world. She might be living her own life, following her own rules, but she wasn't yet ready to be literally caught with her pants down. She reached down to take hold of Matt, lift his head so she could look into his eyes.

He smiled at her. A smile that said, "I know what you want and I know what you're about to say."

"Rain check?" he said.

Liv nodded, reaching behind her and by some miracle not only managing to find both ends of her bra, but to fasten them in one practiced motion.

Matt reached out to snap her shirt, one small click after another. Liv very much wanted to say that she could do it, but she was fascinated by the sight of his strong fingers moving against the red satin.

"Do you think we're really locked in?" Matt asked.

"One way to tell."

He held out his hands and Liv put her fingers in his as she slid off the platform, her thighs brushing over his erection. She almost groaned out loud.

Almost. She had some pride, although apparently not much where he was concerned.

She stepped back to tuck in her shirt, and once Matt was certain she was put back together, he reached out to unclick the lock and try the door. It opened easily. Unfortunately.

And the fact that she was thinking thoughts like that bothered her. But not so much that she was going to take back the rain check. She liked making out with Matt. She liked doing it on her own terms.

She liked being like Shae.

The thought came from nowhere. An unsettling, sobering thought.

Just because she was looking out for herself, it didn't mean she was anything like her stepsister.

IT'D BEEN A DAY, all right. After the encounter in the trailer, Liv had hightailed it off to visit her father, and Matt had gone back up into the stands to watch the rest of the rodeo. But he couldn't get Liv out of his mind.

He'd watched her ride Beckett in the drill, and even though he couldn't say it'd been easy to watch his horse doing something besides the job he was bred to do, he was making his peace with the issue.

He missed the gelding, wanted him back, but he was done trying to strong-arm him away from Liv. If anyone was going to own the horse other than him, he'd just as soon it was her.

Which was something to think about.

He'd expected sleeping with Liv to be…well, interesting…but he hadn't expected her to knock his socks off. She'd surprised him, and he'd surprised himself. He'd slept with women since Trena and had enjoyed each and every encounter, but he hadn't really felt a lot beyond the physical. With Liv he was feeling something he couldn't quite put a name on—or didn't want to put a name on. What he did want was more—more time with Liv, both in and out of bed.

Which led him to wonder, for about the fiftieth time that day, what did Liv want?

"Hey." Matt turned to see Jed hailing him from higher up in the stands. He waved, then worked his way up to where Jed and his small family sat under the shade of the bleacher cover.

"This is Eva," Jed said with a note of quiet pride as Corrie moved the blanket so that Matt could see her tiny face. Her incredibly small fists were clenched as she slept. Matt frowned a little, wondering what it felt like to be responsible for such a delicate being.

"She's four days old," Jed's son, Tyler, announced. "And I'm four years old."

Matt made an impressed "whoa" noise at Tyler, who beamed with pride, then Matt glanced up at Corrie. "Should she be out at this age?"

Corrie laughed. "We want to start her rodeo career off as soon as possible, and Mama wanted to get out of the house."

"So did Papa," Jed said, dragging Tyler up onto his lap.

"We saw your horse!" Tyler announced just before Jed put his fingers over his son's mouth.

The boy rolled his laughing eyes up at his father who whispered, "Shhh."

"So did I," Matt said to Tyler. "He did pretty good, didn't he?"

"I guess," the boy said. "Dad says you got a boy, too. Where is he?"

Matt smiled. "My boy isn't a rodeo fan like you."

"I'm a big fan," Tyler agreed.

"And he'll talk your ear off," Jed said. "So...everything okay?"

"With?"

"Tim. I heard you took him to the hospital."

"A little touch-and-go, but I think he's going to be fine. Liv is keeping me posted."

"So I saw," Corrie said. Jed frowned at her, but she merely smiled and turned her attention back to the action in the arena. Matt wondered just what she was talking about—until he turned to go and saw that the family had a clear view of Liv's trailer from where they sat.

Well, so be it. Maybe he and Liv had simply been inside discussing business—in a room the size of a small closet.

MATT KNEW TIM would be coming home anytime, but he took a chance and drove over to Liv's house while Craig played some interactive game with a kid in some faraway city. He figured the kid had better get his fill of that kind of stuff because the internet at the dude ranch was not very fast.

Liv came out onto the porch as he parked, wearing a long silky red robe and carrying a towel that she'd obviously just taken off her head since her hair hung in damp waves around her face.

"Hmm," he said as he came up the walk. "I should have gotten here earlier."

Liv clutched the towel in both hands and tried to smile, but instead got the same look she'd worn when he'd teased her while she tried to tutor him.

Ah. The roosters had come home to roost. But that didn't stop her from checking him out, which made him think an interesting conversation lay ahead.

"Matt."

"Olivia." Now that they'd identified each other, he was curious what came next.

Her lips twitched, but she made no reply. Matt waited for a second or two, then decided to do the gentlemanly thing and help her out. "I can see that you're itching to lay out some ground rules."

"How can you tell?"

He leaned his shoulder against the newel post, for some reason finding her barriers less intimidating than usual. Maybe because he now knew that those walls could come down. In fact, he couldn't wait to see them come down again. So if she needed ground rules to feel safe, so be it.

"You're…different…than you were in the trailer."

She smiled a little, but she didn't relax. Not one bit.

"Yeah. No doubt." She cocked her head and met his eyes directly. "The other night, with you, was my first…casual encounter." Her eyebrows went up slightly as if she were unsure she was getting her point across. Oh, he got it.

Matt couldn't exactly say the same, but he hadn't considered last night all that casual. Liv needed to, though, and he was curious as to why.

"So what are the ground rules, Liv?" He found himself focusing on her more intently than he wanted to, waiting for her answer with a touch of unexpected impatience. He might be impatient in the professional areas of his life, but in his relationships, he was happy to take things slowly after the train wreck that had occurred after his hasty marriage to Trena.

Her eyebrows drew together slightly. "I'm not making rules," she finally said. "But I will tell you my limitations."

"Shoot."

"I think we're developing a decent friendship here, but I won't let it go past friendship. We will live our own lives."

Limitation number one. "And what we did the other night?"

"I can see it happening again."

"So we'd basically become screw buddies?" He avoided the cruder term, but just barely.

"That sounds so crass," she said.

"Probably because it is." When had he developed these high standards?

"I don't believe this is an uncommon occurrence."

"So what you're saying," he said, "is that we'll do our own thing, go our own way and if we happen to find ourselves in a similar situation to last night, we might screw again."

She blinked. A cool blink that relayed a wealth of repressed emotion. She did not appear happy with the way the laying down of the rules was progressing or with hearing them translated into plain English.

"I guess so," she finally said.

He considered for a moment before saying, "Good for now, but I can't guarantee that I won't ever need more than that."

Alarm flashed in her blue eyes. "I can't offer more."

"You don't know that."

"I'm pretty sure of it."

"Why?"

Liv swallowed. He didn't think she was going to answer, but she surprised him. She swung the towel up over her shoulder, still hanging on to one end as she said, "I've had two serious relationships since high school. The first was not good and I was too sub-servient to do anything about it. He finally dumped me for someone else and I was devastated. And stu-

pid for being devastated. The second guy...I almost
married. I thought we were partners, until it finally
struck me that yeah, he pretended we were partners,
until push came to shove. After that it was his way
or the highway. I finally took the highway." She lev-
eled a serious look at him. "I am never going through
that again."

"Noted."

"I'm serious, Matt. I just want to live my life."

"I wouldn't stop you from doing that."

"Yes, I know."

"Because I won't have a chance. Right?"

"This isn't working," she said softly.

"But it might, given a chance."

She shook her head. "Not unless we understand
each other."

"Play it your way, in other words."

He was more than willing to play it her way. Liv
had some scars he hadn't known about. He didn't
quite understand why she was so militant, but she
was and there was no getting around it, so he had to
work with it.

And right now he wasn't going to sign on as a
screw buddy. Maybe it was ego, maybe just stubbornness, but he didn't think that what they were
developing between them was simply a friends-with-
benefits deal. Liv was skittish, but that didn't mean
that she wouldn't eventually see that the two of them
did pretty damned well together.

"That's all I can offer," she said.

Matt let out a breath—he was a little pissed, a little intrigued. A lot uncertain.

At least he knew more than he'd known before. Liv wasn't up for another bad relationship.

Matt wasn't, either, so they had that in common, and if they ever did get to a point, slowly, that they wanted to embark on something…more…then the last thing he would try to do would be to control her life and her decisions. As long as she understood that, then there shouldn't be a problem and he'd been clear enough on the matter.

Clearer than he and Trena had been with each other.

He looked up at the starry sky for a moment, thinking about the asshole guys who'd had a hand in shaping Liv's outlook on relationships, even causal ones, and felt a deep need to beat the crap out of someone. Then he shook his head and started back for the porch, where Liv stood, rolling the towel into a ball. He'd never felt like this about a woman before and had no idea how things were going to go. This was new territory for him. Territory he wanted to explore.

He started up the steps, taking them slowly. Liv's lips parted when he reached the one just below her, as did her robe when she dropped her hands to her sides, giving him a very good look at why he wasn't in his truck right now, driving away. But it was more than that, and he didn't want to blow this. He stopped a good two feet away from her, resisting the urge to touch her. "Liv, couldn't we just…*be*…for a while? Keep an open mind? Not be so quick to define things?"

She didn't answer immediately, and the conflicting emotions—fear, desire, curiosity, caution—played openly across her features. "And if I try, but can't?" she finally asked.

"We pull the plug."

Her eyes were wide. Wary. "And until then?"

He moved a step closer. "I think you know what happens until then." What she obviously wanted to happen until then.

He saw her swallow, felt again like reaching out to her, but didn't. "I want to be fair," she said. "Tell you the truth...about me."

"You've done that. Now what else do you want?"

She sucked a breath in through her teeth and then slowly planted both hands, one still holding the damp towel, on his chest. "I guess I'd really like to make the most of the last night my father isn't going to be home."

CHAPTER SEVENTEEN

HAVING LIV IN his life—even on her rather strict terms—was a distraction that Matt probably didn't need, but one that he enjoyed all the same. During the two weeks that they'd been together, she both drove him crazy and helped him stay sane. An odd situation, but when he was around her, he didn't think only of roping, of beating his brother to start his comeback, of how long his knee would hold out. He thought of all those things and Liv, too.

Hard to believe this woman who was all but eating him alive was the same girl too shy to talk to him about anything except for the area under curves when she'd tutored him.

He had no idea where this relationship was going, but he had no doubt at all that they did have a relationship, no matter what spin Liv wanted to put on it. They were not simply screw buddies, because if they were, he wouldn't be wondering what he could do to make her happy. He would be satisfied with an evening of hot sex here and again. She wouldn't be on his mind when he wasn't with her.

Craig wouldn't be giving him that people-in-love-are-disgusting look every time she came over to the place—which she did fairly frequently.

So was he in love?

This wasn't what he'd felt for Trena. He'd cared about her, been blown away by her beauty and sensuality, but the protectiveness he felt toward Liv hadn't been part of the deal. That didn't mean he hadn't loved Trena, because he had. An immature love, but love all the same. This was different. Liv was different.

One thing was certain—he didn't need to be in any hurry to answer that question, because the instant he said anything at all that smacked of being a couple, Liv backed off. Sometimes she practically left skid marks. But she was not indifferent. Of that he was sure.

Patience.

And since he was practicing such patience with Liv, perhaps his impatience was spilling out in his professional life. Now that he had Snigs, he could practice more. Snigs one night, one of the practice horses the next, so he didn't overdo it with her. But although Snigs was a fine horse, she wasn't the horse Beckett was. He'd come to a place where he could live with that. Beckett was never a subject of conversation, and the few times that Liv had mentioned him, the moment had felt awkward and she'd quickly changed the subject.

The fact that he was leaving the matter alone was another reason he knew he had it bad for Liv. Anyone else and he would have probably kept pushing. He would have been subtle, but push he would have. A testimony to his feelings, although he didn't know if Liv knew, or would acknowledge it if she did.

Patience.

"Hey, Matt!" Craig's voice came through his closed door loud and clear.

Patience.

"Yeah?"

"Don't you think you should start practice?"

Matt threw back the covers. Of course. It was almost 7:00 a.m. Of course he should start practice. Craig just loved opening the chute and giving him pointers he picked up off of YouTube training videos.

"Be right out."

Craig had the toaster waffles on a plate by the time Matt came down the hall, tucking in his shirt.

"You're walking better," Craig said offhandedly.

"Feeling better," Matt replied.

"Maybe you won't have to get fake knees after all."

"Maybe," Matt said, truly hoping he didn't. All he wanted was one more season, one more win. One more year to figure out what he was going to do with his life that didn't involve ranching with his father.

For the first time ever he wished he'd finished a college degree and had something to fall back on as Wes had mentioned.

So maybe he might go back…but not if he didn't have to.

One more year and maybe he could become a

knee-replacement spokesperson. All he knew was that while he had his knees he was going to use them. If he had to get a replacement, he would, but life would change then and he wasn't ready.

Matt Montoya was going down fighting.

"Hey, don't take all the syrup." Craig held his hand out and Matt handed over the bottle. He was going to miss Craig when he left.

"CRAIG SAYS YOU'RE practicing too hard." Liv's hand paused on Matt's battle-worn knee. The right was worse than the left, crisscrossed with scars from where he'd had the cartilage cut away. The left was not that scarred, but Liv recognized needle marks that shouldn't have been there.

"Still seeing him, aren't you?"

"It's not illegal."

"It should be."

Matt reached down to tilt her chin up so she had to meet his eyes. "I'm not overdoing things."

"Then why do you need to inject painkillers?"

"So I can do my job."

Liv sat up and hugged her knees to her chest. Matt placed the flat of his hand on her back, but it didn't comfort her. It only intensified the sadness she felt that he was doing this to himself and she had no right to ask him to stop.

His life. You want to live your life, you have to allow him to live his.

But what he was doing to his body was so wrong.

"Why is roping so important?"

The hand on her back stilled for a moment, then started moving again. "It's what I do."

"You've said that before."

He brought his lips down to lightly kiss her shoulder blade, sending tingles shooting through her body. "Maybe it's more like it's who I am."

She turned on him. "No. It's not who you are. Something is driving you. I mean, it's not logical to risk destroying your knees for a sport."

"Football players do it all the time."

She dropped her head back down to her knees. Useless.

"Roping…" he began, then fell silent again. She squeezed her eyes shut, hoping he would continue, afraid he would not.

"Roping is the way I express things."

"Like what?"

"When I first started, back in junior rodeo days, it was the competition that I loved. Competing against myself almost more than competing against other people." He paused to clear his throat. "Pleasing my dad when I won."

"Did that change?"

"Oh, yeah."

Liv waited for a moment, then rolled her head so that she could see him. "How?"

"When I was fifteen years old, I took a trip with my dad to a roping clinic in Butte. I got done with my section and headed to the trailer to meet up with him.

When I got there, I could hear him talking to some woman on the other side. I was about to walk around and tell him I was done when I heard her say, 'Ryan needs braces.' And there was something about the way she said it…"

Liv had no idea where this was going, but wherever, it was serious. Matt wasn't looking at her and his hand had once again stopped.

"So I'm wondering to myself why my dad would care if Ryan needed braces."

"Did you know Ryan?"

He gave a soft snort. "Oh, yeah. Ryan was the kid who was my toughest competition. A year younger than me, but we were in the same divisions."

"So why would your father care if Ryan needed braces?"

"Because, come to find out, Ryan is my half brother."

Liv tossed her hair back as she sat up straight. "No."

"Oh, yeah. Not the best thing for a kid to find out about the dad he worshipped."

"My gosh, Matt."

He smiled tightly and she could see what this cost him to tell her this…this secret. More than that, she wondered what this was costing her. "Who knows about this?"

"Me. Dad. Ryan's mom. I don't know if he knows. I don't think he does."

"Your mom?"

Matt shook his head. "As far as I know, no. Which is why I've never let on that I know. I just stood on the other side of that trailer, listening when I should have walked away, and since that time I've never said a word."

Liv simply stared at him, knowing exactly what he was talking about, since the same thing had recently happened to her, and trying to think of what on earth she could say, when all she wanted to do was to put her arms around the fifteen-year-old boy who'd just had his world destroyed.

"You've never talked to anyone about this?"

"How? What if it got back to my mom?"

"Maybe she knows."

"And what if she doesn't?"

Liv could see his point. So for over fifteen years he'd carried the secret…no wonder she'd sensed that there were issues between him and his father.

"And your dad?"

"I…try to have a relationship."

"Never the same?"

"How could they be?"

Liv reached out to touch him. He caught her hand before it landed on his arm, held her fingers. For contact? Or to keep her from touching him?

All these years and he'd never told anyone. But now he was telling her.

She would think about how much that frightened her later. Right now…right now she needed to think about Matt.

"You know I'll never whisper a word."

"If I didn't I wouldn't have said anything."

Emotion tinged again with fear swelled inside of her. She was touched that he'd told, afraid that it meant he was seeing her as more than a friend.

"So you handled the stress by roping," she finally said.

"I needed to be the better son," Matt said simply. "I needed to beat my brother, who shouldn't even have existed."

But he did and he was Matt's greatest competition, then and now.

"I couldn't understand why he—my dad—would knock someone up when I was less than a year old. Wasn't I enough for him?"

"I'm sure it was an accident."

"That he was boinking someone in a nearby city?"

"The pregnancy."

"Maybe. Maybe not. Back then, I guess, it pissed me off that my mom and I hadn't been enough. Then, well, Ryan was so damned good, but he didn't even try to go national. Until last year he was content staying on the Montana circuit, dominating there. And then when he did go national, he was great."

"You won world titles."

"And he came close last year, but I didn't make enough money to qualify for the NFR. I don't know if he would have beaten me."

"So all this is just to beat your brother?"

"Half brother, and no. Some of it is because I don't

have anything else to do for a living. I can't come back here and ranch with my dad and I don't have any other training." A good point. "I can probably land a job, but—" he gave a faint scoffing laugh "—I've been spoiled. I want to keep doing what I do well. I like being me."

Liv laughed a little, trying to take the edge off Matt's tension. "You are going to have to build a bigger house—one that can contain both you and your ego."

Matt took her shoulders and gently pushed her back onto the pillows. "Maybe not," he said as he supported himself with elbows planted on either side of her head. "Craig is supposed to be heading north in another week. That should free up some space for my ego."

"Will you miss him?" she asked.

He surprised her by saying, "Yes."

"My heart just officially melted."

"That's the way I want you. Melting all over me."

"Then I'd better be on top."

"No way, sister," he said before kissing her long and hard. "You can have the top tomorrow."

MATT'S CONFESSION ATE at her. This was supposed to be a casual affair, and Liv promised herself before it began that she would not ignore the red flags as they appeared.

Red flag number one: Matt had told her a secret he'd told no one else. That smacked of deep trust.

Fine if she were simply his friend, but when she was also his lover, that muddied the waters—at least as far as she was concerned.

Red flag number two: her heart was breaking for him, both as a boy whose world had been rocked and as a man who was still working out a way to deal with the anger.

He'd never told anyone, except for her.

What did she owe him in return? A shoulder? Moral support? Silence?

The latter would have to do because feeling the need to make it all better for him was seriously seizing her up. Making things better, smoothing the waters were the hallmarks of falling back into the old habits.

Old habits would destroy her. She could not live her mother's life.

So the next move will be...

Liv hadn't a clue. She looked forward to her time with Matt. Every time they were together and every time she was able to part company without asking when they might see each other again, or making plans for the next day, made her feel more in control of her own destiny.

But it didn't stop her from looking forward to seeing him whenever she could. And it didn't stop her from getting angry every time she saw those needle marks in his leg.

After the confession, things changed between them. Matt withdrew somewhat, as if he regretted telling her about his half brother—which actually comforted her. He'd slipped up, trusted her with more than he should have and now he regretted it.

But when he made love to her, things had changed there, too. He was quieter than before. He saw to her pleasure, seemed to enjoy himself, but some of the abandon was gone, and Liv wasn't certain what—if anything—to do about it.

MATT HADN'T EXPECTED the house to feel so empty after Willa picked up Craig five days after her I-got-the-job email. He missed the kid, but it'd been easy to see how happy Craig was to be reunited with his mom—even if he was going to have to continue fighting the Crag/Craig battle. Maybe someday when Matt went to visit—as he'd promised he would—he'd have a serious talk with Willa. None of his business, and he didn't want to hurt his cousin's feelings, but, really? Crag?

The only truly positive aspect of Craig leaving was that Matt and Liv had a safe place to rendezvous. And rendezvous they did—which only served to convince Matt that he sucked at no-strings.

He'd never had a problem with strings—as long as he found a woman he wanted to be tied to. If he didn't find her, he was quite happy exploring, but once he did, he was the settling kind. Ironically, Liv was not and she showed no signs of weakening her resolve. It was killing him in a way. And she was concerned about someone controlling her.

She also had a major problem with his knee treatment. They hadn't talked about it in the days since he'd told her about Ryan, but it still bothered her and he wondered if that was a huge part of the unspoken problem between them. Maybe if she just watched him go through his paces, it might reassure her that he wasn't numbing the pain so he could bend the joint backward or anything. She could see he avoided lateral movements and that the brace did most of the work supporting the joint; then maybe she'd see that the injections merely helped him get through this rough patch and allowed him to train.

With that in mind, he approached the subject as she left his place after eating dinner with him.

"I thought you might come watch me rope," he said as he walked her out onto the porch.

"I don't think so." And before he could say anything, she added, "You know why."

"The *why* is the reason I want you to watch. What I'm doing is the same thing I've always done. I wear the brace, the knee is protected. I'm not destroying myself."

"Then why does your knee have to be numbed?"

"Because it makes practice easier. And it's not totally numbed. I can still feel and it still hurts like a son of a bitch sometimes."

"Pain is nature's way of saying stop. You're too stubborn to get the message."

"Liv…" He put his hands on her shoulders and

felt her muscles tense. "Walk over to the arena when you're done with practice. Just watch. Once."

She opened her mouth, then thought better of whatever she'd been about to say. Instead, she swallowed and made an obvious effort to relax. He kept his hands right where they were, drawing strength, which was an irony, since he needed the strength to hold his own against her resistance to letting their lives mesh any further than they already were.

Liv was on a journey. Would he be left along the road at some point?

He had a strong feeling that was part of her master plan. After Trena he'd pretty well sworn never again, but here he was, with a woman who responded to him passionately when they made love, but refused to let the relationship move past friendship. And he didn't even have the satisfaction of getting to beat the shit out of the guy who'd given her the wakeup call. In his opinion, she was going overboard, but it was the only way she felt secure and it was hard to argue with that.

"Forget I said anything," he said, stepping back. His words were clipped, the result of frustration over things he couldn't control but had to deal with.

"I can't condone what you're doing."

"I'm not asking you to condone it," he said, honestly wishing now he hadn't said anything. "I'm asking you to gather some information instead of proceeding with a closed mind."

"Really," she said stonily. "A closed mind. Which of us has a bit more training in the field of physiology?"

"If we have this no-strings relationship you say we have, then why do you even care?"

"Professional ethics."

"Ah. A matter of principle."

"I would have the same concerns regardless of who you were."

"Who am I, Liv? To you?"

"Don't make me label this."

"That's right. You don't like labels, even if they're accurate. I remember that *screw buddy* was off-limits."

"Look—" she rounded on him "—I told you what I could give. You said you could accept that."

"And now I want to know why that's all you can give. You didn't make any rules about that."

"I have to go," she said.

"I'm sure you do."

"I'm not a coward, Matt. I'm a realist. I've made some decisions about my life and I'm standing by them."

"No matter who you hurt in the process?"

Her mouth went flat and then she turned and walked out the door. It'd be great to call her back, to tell her he was sorry, but he wasn't certain he was.

THAT HAD BEEN uncalled for. She'd been nothing but up-front with Matt and he'd said he agreed and now...

Why on earth was this happening? And why

couldn't she have been like Shae and told Matt she was attracted to him back when she'd wanted so desperately to date him? Then this would all be over and done with and she'd have moved on with her life.

Except the thought of moving on didn't feel so good.

Red flag of the highest order.

Liv drew in a breath, told herself she was over-thinking, overreacting. She was angry at what she saw as Matt breaking the rules, but really, what had he done except ask her to come and watch him? She made a quantum leap into thinking she was being controlled. He'd just asked. Not cajoled, not implored, but simply asked. And he'd had a solid reason—from his point of view. Nothing was going to change her thoughts on what he was doing and why it was wrong.

Bottom line, she'd overreacted, but she still wasn't going to watch him rope. Not while he was shooting painkillers into himself.

Tim was finally up and around and for once in his life not ignoring the advice of others. He allowed Liv to do what she had time to do around the place, hired Walter across the road to do the remaining chores. He never mentioned asking Matt to come back and wondered just what he might have heard via the grapevine. It didn't matter because it was her business, not his, and she didn't need to live her life to please him any more than she needed to live it to please anyone. She could be a respectful, loving daughter and have her own life. If nothing else, Tim modeled that behavior more than anyone she knew. True, it'd gotten him in trouble, but he certainly didn't bend over backward to please anyone, and everyone knew where they stood with him.

After four days of not seeing or hearing anything from Matt, Liv had to admit she missed him. A lot. But she didn't seek him out. No. She bumped straight into him in the last place she expected—at a discount store in Butte while she was shopping with Shae for wedding doodads.

Shae was still in the next aisle over and Liv was more than grateful that, for the moment, it was just she and Matt. Alone, except for the grandmotherly lady perusing the paper goods a few feet away. Shae didn't miss much and the vibe between Liv and Matt was instantly awkward. No. *She* felt awkward. Matt seemed fine.

"I didn't expect to see you here," she said, hoping they parted company before Shae found them and started asking questions.

"I'm kind of putting together a care package to send to Craig." He gestured down at the batteries and USB cables and other assorted electronics in the cart. Liv almost smiled. Matt was more softhearted than she'd given him credit for.

"You miss him."

"It's not the same with just me and my ego crammed into the house." There was no amusement in his eyes as he spoke.

"Liv?" Shae's voice carried down the aisle. Liv and Matt turned in unison to see her come around the corner. She stopped short when she saw Matt, her eyebrows going up. "Matt! Wow. It's been a while."

He smiled easily. "Shae. I hear congratulations are in order."

"Yes." She beamed as she held out the rock on her hand. She gave him a slow once-over. "You're looking good. I guess world championships agree with you."

"I'm not a champion anymore, Shae."

"You'll always be a champion in my book," Shae said in a way that made Liv, the most nonviolent of people, want to reach out and smack her one. Then Matt cut a subtle sideways glance her way, caught her eye, and Liv suddenly wanted to laugh. Maybe Shae didn't always outshine her. She and Matt might be on the outs, but at least he took her seriously.

CHAPTER EIGHTEEN

LIV MISSED MATT. As a friend. As a confidant. As a lover.

There were matters, such as her father, that were easier to discuss with Matt than with Andie, and after five days of silence, she knew that the ball was in her court. She had to be the one to reestablish contact—hopefully out of hearing range of Tim.

On the night that the drill team practiced in the slack arena while the ropers commanded the larger one, Liv decided to make her move. She told herself that it was crazy to give up on a decent friendship when they might be able to iron things out. She fully admitted to herself that she missed the sex—and that she'd been stupid to draw a line in the sand.

She also realized that what she'd been doing was wrong; she had tried to do to him exactly what she'd refused to let him do to her—have a say in his life. Yes, what he was doing to his knee was wrong and crazy, but so what? It was his life. She couldn't control him. In fact, she was a bit ashamed that she'd tried. The pot calling the kettle black and all that.

After her practice was over, about midway through the roping, Liv led Beckett through the trailers to

Matt's, where she found a roan and a bay tied side by side. No Matt.

She thought about waiting, changed her mind, walked a few steps back in the direction she'd come and then stopped when he called her name.

"Hey," she said as she turned around, feeling awkward. She and Beckett walked back to the trailer where he was coming out of the tack room. "I...uh—" she peeked into the tack room and her mouth went a little dry as she remembered their last experience in a trailer "—just wanted to see you."

There. Out and honest.

"Yeah?" he asked in that voice that just kind of did things to her—a marked change from the cool tone he'd used in the discount store a few days ago.

"I shouldn't be trying to tell you what to do. With your knee." Matt slung the bridle he was carrying over his shoulder. Before he could say anything—if he was going to say anything—she added, "I was doing exactly what I asked you not to do."

"What shall we do about that?" he asked reasonably.

"Start again?" Liv pulled in a breath. "I...miss talking to you."

A slow, knowing smile curved his mouth. "Is that all?"

"You know it isn't."

Matt glanced over at the arena, then back at Liv. "Can we talk after the roping? Can you hang around that long?"

Liv nodded. "I can do that." Because she wanted to talk to Matt and get things back the way they'd been before she'd made her error.

Matt smiled and Liv's stomach did a bit of a free fall as he said, "I missed you, too, Liv." A simple statement that held a wealth of meaning, as in, he accepted her apology.

Without thinking, she reached up to touch his stubbled cheek. He caught her hand, kissed the palm, making her breath catch as she thought once again of tack rooms, and then Beckett gave her a nudge from behind, knocking her forward half a step. Matt laughed and reached out to pat Beckett's neck.

"How's the drill horse?" he asked.

"Good." A lot less tense than she was at the moment.

"I miss him, too," Matt said matter-of-factly, sliding a hand under the horse's mane. "But...you know."

Liv did know. He hadn't asked to buy the horse back since his second failed attempt. He had other horses and seemed satisfied to use them. Maybe the only reason he'd been so driven to get Beckett back had been because of Trena. The woman had not played fair, but Matt seemed to be moving on.

Beckett bobbed his head and leaned into Matt's hand as he stroked the horse's neck.

"Someday you'll have to let me take him out. For old time's sake."

"Go ahead," Liv said.

Matt shot her a startled look.

"Get on him," she said.

Matt grinned widely. It took him less than a minute to change the stirrup length and mount. Her saddle was slightly too small for him, but Matt didn't seem to care. It was a roping saddle and that was all he needed.

He lifted the reins and Beckett's head came up. Liv watched the change in her horse with both amazement and a twist of jealousy. Beckett was alert, ready to go, an expression of equine anticipation in his amber eyes. The damned horse was practically smiling.

"One calf?"

Liv shrugged, her gut tightening. "Sure."

Matt rode toward the arena gate and Liv followed, stopping close to where Margo was seated on the end of the bleachers. She smiled coolly at the woman who was making her father crazy, and then tried to find Matt and Beckett.

"He once owned the horse?" Margo asked. It was the first time the woman had spoken to her, other than a quick word during practice, since Tim had come out of the hospital.

"Yeah."

"You can tell."

Damn it, she could. They hadn't been together in almost two years and man and animal were in total sync.

"I'd hate to lose him," Liv said more to herself than to Margo.

"There's nothing saying you have to."

"I kind of got him in an underhanded deal."

"I know." Liv shot Margo a glance and the older woman said, "People talk."

That's right. They did. And now she was going to talk, or rather ask a question. "What happened with you and my father?"

Margo's expression didn't change. She'd been expecting the question. "A lot of stuff a long time ago."

"Must have been some incredible *stuff* if you paid his hospital bill." Liv lifted her chin as Matt and Beckett came into the arena through the small gate on the opposite end, half wishing she'd kept her mouth shut.

"That's between Tim and me," Margo said.

Liv kept her eye on the arena. It *was* between Margo and Tim. She may never know what their relationship was, but she wished that whatever it was, that they either buried it or dealt with it because she'd never seen her father like this in her life.

Matt maneuvered Beckett into position next to the chute. He nodded and the calf came charging out. A second later, Beckett went after him, switching his tail as he thundered after the animal. Her horse was fast.

Matt swung a loop and it settled over the calf's head, then he released the rope and the calf continued on his way around the arena, the rope trailing after him.

She could see Matt's triumphant smile from where she stood. He must have roped the beast in three flat and she had to give him bonus points for not throwing the calf, knowing how she felt about his knees. The calf ran to the chute and the guy keeping the gate snagged the loop off its head. Matt rode up, took the rope and coiled it as he and Beckett headed to the gate.

"Some team," Margo said.

Liv couldn't bring herself to answer. Beckett had loved every second of that run, in a way that he didn't love doing drill work.

"Matt shouldn't be roping," she said.

"Honey, what a man should do and what he does do are very different things sometimes."

Liv didn't need to be hit over to the head in order to know that Margo was talking about her father. And she really wanted to know what Tim hadn't done that was keeping him awake at night.

Matt was still smiling when he rode Beckett back up to Liv's trailer. "I don't imagine you watched."

"I did," she admitted.

Matt dismounted and handed the reins to Liv. "Finally."

Matt ran a hand over Beckett's neck. "You did good for having no practice," he said to the horse.

Liv cleared her throat. "And you two did well together—just like you said." She pulled in a breath, then realized that after stating the obvious, she had nothing else to say. He put a hand on the back of her neck, his fingers caressing over the smooth skin beneath her ponytail.

"You don't need to sound so sad. I'm not going to steal him."

The thought of letting Beckett go made her gut twist…as did the memory of how excited the horse had been to charge after that calf. That was what he'd been bred to do and he loved it. As did the guy who'd been riding him.

Beckett belonged to Matt. He really did.

I can't let him go.

She wanted very much to say the words out loud, but instead she smiled at Matt. "I'd send the sheriff after you if you did."

Matt took a step closer, sending her senses into high alert. "It'd work better if you…came yourself."

Liv's pulse jumped and she leaned toward him, maybe just so she could draw his scent into her lungs, maybe just because he did crazy things to her hormones.

"Any chance you could stop by later tonight?" Matt asked.

Liv's heart stuttered even as she calmly met his eyes. "With or without my horse?"

"It's not roping I'm interested in."

"I'll see what I can do."

He kissed her, right there, in front of anyone who cared to see. And Liv didn't step back. She met his kiss, answered with one of her own. Quicker and less lingering than his, but a kiss all the same.

So now she was kissing him in public, but calling him a friend. There was something off about that, just as Matt had said. Something that she was going to have to think about.

And think she did—not that it got her anywhere.

She enjoyed being with Matt, enjoyed being in his bed. Enjoyed everything about her time with him except for the gnawing fear that she would get herself in over her head and lose control. She was so damned afraid of losing control…every relationship in her life, except for maybe that with her mother, had consisted of Liv eventually giving in to keep a peaceful status quo. No, she even did that with her mother—just look at the things she did to keep Shae happy—but she did those out of love and understanding. To keep her fragile mother happy…

But was that so different from what she was afraid of doing with Matt?

As long as they continued as they were, she told herself over and over again, she was safe. She wasn't going to lose herself. And in those moments when she found the old Liv wishing that she could have more of a committed relationship with Matt, the new Liv sternly reminded the old Liv of just what her life had been like in every other committed relationship she'd ever had.

Which made it all the more difficult, and threatening, when she sometimes wondered if she were actually falling for Matt.

Even if she did…well…she wouldn't.

But what if…

Damn, but Matt Montoya scared her.

She laid a hand on Beckett's neck. "You brought us together, big guy. Now…would you mind telling me what to do?"

Most of Matt's days were spent practicing. He roped, he tied, he threw. His knee was getting stronger, not weaker, as all the naysayers had predicted. He and Snigs were developing their rhythm and overall he felt confident about his comeback.

And when Liv was with him, his world felt complete, as sappy as that seemed. But it was true and Matt thought that maybe she was feeling the same. They didn't talk about limitations and rules and parameters anymore—or at least they hadn't during the past three weeks. Liv came over as often as she could and they'd spend the evenings horseback riding or cooking or sometimes playing one of the video games Craig had left that they were both really bad at. A couple of times she'd brought Beckett by on her way home from practice and had let him ride his old buddy. It gnawed at him to do so, but he knew she thought she was doing him a favor.

In some ways the past weeks had been the most peaceful and fulfilling in Matt's life. And in others the most frustrating—because he didn't know where he stood with Liv. Didn't know if things were only shifting on his side. What really bothered him was that he was afraid to bring up the topic, afraid of upsetting the balance. And because of that he was getting antsy.

He wanted reassurance that he wasn't alone in the feeling that they were developing something special. He was more than willing to go slowly, for Liv's peace of mind, but he wanted to make sure they were on the same page.

"Don't rush" became his mantra, but being the guy he was, of course he screwed it up.

One Thursday night, after Liv had stopped by after drill practice and put him through a few paces of her own, he opened his mouth and risked turning his world upside down.

"We do well together," he said as he pulled her up against him, running a hand over her hair and letting his fingers tangle loosely in the reddish-brown strands.

"I'd say there's some chemistry," she agreed.

"Chemistry is important. Look at me and Beckett. We've had chemistry since day one."

"I can see that," Liv said.

"Don't worry, Livvy. I'm not asking to have Beckett back."

"Then what do you want?"

He casually stroked his hand down the side of her face. "I want you to give us a chance."

"By chance you mean..." He made a slow you-know gesture with one hand. "Damn, Matt." She put some space between them, gathering the sheet up to her neck with both hands. "I made myself clear on that point from the beginning. You can't ask for change now."

322   ONCE A CHAMPION

"Why the hell not?"

"Because we agreed."

"We agreed according to the way things were then. Whether you will admit it or not, things have changed."

"For you, maybe."

"I don't believe that."

"Believe it," she said, scrambling out of bed and searching for her clothes on the floor. She pulled up a pair of jeans—his—and dropped them before going for the pair underneath it.

"Liv!"

Something in his tone made her stop, her jeans clutched in one hand.

"There is something very wrong here."

"Yes. I agree." She went for her shirt.

"With you."

That got her attention. "There is nothing wrong with me."

"Yeah. There is. Why are you denying you feel anything for me?"

"I'm not admitting or denying. The way I feel is my own business. I'm just telling you that I do not want a relationship."

"Like it or not, you have one."

"Not anymore."

"Meaning?"

"What does it sound like I mean?" She pulled her pants up and buttoned the waistband, then jammed her arms into her shirt without bothering with her bra.

Once covered, she reached down for her socks and underwear, holding them loosely in one hand as she spoke as clearly as she possibly could, so he would make no mistake in her meaning.

"I mean that this—" she pointed to first him then back to herself "—is no more."

"Liv…" His voice was a low rumble, but she ignored what it did to her.

"I can't do this anymore. I can't fight you. I won't fight you."

"I'm not fighting with you! I'm trying to clue you into reality."

"Okay. Let's talk reality. In all my relationships, I've been the giver. The one that bends, the one that changes. It's not healthy, but I will keep doing it. Even though I don't want to."

"Then don't."

"I don't intend to."

It took a moment for her meaning to sink in. He was about tell her that he wasn't interested in a relationship with someone who always bent, when she said, "Take Beckett."

"What?"

"Take Beckett and then there's no more reason for us to share anything. You'll have what you wanted from the beginning and I'll have—"

"What, Liv? What will you have?"

"Peace of mind," she said fiercely.

"I am not some jerk who'll take over your life."

"That's not a chance I'm ready to take."

ONCE A CHAMPION

LESS THAN THREE minutes later, Liv numbly stepped out into a windy July night. The moon was full, bathing her truck in a yellowish light.

You're fine. You did the right thing.

Of course, she had.

You gave away your horse… .

As if Beckett had ever truly been hers. She loved him, but he was Matt's. The ties between her and Matt were now severed. Matt had told her he wasn't taking the horse without paying for him. Liv had told him that was fine. She'd take the money; he could take Beckett. It would have been difficult to ride Beckett now anyway, because he would remind her too much of Matt.

Matt, who should never have lost the horse in the first place. If she hadn't bought him from Trena, none of this would have happened. She wouldn't now be turned inside out over a man who was ignoring the ground rules, trying to get her to agree to something she'd told him from the beginning she wouldn't agree to. Just as Allen had done. Just as Greg had done.

Only this was worse, because, unlike with the other men in her life, she'd laid everything out to Matt from day one, told him how far she was willing to go, and he'd still tried to push her into a corner.

"MATT PICKED UP your horse this afternoon," Tim said as soon as Liv walked in the door after work. "And left a healthy check."

"Let me see that," Liv said, striding across the

room. She coughed when she saw the amount—about five times what she'd paid for Beckett. "Great. Just great," she muttered, dropping the mail on the end table next to her father so he could go through it. Now she'd have to hammer this out with Matt.

"I don't understand one thing about this," Tim said. "You broke up with the guy. Why does he get the horse?"

"Because he should have always had him," Liv said wearily. Her father did not look as if he were buying her statement, but went back to reading his paper, his expression morose.

Liv was having an increasingly hard time being around her father while he was in this funk, induced no doubt by both his illness and Margo.

Figuring he couldn't feel any worse than he did now, and desperately needing to distract herself from Matt and this check, Liv fired out the question that she'd been holding back for so long.

"What happened with you and Margo?"

"There was a time you didn't ask questions like that," Tim said irritably.

"I've changed." Which was why Matt was out of the picture. So that she could maintain her changes without being tempted to fall back into her old patterns.

"What's to tell?" he said with a shrug.

"Were you involved when my mom was in the picture?"

"Who said we were involved at all?"

"Give me a break, Dad. It's obvious that something happened between you." He sent her a baleful look, which she ignored, feeling very much like she was dealing with one of her patients. She had to help them learn to deal with pain in order to get better. Maybe it was time for Tim to do the same.

"Before."

"So...thirty years ago?"

"Thirty-two. She helped me build this house."

Liv looked around the room. "*This* house." She pointed at the floor with her index finger.

"The same. She drew up the plans."

"Wow." Liv sat in the chair opposite her father. "What happened?"

Tim made a helpless gesture. "I did, I guess. Margo never kowtowed to me. We saw eye-to-eye on most everything, except for one thing. Money. She had it. I didn't."

"And..."

"And I wouldn't let her bankroll me," he said as if it were obvious.

"First she wanted to pay for the place herself, but I said no. Then she wanted to go fifty-fifty."

"Fifty-fifty seems fair."

Tim's jaw clenched tight, making the cords in his neck stand out for a moment before he spoke. "My dad never did shit around the place when I was growing up." Liv blinked. "My ma did everything, paid for everything. I decided clear back when I was a kid that I was never going to be that kind of man. Having other people do things for me. I was going to be the doer. The provider."

"You've done that," Liv murmured. Tim gave a jerky nod and Liv began to wonder if maybe she shouldn't have opened this particular can of worms. She'd never met her grandfather—he'd passed before she was born and Tim rarely spoke of him. Now she knew why. Tim had no respect for him.

"That's why you broke up?"

"There were other reasons, but that was one of them. She told me I was stubborn and if I couldn't learn to bend a little, then she wouldn't want to bend, either. So she left."

"Damn, Dad."

"I screwed up, although, looking back, I don't think I could have done it any differently at that age. I was still so damned mad at my dad for working my ma to death." His head fell back against the headrest. "So Margo married Bill Carlton and moved to Wyoming."

"And you?"

"I married your mom."

"Why?" The question she'd wondered about for at least two decades slipped right out of her mouth.

"Your mom was…is…beautiful and bubbly and she was the picture of cooperation. She agreed to whatever I said." Tim's mouth tightened slightly. "And I liked that, at first."

"Not so much later?"

"I don't like talking about this."

"That's okay. I don't blame either of you. I could just never figure out why you got married."

"Now you know." He sounded bitter, but Liv was relieved to finally know the score. Her dad had screwed up. So had Margo, in a way. Neither had been willing to bend.

"So…no chance of you and Margo ever becoming friends again?"

Tim snorted. "Let me put it this way…can you think of anything that would piss me off more than paying my hospital bill?"

Excellent point. Margo played hardball.

"Thirty years and she's still pissed," Tim grumbled, reaching for the TV remote, a sure sign that this uncomfortable but illuminating conversation was over.

Liv stood up and went to the back of her father's chair and lightly put her hands on the headrest. "You might want to ask yourself, Dad, *why* is she still so angry after thirty years?"

CHAPTER NINETEEN

CRAIG SENT MATT an email every day, asking about the animals, the roping, offering a few cleaning tips. Matt smiled every time he read one. Damn, but he missed that kid. The house was empty without Craig and right now his life felt empty without Liv—although he was doing his damndest to move past that. He'd cared for her; she hadn't cared for him. Not enough anyway.

He rode Beckett daily, getting the horse back into shape as quickly as possible without souring him, and the rest of the time he roped off from one of his practice horses. In the evenings, he headed into Dillon and drank too much with Pete and sometimes Wes, although Wes rarely drank more than one beer. Occasionally Etta joined them, and Matt soon realized that she did not hold a grudge. In fact, now that he was no longer seeing Liv, she was game for another round. So far, Matt had put her off. He enjoyed her company, but was not interested in what she had in mind. She was funny, though, and could hold her own with the guys, which he'd always admired in a woman.

Jed never came out with them because he was now

a worn-out but proud papa of two. Matt was amazed to feel stirrings of envy, which was stupid, because he was about to go back out on the road and if there were one thing he had figured out over the past few years it was that traveling and families didn't mix—unless the families came along.

Wes let it be known whenever the subject of injury came up that he was of the same mind as Liv when it came to numbing pain—which might have been why Matt lowered the dosage. Once, then twice, then finally gave it up altogether.

Now his knee hurt, but it didn't swell as much as before and the brace seemed to be doing its job. He was slower than he should be, but Beckett could help him add seconds to his time and thus compensate. Would he win the championship this year? Probably not. Would he beat his smart-ass brother in front of his dad and the hometown crowd?

Oh, yeah. He would make Ryan eat his words. Focusing on time and his knee helped him not focus on the one area of his life that was totally ruining him. The relationship part.

In the long run, it might be for the best that Liv kicked him out of her life. He was now deep into the competitive zone; his days revolved around roping. Despite what he'd told Liv, he'd probably have tried to put competition above his relationship. And Liv had been afraid that she'd let him do that, at her expense.

As if.

What Liv seemed to be missing here was that she

hadn't given an inch in the relationship that she pretended they weren't having. If anyone had bent it was him. He'd shown her he cared, in every way he knew how and it hadn't been enough. He was tired of sleepless nights, tired of his gut being all tied up. They could have had so much more, did have so much more when Liv forgot herself and let her guard down, but now he was done. Frustrated, angry and done.

LINDA, WHO WAS horrified when she discovered that one of her team members was unmounted, lent Liv a horse. A small fine-boned bay Paso Fino named Queso, who felt like a pony after riding sturdy Beckett. No one to blame but herself. She was once again perusing the ads, looking for a big quarter horse gelding, knowing that none would be the same as Beckett.

She'd had to let him go, though. She wanted no ties to Matt. No strings. It was him wanting those things that had gotten her into trouble in the first place.

Why couldn't they have continued as they were? When had Matt become a relationship guy?

A one-woman guy. And she could have been that woman.

She didn't want to be anyone's woman.

But she was also stunned at how much she hated seeing Matt with another woman—and of all people, it was Etta she saw sitting on the hood of his truck during the roping practice cheering him on. Etta, who'd been quite open about finding Matt *H-O-T*. Hot.

Well, fine. Etta. Have at him. It's only fair since I can't give him what he wants.

Liv was not one for sour grapes.

Much.

The next three rodeos were going to be interesting and unsettling because, according to Etta, Matt would be roping in all of them. Such was life. She'd tackle the situation one rodeo at a time and hopefully, by the Bitterroot Challenge, the awkwardness would be gone.

She hoped.

THE DAY OF the Newport rodeo arrived, the first of what Liv had come to think of as the dreaded Big Three, rainy and nasty. Liv went out to hook up the trailer and load Queso, only to find Tim had beaten her to it.

"I thought you were in the bathroom," she said as rain poured down her face.

"I'm not. I'm out here hooking up the trailer."

"Why?"

"I'm going."

"Again, why?"

"I have some business to attend to and this is the first step."

Liv decided that she knew enough. The business probably had something to do with Margo, and she was not getting involved. Asking questions about the past was one thing. Watching her father deal with an old flame in real time, another.

"I thought maybe you didn't trust me to drive in the rain."

"Yeah. Right."

Liv smiled at that. Tim met her eyes, but didn't smile back. He looked...nervous. Well, she was nervous, too. She had no intention of watching Matt rope, but she was facing the possibility of their first post-breakup encounter, and so not looking forward to it.

The rain had let up by the time they reached Butte and a watery sun hung low in the eastern sky when they arrived in Newport. Liv had asked Tim to drive because the few times she'd driven him to see the doctor, watching him fidget in the passenger seat had made her crazy.

Would Tim want to leave early today? As soon as her performance was done? Would he be done with his "business" by then?

Damn. She hoped so. She could talk all she wanted about living her own life, but just being in the same place as Matt was unsettling, which only added to her conviction that she'd made the right choice.

The only choice.

Then why do you keep chasing it around your head?

Why do you feel so miserable?

Because she'd let it go too far. Because Matt hadn't played by the rules. Because she missed what they had had. She missed the feel of his hands on her body. Missed their lighthearted conversations, the way he'd gently tease her and smile as if he'd scored a point when she retaliated.

Sex and laughter.

The best.

And how very superficial.

Liv shoved the niggling thought out of her mind.

THE PARKING AREA WAS packed with trucks and trailers. Tim easily maneuvered into a parking spot toward the west edge where the Rhinestone Rough Riders had agreed to meet, parking in the last spot next to Andie's outfit. Margo, who had the only trailer with living quarters, was parked two spaces down, and Liv noticed Tim eyeing the trailer as he drove by.

This was going to be one interesting day. Liv reached for the aspirin in the side panel of the door, popped two into her mouth, then one more for good measure and washed it down with what was left of her coffee.

Tim's expression was grim as he parked, but he didn't say a word as he went back to open the trailer and hold the door while Liv lead Queso out onto the muddy grass.

"Hey, Liv." Linda walked by leading her buckskin, whose back was damp. "Do you have that extra tail barrette?"

"Yes. Let me grab it from the tack room."

Liv handed off the barrette to Linda, then busied herself decking Queso and herself out in Rough Rider finery, trying not to think about Matt, or worse yet, seeing Beckett and bursting into tears, because even though giving him back had been the right thing to do, she really, really missed her horse. She also tried not to wonder where her father was, because shortly after closing the trailer door, he disappeared. Liv didn't know if he'd gone to get a seat in the stands or a cup of coffee. Margo had her horse tied to her trailer and every now and then Liv saw her moving around the animal, so if Tim had come to settle some things with her, then he wasn't doing it now. Thank goodness.

"Hey, Liv," Susie called from the front of Liv's truck where she stood with Linda and Ronnie. "We have over an hour before warming up. Want to go watch the action with us?"

"I'm going to stay here," Liv said, her fingers busy in the horse's mane.

Susie waved an acknowledgment and the group ambled on, their long, sparkly pant legs rolled up four or five times to keep them out of the mud.

Liv continued to work on Queso. Once his mane was braided, maybe she'd sit in the truck and read a book. The last thing she wanted to do was to leave the safety of her trailer.

The thought made Liv's fingers stop.

The safety of her trailer. Really?

This was living life on her own terms? Hiding from Matt and camping out in her truck reading a book? That sounded more like avoidance than empowerment.

Was she never going to get it right?

She wasn't going to hide. She finished Queso's mane and was on her way to the stands to look for her father when Margo emerged from her trailer. She stumbled coming down the trailer steps, grabbed the handle and caught herself just before she fell. Liv hurried over to her.

"Are you all right?"

Margo pulled a quick breath in through her nose, then raised her face. She'd been crying.

"No. I'm not all right," she said brusquely.

"Is there anything…" And then it struck her. She'd been talking to Tim. Liv was probably one of the last people she wanted to see. "I can do?" she finished weakly.

"Got a tissue?"

Liv reached into her pocket and pulled out a pink bandana, handing it over to Margo without a word. The older woman took it and dabbed at her eyes, sniffing a little. "Damned allergies," she said, meeting Liv's gaze dead on, daring her to contradict her.

Unfortunately for her, Liv was getting used to crossing lines drawn in the sand. "Do you guys still have feelings for each other?"

Margo's chin snapped up a half inch higher as she wadded the bandana in one hand. "Yes. Your father pisses me off to no end." She spoke without a hint of apology. Margo shoved the bandana back at Liv, who automatically took it.

"I think he still has feelings for you."

"Well, bully for him," Margo said. "Excuse me. I need to check on something."

Apparently, something in the ladies' room because that was where she headed.

Liv watched her go.

Damn. Thirty years had passed and her father could still piss off the woman to the point of tears.

"DID YOU WATCH Matt rope?" Tim asked on the drive home.

"No," Liv said, keeping her eyes straight ahead. She wasn't ready to do that yet. "But I heard the crowd."

"He was pretty damned impressive."

"He should be," Liv said coolly. "He's dedicated his life to the sport." By his own admission, for years it was the only thing that really mattered to him. "Did you, uh…conduct business?" she asked, deflecting the conversation away from Matt in the most effective way she could think of.

Tim was silent for a moment and then he cleared his throat. "Yes."

"Did it go well?" Liv asked innocently.

"As well as could be expected." Tim's knuckles appeared to be turning white on the steering wheel.

"Will you…be conducting more business later?"

Tim inhaled deeply, obviously hating the way the conversation was going. "Maybe."

Liv shrugged nonchalantly. "Good."

"Matt's knee seems to be better," Tim said. Liv

was aware of the muscles in her shoulders tightening at the second mention of Matt's name.

"Yeah. Painkillers will do that."

"He wore the brace."

I don't give two hoots for what he was wearing— or how well he roped. I don't want to think about him! But she was having a hell of time not doing that. When she'd left Greg, it had felt totally right, as if she were walking from a poisonous environment into fresh air. She was still fighting to get that feeling with Matt.

"Too bad Ryan Madison wasn't at this rodeo," Tim continued, determined to talk about Matt, probably to head off mention of Margo. "I would have liked to have seen the two of them go head-to-head."

Liv was saved from answering by the buzzing of her cell phone. She dug it out of her pocket, grateful for the interruption until she saw the number. What now?

"Hi, Mom," she said lightly. Tim gave her a quick glance, before fixing his attention back on the road, giving Liv the distinct feeling that he was happy not to be in her shoes at the moment.

"Oh, Liv…" A hiccupping sob followed her name.

"Calm down." Liv stared down at her lap as the blood started to pound in her temples. She was going to be so happy when this wedding-to-end-all-weddings was over.

"I'm trying, but the stress. You're the only one I can talk to."

"I know." Talking to her husband would be out of the question, because Vivian would not make waves.

"David is talking about taking out a loan now. Once the magazine got involved, well, he's just determined to really put on a show. In some ways he's worse than Shae."

"I'm so sorry, Mom." Tim glanced her way again and Liv shrugged helplessly at him. For several minutes Vivian unloaded, her words so rushed at times, as if she'd held them in for way too long, that Liv could barely understand her.

"Have you told David you don't want to take out a loan?" she finally said. "Have you discussed this with him?"

"This wedding is so important to both him and Shae. How could I possibly—"

"Mom, you have a say in this. This is your money, too." But even as she spoke, she knew that Vivian would never have a much-needed talk with her husband. She just needed to talk now, and Liv was her sounding board. Liv wasn't supposed to offer ways to solve the problem, she was supposed to give moral support.

So damned hard.

But Liv sucked it up and continued to listen until, finally, her mother had talked herself out, convinced herself that everything was going to be fine if she just let Shae and David have their way.

"Thanks for listening, Liv." Vivian sounded tired,

a bit self-conscious and relieved. "I hope you're doing well. I didn't even ask."

"I'm fine, Mom." *I'm not all that directly involved with Bridezilla and her father.* "I love you and I'll talk to you soon." Liv pocketed the phone.

"Everything okay?" Tim asked.

"Why won't she just grow a backbone," Liv muttered as she leaned her head back against the headrest.

"Because in this life there are givers and takers, Liv. Your mom is a giver." Liv gave her father a frowning look. Sometimes Tim surprised her and he continued to do so by expounding on the matter. "With me she gave and gave and gave, to the point that it made me uncomfortable."

"You felt like your dad?" The guy that Tim said had dedicated his life to taking and giving nothing in return.

He gave her a curious look. "I never thought about it, but yeah, maybe I did. Anyway, I don't think there's any way your mom is going to grow a backbone at this point in her life. You're just going to have to deal with it." He gave a small snort. "The way I probably should have and didn't."

"What happened with you and Margo? Today?" Liv blurted the question out. It was none of her business, but…maybe it was.

Tim exhaled. "We hashed a few things out." He tightened the corner of his mouth before going on to say, "I planned to present her with a payment plan for the hospital bill, but…it got personal."

Liv had noticed. Personal to the point of making Margo cry. "Dad…is there any chance that you and Margo could maybe forge a new path?"

"I don't know."

"Are you…going to look into it?"

"I don't know."

From the tone of his voice it was obvious that sharing time was over. Apparently, both she and her father sucked at relationships. She did because she was afraid she wouldn't stand up for herself and he did because he adamantly stood up for what he believed. He wasn't a taker. Nor was he a giver.

And maybe that was the problem.

MATT CELEBRATED THE first victory in his comeback with a night out on the town in Dillon. Etta was there, as were Wes, Pete, Jed and Corrie.

"You were *awesome*," Wes said, the sarcasm in his deep voice masking a sincere compliment. Wes was never one to get too mushy.

"Yeah. Awesome," Matt replied, lifting his beer. Awesome or not, Ryan had clocked a better time in the rodeo he'd competed in on the opposite end of the state. Matt knew that because Craig had texted him the times and told him to practice more. He'd also told him that his mom was trying to get a day off so they could come to one of Matt's rodeos. Apparently, Willa was quite pleased with her son's new-

found love of roping—although the dude ranch dogs
weren't of the same mind, since they were occasionally the chosen target.

Etta put her hand on his leg and he realized he'd
probably have to set things straight with her and get
himself wished back to hell again. Right now he was
not up for more female entanglements. Maybe in a
week or two, when he got his head on straight again.

The only problem was, it didn't seem to be straightening out as fast as usual. Even Trena, who'd brought
a lot of trauma into his life, hadn't screwed up his
head in this particular way.

He'd wanted something that he couldn't have.
He'd deluded himself into thinking that given some
time Liv could give it. But she couldn't. Or wouldn't.
Didn't matter which.

Two beers in—diet sodas for Wes and Corrie—and
Jed announced that they had to get the sitter home.
Etta, Pete and Matt had one more beer, then Pete
called it quits and Matt walked Etta out to her car.

He took her keys, opened the door, then turned
around to find himself wearing her.

And he'd be a liar if he said it didn't feel good.

But it also didn't feel right.

He finally untangled himself, took her hands
firmly in his so that they didn't go back on their
seek-and-destroy mission.

"Matt?" she asked, her eyes wide and yet somehow seductive as hell.

"Can't."

She squeezed his fingers. "Why?"

"Not a good time for doing this."

She pulled her hands out of his, frowning. "Someone else?"

"Just me."

She snorted. "I don't think I believe you."

"Why?" he asked, putting a hand on the open door frame.

"Don't play stupid, Matt." She brushed past him to get into the car. "You know why."

She didn't smile as she closed the door and when she started the car, Matt stepped back so as not to get his foot run over. Maybe he did know why, but that didn't mean he wanted to discuss it with Etta. And he didn't want to complicate his life any more by sleeping with her.

But he could have been a bit more honest with himself. Thoughts of Liv were still messing with his head and he didn't like what it was doing to him.

CHAPTER TWENTY

L IV RECEIVED ANOTHER lesson in giving and taking—
or the lack thereof—prior to leaving for the second
rodeo of the Big Three. Her mother had called to
say that she'd actually broached the money matter
with David. Liv could only imagine the amount of
stress her mother must have felt to have taken such
a huge step.

David had not been all that receptive, and Vivian
had apparently instantly backed down, which made
Liv want to tear her hair out. Partly because she
worried about her mother, but mainly because she
recalled doing the exact same thing herself. Over
and over and over. Taking a stab at making a stand
and then backing down. Maybe if Vivian stood her
ground, then David would at the very least compromise. But no.

"You're quiet," Tim said as they passed through
Deer Lodge.

"Just thinking about giving and taking," Liv said
darkly.

"Another call from your mother?"

"Mmm." Liv didn't want to discuss it. The nice

thing about her father was that he was comfortable with silence.

Liv and Tim were the first to arrive at the rodeo grounds on a gloriously sunny day—the antithesis of the weather at the last rodeo. Tim parked at the far west side of the lot, and a few minutes later Susie's trailer pulled up close to them, and Susie and Pete got out. "I told you we left too early," Pete said as he headed to the back of the trailer.

"It won't kill you to get here an hour early," Susie said before raising a hand to Liv and calling, "Hi, Tim. Hi, Liv."

"Hey," Liv called back.

"Hi, guys," Pete said absently before turning back to his wife. "I had some stuff I wanted to get done."

"You can do it when we get back." Susie disappeared into the tack room, so her voice was muffled as she called, "I just wanted to get here early enough to get the damned horse ready so I can watch some of the rodeo before the team meets."

"Fine," Pete muttered in a resigned voice.

Tim unloaded Queso while Liv got out the tack, trying not to listen to the continued bickering at the trailer next door, but finding it impossible not to.

While she'd been growing up, her mother and David had never bickered. What David wanted, happened. The same had been true of her relationship with Greg, although she hadn't realized it until she'd finally stood up for herself. He was smoother than David, but controlling all the same. He took and gave

very little back—only enough to keep her in line—
and she hadn't realized how unbalanced their relationship had been because she was so unfamiliar with
the dynamics of give-and-take. In her experience,
there was no back-and-forth. Except with Andie and
her mom, all of her relationships seemed to play out
that way—even her most recent one. Especially her
most recent one, which was supposed to follow a different path than the others, and obviously hadn't. Despite her being candid about how far she was willing
to go, Matt had tried to push her farther.

Liv frowned slightly, vaguely aware of Pete telling Susie that since they'd come early to the rodeo,
that it was only fair that he be able to stay late at the
poker game on Tuesday.

Yes. Matt had definitely done that. He'd pushed.

"All right," Susie muttered from the other side of
the trailer. "But you better not wake me up when you
get in, and you'd better bring home some money."

"Deal," Pete said.

*Had Matt actually pushed? Or had he stated his
position? Told her what he wanted?*

It had felt like pushing…or had that been her
skewed perspective, colored by the past?

And…had he actually taken anything from her?
Or even attempted to take anything from her?

Liv did not like the answer that instantly shot into
her brain.

*No, he did not. But you took all you could from
him and refused to give back.*

Really?

Liv sat down on the running board of the trailer, next to the open tack room door, the brush still in her hand. Had she become exactly what she'd wanted to avoid? Had she been the taker in the relationship?

Well, there certainly hadn't been a lot to give on her part.

But if there had been a giver...

Matt hadn't scurried around as she and her mother had, trying to make things perfect so Liv didn't come unglued, but he'd definitely been flexible. And, true to her promise to herself, Liv had not bent an iota. She'd been the taker.

"Are you all right?" Tim asked gruffly as he walked by leading Queso.

"Yeah," Liv said vaguely, getting back to her feet.

Well, damn.

THE DRILL PERFORMANCE had gone perfectly, Vivian called before Liv and Tim got home to say that things had settled down and that David was reconsidering the loan. Tim had not made Margo cry, at least as far as Liv knew, but she had seen him talking to her— and they had been standing closer than before.

In addition to those happy circumstances, Liv had not bumped into Matt, which was grand, because she was so not ready for a Matt encounter while she was in the throes of some pretty intense soul searching—soul searching that kept her from falling asleep that night despite being both mentally and physically exhausted after one long day.

She'd been a taker and she was not happy about it.

What could a taker do to make things right?

Should she try to make things right?

Damn it all, what *was* right?

I'm done, Liv. This is it. How many times had she played those words over in her head? Firmly told herself it was for the best?

Why hadn't she believed it?

Because she'd twisted her perception of the situation to make it match what had happened between herself and Greg. Matt wasn't Greg. Yes, he had his faults, but manipulating her wasn't one of them. He'd flat out asked for more of a relationship. She'd flat out shut him down—and not because she hadn't cared for him. She could tell herself over and over that he'd known the score before they hooked up, but deep down she knew that when feelings change, they change.

His feelings had changed, intensified, and he'd been honest about it. That wasn't pushing.

Liv tossed and turned for a couple hours as the recriminating thoughts chased around in her head, then finally she snuck out of the house and went to the barn where she groomed Queso and talked to him while he steadfastly ignored her. Not even an ear flick to acknowledge her words. Sometimes the connection was there and sometimes it was not. With Queso it wasn't there. With Beckett, it was.

With Matt… She leaned her head against the bay's silky mane…with Matt it could have been, but she'd screwed it up. To save herself.

So what could she do now? Matt and Etta were a cozy little couple—or at least that was what Etta seemed to think.

Stay safe and leave things as they were?

What had been the obvious answer a few days ago did not seem so obvious now. If her father, her unsentimental father, had not managed to fall out of love in thirty years, then what chance did she have?

Liv started brushing again with a vengeance. How badly had she screwed up? She'd pretty much done everything possible to burn the bridge between them.

Everything read "too late."

She could still recall Margo coming out of the ladies' room at the Newport rodeo a week ago, her face even redder than when she'd gone in. The picture of too late. Because of stubbornness on both sides, although neither saw it that way. Thirty years of stubbornness and Margo was by all appearances still in love with Tim.

It wasn't the relationship in this case that was driving her father and Margo crazy—it was the loss of relationship.

She could easily live her life alone and independently. Call the shots, be her own person.

As opposed to…?

Losing herself in a relationship.

Losing herself.

Did she have so little faith in herself? All that talk about being strong and she didn't believe for one minute that she was strong enough to hold her own in a relationship without being controlled.

But who had called the shots with Matt?

She had. She'd started it when she'd kissed him back, and she'd ended it. And while Matt hadn't exactly accepted what she'd decided without a fight, he'd ultimately respected her decision.

Even though he'd hated it.

What kind of a person was she?

Easy answer there. One who *still* had no faith in herself.

Nothing had changed since the days when she'd hid behind her studies and hoped Matt would notice her. Since she'd done all she could so that first Allen and then Greg would "keep" her.

Liv stopped brushing and for a moment her arms hung loosely at her sides before she wrapped them around Queso's neck and hugged him, closing her eyes, wishing he was Beckett.

Damn. She missed her horse…and she missed Matt. And it was her fault that he was gone. He'd done exactly as she'd asked and removed himself from her life. She was stupid.

Maybe Matt was done with her, but for the sake of her sanity, she needed to talk to him, to at the very least tell him that she'd come to understand what he'd been trying to show her all along.

LIV GOT UP early the morning of the Bitterroot Challenge, the last of the Big Three, but once again Tim had beaten her out to the trailer and had the little Paso Fino loaded. Queso was a decent drill mount, but he was not a good late-night confidant. Yes, she'd told him her troubles, but since he didn't have any issues of his own, it hadn't been the same. She and Beckett had helped each other heal.

Queso was fine. She was not. A one-sided relationship.

Today she was going to watch Matt rope and she was going to talk to him. Try to nudge open that door, tell him what she'd figured out. Tell him she was sorry for having such a skewed view.

There was a very real chance that he was going to tell her to go to hell. If he did, she'd deal with it, but at least she would end the relationship being honest.

Damn, but she hoped he didn't tell her to go to hell.

"Do you want to leave the rodeo early again?" Tim asked as they got into the truck.

"No. I want to stay for the whole thing. I think I want to watch Matt rope."

Tim glanced over at her and Liv shrugged with a nonchalance she didn't come close to feeling. "I have some…business to attend to."

Tim didn't say another word.

HIS PARENTS WERE THERE. Matt had expected them to be, since they attended all of the rodeos within easy driving distance, but what he hadn't expected was to see his father faced off with Ryan near Ryan's no-frills stock trailer as he'd crossed the lot to drop his phone at his truck.

Matt stopped so suddenly that Beckett stepped on his boot heel. Matt winced and pushed the horse back, his eyes still on Ryan and Charles.

The conversation, it seemed, was not a pleasant one. Ryan pointed a finger at Charles, and even at this distance—too far away to hear more than the tone of their voices—Matt could see that his father's face was red.

What the hell?

Did he want to know?

Then Charles turned on his heel and started striding away, stopping when he saw Matt standing twenty yards away.

Matt started walking toward him. He didn't know why, but it was something he needed to do. Charles stood planted where he'd stopped and then Ryan started to approach from behind.

Caught between his sons.

This son had no idea how this was going to play out, but he kept putting one foot in front of the other, Beckett following behind him on a loose rein.

"Hey, Dad," he said.

Charles had a wild look in his eyes as Ryan came up behind him. Matt met his brother's eyes directly for probably the first time since they'd fought in the men's room all those years ago. Now he could see a little of his father in Ryan. The jaw. The line of the nose.

And for the first time since that fight, Ryan spoke directly to Matt. "I was just explaining to *your* father how much his recent phone call to my mom had upset her."

Matt's blood pressure red-lined. Charles was still in contact with this woman?

Ryan jutted his chin out at Matt, as if Matt were somehow responsible. "If it happens again, I'll make a call of my own."

There was no mistaking his meaning. He'd call Matt's mother, just as Charles had called his.

"Do that," Matt growled, "and I will beat the shit out of you."

"Or try?" Ryan turned his attention back to Charles before Matt could reply and said, "No more calls, you son of a bitch. Leave her alone." With that he turned and strode back toward his thousand-dollar trailer with the forty-thousand-dollar horse tied to it.

Charles face was now more white than red. "Are you still involved with her?" Matt demanded.

"No!"

"Just calling her for old time's sake?" Matt asked with a sneer.

"Calling her to tell her to keep her mouth shut." Charles took on his defensive self-righteous stance. "She was the one who clued you in, right?"

Matt just stared at him. "*I* clued me in. I've known since I was fifteen and she had nothing to do with it." Charles's jaw dropped. "Shit, Dad—"

He needed to get out of there, before he gave in

to impulse and punched his father in the teeth. He turned and abruptly started back toward the warm-up area. He was almost there, rounding the last trailer when he heard his name.

Liv. Oh, man. Liv to front, his father to rear. Who knew where the hell his brother was? It was more than he could handle right now.

"I can't talk."

She reached a hand out toward him, touching his arm, but Matt shook it off and walked on. He had to. If he talked to Liv, he was going to lose it and he couldn't afford that right now.

All he wanted to do was to hole up, get his head on straight before his run. To bury himself in the heat of competition, which had saved him before and would hopefully save him again.

LIV WALKED STRAIGHT back to her trailer, climbed into the tack room and pulled the saddle pad and shiny red cover off the storage bar, stepping back down to the soggy grass just as Tim passed her going into the room to get the saddle.

Matt had shut her down in a spectacular way and it hurt like hell. But what had she expected? A tearful reunion?

No. But she hadn't expected him to be so brutally cold.

Numbly, she helped get Queso ready for the drill, exchanging greetings with her teammates as she worked, watching with a stab of envy as Pete patted Susie on the butt when she walked by in her shiny jeans.

She put glitter on the horse's rump while Tim did the same to all four hooves. She'd never thought she'd see the day. Probably neither did Margo, who was parked a couple spaces down, casting the occasional glance in Tim's direction.

Okay, Matt had every right to brush her off, but Liv was going to have her say. Get the closure she didn't yet have.

She looked up to see her father studying her. "I'm fine," she said automatically.

Tim just shook his head. Apparently, she was a bad liar.

"Okay, I'm not fine. I screwed up with Matt." Tim already knew that, so she may as well confess out loud.

"Talk to him," Tim said gruffly.

I tried. "I will."

Tim's eyes went to Margo's trailer, even though she'd mounted and left a few minutes before. "Do that," he said.

MATT HAD WONDERED if it was a mistake to ride Beckett competitively for the first time in this rodeo, the most important purse in his comeback attempt, but with his nerves still jangled after the encounter with his brother and his father, he was glad to have his old friend with him. A horse he could trust, because he was having one hell of a time focusing.

Ryan had already made his run prior to the big confrontation. Matt had watched from the warm-up pen as his brother had made a perfect catch and tied in record time, wondering briefly if his father had stood up to cheer with the rest of the crowd.

Now he had his answer. No, his father hadn't been cheering. For some reason he'd called Ryan's mother, thus pissing Ryan off. Why?

Matt shoved the thought out of his head. Later.

And Liv. What had she wanted? She'd looked so stressed, haunted almost.

Later.

But somehow the hyperfocus he'd always escaped into eluded him. Liv, Ryan, Charles.

When they entered the box Matt felt Beckett's energy through his legs. Ears forward, ready to go. Beckett was as anxious to do his job as Matt was to do his. A team, as always, which was the reason they were champions and would remain champions. For at least one more year. Maybe more.

Matt exhaled, eyes straight ahead, rope in hand. Beckett practically vibrated beneath him. Matt nodded, the chute clanged open and as soon at the calf hit the advantage point, Beckett charged past the barrier, stretching out with his ears back as he sought his prey. He was on the calf in seconds, but just as Matt released his loop, the calf cut to the left, making a suicidal bound directly in front of the horse. Beckett automatically pulled up, skidding in the mud, and then all Matt was aware of was the odd sensation of the sky being in the wrong place followed by crushing pain as twelve hundred pounds of horse came down on him.

CHAPTER TWENTY-ONE

LIV PURPOSELY CHOSE not to watch Matt's run, but she knew as soon as the collective gasp sounded from the stands, followed by silence, that something very, very bad had happened.

She dropped Queso's reins and ran to the arena fence in time to see Beckett get to his feet and almost go down again as he touched his left front leg to the ground.

But Matt...she couldn't see Matt. Just the men surrounding the area where he lay and then the arena gate opened and the ambulance came in.

A hand settled on her shoulder but she barely felt it, didn't even turn to see who it was. It was only when she realized that she was repeating, "Oh, no, oh, no, oh, no," that she made an effort to get hold of herself.

"He moved."

Margo. It was Margo who was standing with her, and then a second later, Tim was on the other side. The three stood watching as Matt was strapped to a backboard, then loaded into the ambulance. Once the gate was closed, Tim nudged her and said, "Come on."

Liv didn't ask where they were going or why. She

simply followed him to the truck where Queso still stood even though he wasn't tied. Tim unsaddled the horse and loaded him while Liv numbly stored the gear.

"We're going to the hospital, right?" Liv finally asked Tim. Because if he wasn't, then she was going to find her own ride there.

"Yes," Tim said, holding the door open. "Get in."

Liv got into the truck then, without a word, scooted to the middle when Margo followed her in. Tim shot the older woman a quick look. A silent communication passed between them, and then Tim reached down to start the engine.

Liv noted in a distant way that it seemed strange that after all these years they could communicate without speaking, but maybe that was the way it worked when people were in love.

The man she loved had just been crushed by a falling horse. If she didn't get that chance to tell him how stupid and blind she'd been, she didn't know if she'd ever forgive herself.

IT WASN'T THE first time Matt had broken a bone, or the first time he'd gone to the hospital in an ambulance. But it was the first time he'd known for a fact that his career was over.

Before they'd loaded him into the ambulance, the paramedics had cut away his jeans and he'd gotten a great view of a compound femur fracture. Not pretty.

And the fact that he hadn't been able to feel anything from the fracture on down scared the hell out of him.

All the decisions he'd put off making until after he finished his last year—or two—were now front and center. What was he going to do with his life? Would he be doing it one-legged?

An hour after he'd been admitted to the hospital the doctors told him that the feeling would come back to his lower leg, the broken bones—as in more than one—had been set and he was a hell of a lucky guy. Beckett had crushed his left leg, but his pelvis and back hadn't been severely injured. Merely bruised.

Amazing how bad merely bruised could feel.

Matt had clutched the pain pump during the visit with his parents. His mother fussed over him, her eyes red with unshed tears. His father had gruffly told him that if he needed anything, to just give a call. And then he left, taking the elephant in the room with him.

Leaving Matt alone. In pain, mental and physical, clutching the pump and clicking it, hoping the dose was only a matter of seconds away. He just wanted to drift away to a place where he didn't have to think.

He was almost there when the door opened again. He raised his head as much as he could, then let it fall back to the pillow. Liv came closer, moving quietly, as if she were afraid he was sleeping.

"It's all right," he said without looking at her. He'd seen this before, more than once. Estranged wives and girlfriends of his injured rodeo buddies showing up at the hospital. Helping them through the process and then, once everything was close to normal again, realizing that all the problems that had driven them apart were still there. All they'd done was prolong the inevitable.

Not going to happen to him. Not while he had this lovely pain pump to help knock him out.

"I'm really sorry," she said.

"How's Beckett?" he asked without looking at her. If he looked at her, he would regret it. Maybe even do something stupid, like accept comfort.

"Limping, but his leg isn't broken or anything."

"Good," Matt muttered. "I want you to keep him."

"I'll take care of him for you."

"No," he said roughly. "Keep him."

"All right," she said slowly, coming to sit on the edge of the chair next to his bed. "I wanted to tell you something before I went home."

Matt closed his eyes. "Don't, Liv."

"Don't what?" she asked in a startled tone.

"Don't tell me you had a revelation when I got hurt. Okay? Just do me that favor."

She didn't answer, but he could feel the tension radiating from her slim body. "I had it before you got hurt," she finally said, her voice little more than a whisper.

"Yeah. Well…sorry," he said.

"Sorry how?" she asked.

"Sorry as in…sorry." Finally, he looked at her. Painfully rolled his head so that he could see her pale, beautiful face, and for a moment his resolve faltered. But he was having none of this mercy-reunion shit. It never lasted and he had enough on his plate without letting Liv tie him up into even more knots, then cut him loose again. "I'm done," he said.

Her lips parted, then she firmly pressed them together.

"Anything else?" he asked, hearing the rudeness in his tone, and thinking that was probably a good thing.

"I made mistakes," she said with that same stubborn note in her voice that she'd had whenever she told him they would never be a couple.

"Me, too. But I came to my senses. Anything else?"

"No, Matt. Nothing."

She got up from the chair, her back soldier-straight, and left the room without a backward glance. Matt closed his eyes, gave the pump a click. Maybe now he could start to recover. On many fronts.

When the door opened again, he was afraid it was Liv, back for round two, and also very afraid that he didn't have the strength to stand up to her. But the person that walked into the room was not Liv, was not anyone he'd ever expected to see alone in close quarters—especially not in his hospital room.

Ryan Madison pulled his hat off as he quietly closed the door behind him.

"Congratulations," Matt muttered. He clicked the pump. Nothing. "You won, right?"

"Yeah." Ryan turned the hat in his hands and for

a moment Matt studied his brother's face. "I heard that the news isn't good."

"For me. Probably works out fine for you."

Ryan gave his head a weary shake. "I guess."

"Why are you here?"

"Probably not the time for this, but I may never get you pinned down again."

"One can hope."

"How long have you known?"

Although he was distracted by pain the likes of which he'd never before experienced, Matt knew exactly what Ryan meant. "Since before that fight in the john."

Ryan nodded, turning the hat again. "I kind of thought that, but your old man called my mother out of the blue a few days ago and accused her of telling you. It really upset her because she's trying so damned hard to do the right thing."

"Like I said. I knew long before." But his father hadn't known he'd known until recently.

"I think he threatened her," Ryan continued in a grim voice. "She won't tell me everything." Matt exhaled, tried to come up with an answer. "Not that it's any of your concern," Ryan continued before Matt could say anything. "I just wanted some answers so I know how to proceed."

"Do not," Matt said, his voice slurred with pain, "do *not* call my mother. None of this is her fault."

"I hated you for a long time, you know."

Matt shrugged, clicked the pump again. Nothing.

"You had everything I wanted. Excellent horses. A practice arena, roping camp." He pulled in a long breath. "A father."

Matt's eyes narrowed at the last words.

"Or maybe I should say a father that acknowledged me."

Click. *Ahhh. Finally.*

"I don't have a lot to say about fathers one way or the other," Matt said.

Ryan regarded him with a deep frown. Apparently, Matt's answers weren't what he expected. The medication was starting to work and he was beginning to regret clicking the plunger so soon. He wanted to get a promise out of Madison—a promise that he'd keep the secret.

"Don't…" Matt's eyelids started to droop as the medication began to have its way with him.

"I won't," Ryan said softly.

Matt forced his eyelids open, trying to make certain he'd heard right, but they started back down again.

"Well…get better."

"You, too," Matt murmured, realizing even as he said it that the words made no sense at all.

CHAPTER TWENTY-TWO

THREE DAYS AFTER Matt had been released from the hospital, Craig and Willa showed up out of the blue. Willa knocked, but apparently knowing how hard it was for him to move, opened the door before he could struggle to his feet.

"Don't get up," she said. Craig came in behind her, grinning widely.

"Are you out of work?" Matt asked.

Willa laughed. "Not at all. But I thought you might need an extra pair of hands for a week or two until school starts."

Matt smiled, maybe for the first time since the injury. "I honestly could." And some company, too.

"I had a dentist appointment in Butte, and then Craig laid his plan out to me and—" she shrugged "—I figured we may as well stop by and see if you were game."

"Totally," Matt said without hesitation, "although I don't think I can do my share of the cooking for a while."

"That's okay," Craig said. "I can feed the animals, feed the people."

"Welcome aboard," Matt said.

Willa left after making some coffee and chatting about her job for a while and then Craig commenced tidying up the house as he prattled on about his new life on the dude ranch. He was teaching some of the clients the basics of dummy roping and the boss had started giving him a stipend, which pleased the kid to no end. School was starting soon and he'd already made a couple of friends. All in all, life was good for Craig and Matt sincerely hoped it continued that way.

Finally, the kid ran out of steam and headed back to his room to unpack and then settle into a TV show. Matt expected the gut-wrenching uncertainty that filled his days to return once Craig left the room, but somehow, having the kid there had shoved his problems further into the back of his mind.

Matt was half-asleep when a knock startled him awake. He leaned over to look out the window from where he sat on the sofa, his leg propped up, then frowned when he recognized the Bailey ranch rig. Liv? He wasn't ready.

He struggled to his feet as the knock came again.

"Come in," he finally yelled after dropping his crutch.

The door pushed open and Tim, not Liv, walked in. Relief flooded through him. Tim he could deal with.

And then it struck him. Had something happened to Liv? Or Beckett? Was that why he was here?

"What?" he asked drily. "Is Liv all right?"

"I'm not here to talk about Liv."

Well, at least that answered his question.

"Then…" he prompted when Tim didn't say anything else. The older man shoved his hands into his jacket pockets.

"I'm here to talk about me." Matt nodded while at the same time wondering what the hell? It took Tim another couple of seconds to say, "I made a giant mistake when I was a little younger than you." Tim clamped his mouth shut then, took a moment, then managed to get it open again. "I've watched Liv make the same mistake."

The older man looked down and for a few seconds Matt thought it was the end of the conversation, but then Tim brought his eyes back up again. "Now, I'm not saying that you guys are meant to be together or anything like that. I'm trying not to stick my nose in."

"Feel free," Matt muttered, feeling very much as he had as Beckett had taken his fall. The sky wasn't where it should be and Tim Bailey shouldn't be in his living room talking about Liv.

"How do you feel about my daughter?"

"Maybe not that free," Matt said. "And I thought you were here to talk about you."

Tim gave him a fierce look. "I screwed up what could have been thirty years of a good relationship because I was pigheaded. I can see that Liv has probably done the same thing."

The fierce look shifted closer to self-consciousness. Tim cleared his throat, looked at the door as if wishing he were heading back out of it.

Matt struggled to his feet and balanced on his better leg. "As much as I appreciate your visit, Tim, I gotta tell you…I think you've misread the situation."

Tim gave him a long, you-stupid-bastard look, then shook his head and headed for the door. And that was that. A blitzkrieg mission. Matt heard Tim start his truck just as Craig ambled into the room.

"Well, that was awkward," he said.

"You were listening?" Wonderful.

"I'd conked out on the sofa in there, but you guys were loud," he said. "And I didn't want to turn on the TV, because then the old guy would have known I was there and clammed up." Craig sat in the chair opposite and clasped his hands loosely between his knees. "So what are you going to do?"

"About what?"

Craig rolled his eyes. "This big mistake he was talking about. Are you going to go see her? Tell her that she's being stubborn?"

Matt stared at the kid, at a loss for words.

"Because I think she really liked you a lot."

"Not enough," Matt said. "And I really don't think we need to discuss this."

"No. I think we do."

"You're out of line, Craig." Matt spoke softly, but in a tone that did not encourage argument.

Craig raised his hands in surrender. "Things have sure changed since I left."

"I'm not trying to be mean. I just want some privacy in my personal matters."

"That's not what I'm talking about."

Matt frowned. "Then what?"

Craig shook his head. "You guys liked each other. A lot. I mean, it was only obvious." He made kissing noises.

Matt rolled his eyes. "Things change."

"That's what I'm talking about. They changed really fast." He shrugged. "I liked her."

"Me, too," Matt said softly, truthfully. And he'd love to have someone to bounce some of his thoughts off, but Craig, as precocious as he was, wasn't the one.

"Then do something about it," Craig said. "Don't be like Tim. And my mom."

Matt's eyebrows went up.

"Oh, yeah. Mom and the cook had a long talk the other day."

"And you listened."

Craig shrugged. "Now, here's the thing…" Craig sliced the air in front of him with both hands held parallel. "You need to *tell* the other person what it is you want, so that they know. You can't expect them to guess at it."

"I did," Matt said, wondering what other nuggets of wisdom Craig had picked up from his mom and the cook.

"And?"

"None of your business."

Craig exhaled loudly. "I can't help you if you don't cooperate."

Matt laughed. "I don't need help." Liar. If he didn't

need help, then he'd be able to stop thinking about all the *if onlys*.

Craig threw his hands into the air and got to his feet. "If you like her, you should do something about it and not wimp out."

"Craig—"

The kid jabbed a finger at Matt, cutting him off. "It's a good thing you didn't treat your roping career like this, quitting at the first sign of trouble, or you wouldn't have come close to being a world champion."

With a disgusted snort, Craig started down the hall, only to stop and turn back. "You know," he said in an intense un-Craiglike tone, "you need to think about what it means to be a champion."

After one final dark look, he continued on down the hall, leaving Matt staring after him.

How old was this kid?

"HE'S GETTING BETTER," Etta chirped to Andie as Liv came in the back door of the clinic. "When I stopped by last night, he was up and around. Of course, I made certain to get him *off his feet,* if you know what I mean, as soon as possible…."

Liv stopped, drew on her rapidly dwindling reserves of inner strength and then continued into the front office.

"Hi," Etta said in her upbeat voice.

"Hi," Liv echoed. "When's my first patient?"

"Almost immediately."

Good. Something to focus on. Liv was no longer certain of her course of action. She wanted to do something, but what? Matt had made it pretty damned clear that he thought her "revelation" as he called it, was due to pity and would evaporate as soon as he got better.

And then there was Etta. How serious was that?

Her gut told her it wasn't. Etta was just a bit too shifty when she talked about Matt, as if by acting that they had a deep relationship she could make it true.

Liv was only working a half day since Dr. Hoss was coming to treat Beckett's injured leg. She saw two new patients, did a consultation with a third, then instead of heading out the side exit for the parking lot when it came time to go, she walked into the reception area where Etta was entering data into the computer.

"How serious are you and Matt?" she asked.

Etta's gaze flashed up. "What?" Liv couldn't blame her for being surprised. The old Liv had never been that direct, but damn it, she needed to know the score.

"Are you two dating?"

"Liv…" There was a note of pity in Etta's voice. "Even if we weren't, Matt's not the right guy for you."

Funny. He'd felt pretty right.

"It's probably hard, what with him being friends with Tim and all—"

"Friends with Tim?"

Etta batted her eyes. "I saw Tim's truck there on my way home the other night."

Liv almost choked. What? Thankfully, she kept the question to herself, so Etta prattled on. "But, really… you're the settle-down kind and Matt isn't."

Liv almost laughed. Etta had it so very backward, but that was secondary to the fact that Tim had been at Matt's.

"He'll hurt you," Etta called as Liv started down the hall to the side exit.

"Already has."

So what did she have to lose? Nothing.

Which was a rather freeing thought.

At the Y in the road on the way home, Liv had a strong urge to turn left instead of right. She went right because the vet was coming. Besides, she had some questions for Tim—who wasn't home.

A reprieve for him.

Dr. Hoss showed up as soon as she'd changed out of her scrubs and she lead the way out to the barn where he gave Beckett a thorough once-over.

Dr. Hoss ran a hand over Beckett's rump after his examination, shaking his head.

"That tendon is probably permanently damaged. I'll know more in a few days when more of the swelling has gone down," Dr. Hoss said, giving her a sympathetic look. "Sorry about this. He was a hell of a horse."

"Still is," Liv said as she walked the vet to his truck.

"How's Matt?" Dr. Hoss asked after stowing his equipment.

"I, uh, don't know." Which killed her.

"Oh." The guy's color rose. "I thought...never mind."

"That's okay," Liv said simply. "We were." Past tense, thanks to her skewed perceptions and stubbornness.

A few minutes later she watched the vet drive away, depressed about Beckett, and more depressed about Matt. So, what was she to do here? Follow the same path as before, sit and wait for Matt, who wasn't going to make a move—this time because she'd been so ridiculously unyielding? When Liv had been younger, she'd made the mistake of overthinking, of not following her gut, because she had no faith in her gut. Today she was trying to have faith in her gut, which told her that if she didn't try one more time to discuss how she felt with Matt, she was going to regret it forever.

Tim was still gone, so Liv fed the steers, then went into the house and showered. She put on makeup while her hair dried in natural waves. In this life there were, in addition to givers and takers, winners and losers. She may not be a winner when this was all said and done, but if she didn't do something, then she would be a loser by default. The new Liv wasn't going to default. She wasn't going to sit silently and hope that the man she cared about noticed her, as she'd done in high school. She wasn't going to tamp down her feelings, but she wasn't going to take a my-way-or-else attitude. She was going to find a middle road if it killed her.

She picked up her phone to see if there was a message from Tim when she heard his truck bump over the cattle guard. She kind of hoped to slip away without announcing her mission, but if she had to, so be it. And she wasn't going to ask why he'd been at Matt's place, because, really, did she want to know?

She grabbed her purse, headed for the door, then stopped when she saw Matt hobbling up the front steps.

Dear heavens.

She jerked the door open, not quite able to process the situation. Matt was here, why? She looked past him to the black-and-silver Dodge, which was not parked under the elm like usual. No, it was parked next to the barn and…was that Craig in the driver's seat?

Her mouth fell open, and after clearing the top step Matt turned to follow her gaze. "He's practicing for his learner's permit."

"Oh." Liv focused back on Matt, a slight frown forming as she gave him a quick once-over. He'd lost weight, which accentuated the hollows under his cheekbones. He needed a shave, and his hair had grown a little too long. He was hunched over on crutches, his left leg encased in plaster up to the top of his thigh…and looked better than ever. Damn, but she wanted to eat him alive—if he'd let her.

Instead, she looked him square in the eye and said, "I don't know if you remember our conversation in the hospital. You were pretty doped up—"

"I remember."

Liv's gaze did not waver even though she felt her cheeks growing warm. "I meant what I said."

"I didn't." The expression in his dark eyes was intense and Liv's heart knocked against her ribs as the words penetrated. "Okay, I meant the part about not wanting a mercy reunion, but—" he looked down at the ground "—if you were there for real…"

"I was there for real, Matt." He raised his eyes to hers. "Honest," she said. She didn't know what else she could say.

"Honest," he repeated.

"Yeah. I…I was so over-the-top as far as maintaining my independence, but I figured a lot of stuff out after you left. I was…afraid."

"I know," he said simply. "I finally figured that out. And I was angry."

"I know…I finally figured *that* out."

Matt reached out to cup his hand around the back of her neck, his crutch falling away and hitting the porch with a hollow clatter. Neither of them seemed to notice or care as his mouth settled on hers.

"Still afraid?" he muttered before kissing her again, more deeply. It felt like a homecoming and if she wasn't so afraid of hurting him, she would have wrapped herself around him.

"Massively. But willing to take the chance."

He smiled against her lips. "The trick to this relationship thing, I hear, is to tell the other person exactly what you want."

"I did that," Liv said. "It didn't work."

Matt kissed her again, making her wonder how one had sex with a full leg cast. "Maybe you didn't totally mean what you said."

"Maybe," she agreed, kissing his upper lip, then gently nipping at his lower. "But I thought I did."

"I know."

"I have a lot to learn about compromise," she said.

"I know," he said with a soft laugh. He leaned back then. "Do you trust me not to take over your life?"

"I'm trying."

"Trying?"

"I might have my moments, you might have to talk me down, but…I'm working on it. I…don't want to lose what we have."

Matt reached out to pull her against him, the other crutch falling away as he lowered his head to kiss her again. "Now we've done it," he said when he finally raised his head and smiled down at her. "I'm helpless. I hope you won't take advantage."

Liv then took his face between her hands to answer him with actions rather than words. When the kiss ended she looked past him at the truck where Craig was staring up at the ceiling.

"Your chauffeur appears to be grossed out."

"My chauffeur is just fine. I'm just fine."

Liv stroked his dark hair away from his forehead. "Funny thing…I think I'm just fine, too."

EPILOGUE

IF PLANNING ONE wedding was hell, it stood to reason that planning two would be doubly hellacious. Not so.

Shae had pushed her wedding back two months, just before the ultraexpensive invitations had been sent out, because she simply needed more time. Tim and Margo, on the other hand, had pushed up their date. At first they'd talked about marrying in two years' time, if all went well. Two years had become one year, and then nine months.

So exactly half a year after Tim had conducted his "business" with Margo at the Newport rodeo, he had a new bride. The wedding plans had been as simple as Shae's were extravagant, taking place in the living room of the house Margo had designed, with a justice of the peace, Liv, Matt, a few of Tim's old buddies, Walter from across the road and all of the Rhinestone Rough Riders.

After the I-dos, the party commenced, and Liv discovered that her teammates could be a wild bunch under the proper circumstances and the marriage of one of their own fit that bill. After the third champagne toast, which involved a cork flying down the front of Linda's shirt, Matt took Liv's hand and they escaped out the back door.

Without a word, they walked to the barn, hand in hand. Beckett nickered a greeting when they went inside and Liv automatically picked up the brush.

"You'll get hair all over your dress," Matt said.

"It'll shake off," Liv replied, opening the stall gate. Matt closed the gate for her and propped his arms on it.

"Sometimes I think you like him more than me," he observed with a tolerant half smile.

"Sometimes I have reason," she said with an answering smile, then after a couple quick strokes of the brush, she walked back to the gate, raised herself up on her toes to kiss Matt's sexy lips. "But not too often."

He growled deep in his throat and took her face in his hands, kissing her back. That evening they were going to his parents' house for Sunday dinner, a semiregular occurrence for the sake of his mother that Matt dreaded. But he put on a good front, as did his father, and Nina seemed happy…although sometimes Liv wondered how much her future mother-in-law knew.

"Let's go home," he said, leaning his forehead against hers. "I need to study for an hour or two before we go to the ranch." Going back to school to start work on a pre-vet degree hadn't been an easy decision, but once made, Matt had thrown himself into his studies with a vengeance. "And—" he smiled wickedly "—I wouldn't mind working some other stuff in."

Liv caught her breath before he gave her one last kiss. Oh, yeah. Time to go home.

She'd looked into renting a house after Tim's engagement so that he and Margo could have privacy, but before she signed the lease, Matt had offered her a bed and more. After a moderate amount of cautious hesitation, she'd accepted—a decision she hadn't come close to regretting. She'd eventually been the one to suggest making their relationship more permanent.

Matt had accepted.

Craig was going to be the best man.

* * * * *

Look out for the next installment of
THE MONTANA WAY series by Jeannie Watt,
coming in January 2014
from Harlequin Superromance.

LARGER-PRINT BOOKS!

GET 2 FREE LARGER-PRINT NOVELS PLUS

2 FREE GIFTS!

HARLEQUIN®

Romance

From the Heart, For the Heart

YES! Please send me 2 FREE LARGER-PRINT Harlequin® Romance novels and my 2 FREE gifts (gifts are worth about $10). After receiving them, if I don't wish to receive any more books, I can return the shipping statement marked "cancel." If I don't cancel, I will receive 4 brand-new novels every month and be billed just $4.84 per book in the U.S. or $5.24 per book in Canada. That's a savings of at least 19% off the cover price! It's quite a bargain! Shipping and handling is just 50¢ per book in the U.S. and 75¢ per book in Canada.* I understand that accepting the 2 free books and gifts places me under no obligation to buy anything. I can always return a shipment and cancel at any time. Even if I never buy another book, the two free books and gifts are mine to keep forever.

119/319 HDN F43Y

Name _____ (PLEASE PRINT) _____

Address _____ Apt. # _____

City _____ State/Prov. _____ Zip/Postal Code _____

Signature (if under 18, a parent or guardian must sign) _____

Mail to the **Harlequin® Reader Service:**
IN U.S.A.: P.O. Box 1867, Buffalo, NY 14240-1867
IN CANADA: P.O. Box 609, Fort Erie, Ontario L2A 5X3
Want to try two free books from another line?
Call 1-800-873-8635 or visit www.ReaderService.com.

* Terms and prices subject to change without notice. Prices do not include applicable taxes. Sales tax applicable in N.Y. Canadian residents will be charged applicable taxes. Offer not valid in Quebec. This offer is limited to one order per household. Not valid for current subscribers to Harlequin Romance Larger-Print books. All orders subject to credit approval. Credit or debit balances in a customer's account(s) may be offset by any other outstanding balance owed by or to the customer. Please allow 4 to 6 weeks for delivery. Offer available while quantities last.

Your Privacy—The Harlequin® Reader Service is committed to protecting your privacy. Our Privacy Policy is available online at www.ReaderService.com or upon request from the Harlequin Reader Service.

We make a portion of our mailing list available to reputable third parties that offer products we believe may interest you. If you prefer that we not exchange your name with third parties, or if you wish to clarify or modify your communication preferences, please visit us at www.ReaderService.com/consumerschoice or write to us at Harlequin Reader Service Preference Service, P.O. Box 9062, Buffalo, NY 14269. Include your complete name and address.

HRLP13R

LARGER-PRINT BOOKS!
GET 2 FREE LARGER-PRINT NOVELS PLUS
2 FREE GIFTS!

⊕ HARLEQUIN®

INTRIGUE®

BREATHTAKING ROMANTIC SUSPENSE

YES! Please send me 2 FREE LARGER-PRINT Harlequin Intrigue® novels and my 2 FREE gifts (gifts are worth about $10). After receiving them, if I don't wish to receive any more books, I can return the shipping statement marked "cancel." If I don't cancel, I will receive 6 brand-new novels every month and be billed just $5.49 per book in the U.S. or $5.99 per book in Canada. That's a saving of at least 13% off the cover price! It's quite a bargain! Shipping and handling is just 50¢ per book in the U.S. and 75¢ per book in Canada.* I understand that accepting the 2 free books and gifts places me under no obligation to buy anything. I can always return a shipment and cancel at any time. Even if I never buy another book, the two free books and gifts are mine to keep forever.

199/399 HDN F42Y

Name	(PLEASE PRINT)

Address	Apt. #

City	State/Prov.	Zip/Postal Code

Signature (if under 18, a parent or guardian must sign)

Mail to the **Harlequin® Reader Service:**
IN U.S.A.: P.O. Box 1867, Buffalo, NY 14240-1867
IN CANADA: P.O. Box 609, Fort Erie, Ontario L2A 5X3

**Are you a subscriber to Harlequin Intrigue books
and want to receive the larger-print edition?
Call 1-800-873-8635 today or visit www.ReaderService.com.**

* Terms and prices subject to change without notice. Prices do not include applicable taxes. Sales tax applicable in N.Y. Canadian residents will be charged applicable taxes. Offer not valid in Quebec. This offer is limited to one order per household. Not valid for current subscribers to Harlequin Intrigue Larger-Print books. All orders subject to credit approval. Credit or debit balances in a customer's account(s) may be offset by any other outstanding balance owed by or to the customer. Please allow 4 to 6 weeks for delivery. Offer available while quantities last.

Your Privacy—The Harlequin® Reader Service is committed to protecting your privacy. Our Privacy Policy is available online at www.ReaderService.com or upon request from the Harlequin Reader Service.

We make a portion of our mailing list available to reputable third parties that offer products we believe may interest you. If you prefer that we not exchange your name with third parties, or if you wish to clarify or modify your communication preferences, please visit us at www.ReaderService.com/consumerchoice or write to us at Harlequin Reader Service Preference Service, P.O. Box 9062, Buffalo, NY 14269. Include your complete name and address.

HILP13R

LARGER-PRINT BOOKS!

❀HARLEQUIN *Presents*

PASSION GUARANTEED SEDUCTION

GET 2 FREE LARGER-PRINT NOVELS PLUS 2 FREE GIFTS!

YES! Please send me 2 FREE LARGER-PRINT Harlequin Presents® novels and my 2 FREE gifts (gifts are worth about $10). After receiving them, if I don't wish to receive any more books, I can return the shipping statement marked "cancel." If I don't cancel, I will receive 6 brand-new novels every month and be billed just $5.05 per book in the U.S. or $5.49 per book in Canada. That's a saving of at least 16% off the cover price! It's quite a bargain! Shipping and handling is just 50¢ per book in the U.S. and 75¢ per book in Canada.* I understand that accepting the 2 free books and gifts places me under no obligation to buy anything. I can always return a shipment and cancel at any time. Even if I never buy another book, the two free books and gifts are mine to keep forever.

176/376 HDN F43N

Name _____ (PLEASE PRINT)

Address _____ Apt. #

City _____ State/Prov. _____ Zip/Postal Code

Signature (If under 18, a parent or guardian must sign)

Mail to the **Harlequin® Reader Service**:
IN U.S.A.: P.O. Box 1867, Buffalo, NY 14240-1867
IN CANADA: P.O. Box 609, Fort Erie, Ontario L2A 5X3

**Are you a subscriber to Harlequin Presents books and want to receive the larger-print edition?
Call 1-800-873-8635 today or visit us at www.ReaderService.com.**

* Terms and prices subject to change without notice. Prices do not include applicable taxes. Sales tax applicable in N.Y. Canadian residents will be charged applicable taxes. Offer not valid in Quebec. This offer is limited to one order per household. Not valid for current subscribers to Harlequin Presents Larger-Print books. All orders subject to credit approval. Credit or debit balances in a customer's account(s) may be offset by any other outstanding balance owed by or to the customer. Please allow 4 to 6 weeks for delivery. Offer available while quantities last.

Your Privacy—The Harlequin® Reader Service is committed to protecting your privacy. Our Privacy Policy is available online at www.ReaderService.com or upon request from the Harlequin Reader Service.

We make a portion of our mailing list available to reputable third parties that offer products we believe may interest you. If you prefer that we not exchange your name with third parties, or if you wish to clarify or modify your communication preferences, please visit us at www.ReaderService.com/consumerschoice or write to us at Harlequin Reader Service Preference Service, P.O. Box 9062, Buffalo, NY 14269. Include your complete name and address.

HPLP13R

Reader Service.com

Manage your account online!
- Review your order history
- Manage your payments
- Update your address

> ### We've designed the Harlequin® Reader Service website just for you.

Enjoy all the features!
- Reader excerpts from any series
- Respond to mailings and special monthly offers
- Discover new series available to you
- Browse the Bonus Bucks catalog
- Share your feedback

Visit us at:

ReaderService.com

RS13